Praise for *Jane & E*

"Instantly captivating and utterly charming. I found myself smiling (sometimes through tears) from start to finish. This sexy, funny, razor-sharp rom-com is one of the best books I've read all year. Melodie Edwards delivers a first-rate, modern take on the classic *Jane Eyre*, so deliciously romantic that Charlotte Brontë herself would be dazzled."

—Lori Nelson Spielman, *New York Times* bestselling author of *The Star-Crossed Sisters of Tuscany*

"Razor sharp, wickedly funny, and touchingly poignant, I was thoroughly beguiled by Melodie Edwards's debut novel *Jane & Edward*. Rarely have I been so thoroughly invested in a novel's outcome. This is an absolute must-read!"

—Jenn McKinlay, *New York Times* bestselling author of *Wait for It*

"Melodie Edwards' witty reimagining of *Jane Eyre* gives us a pitch-perfect protagonist who's somehow even more endearing than the original. . . . This book is brimming with heart; characters that stick with you; and smart, timeless insights about life and love."   —Ashley Winstead, author of *Fool Me Once*

"A jaunty homage to the beloved classic novel."

—Danielle Jackson, author of *The Accidental Pinup*

"A charming and delightful debut. Melodie Edwards seamlessly balances depth with smart and witty dialogue and straight-up laugh-out-loud moments."

—Meredith Schorr, author of *As Seen on TV*

Jane & Edward

Jane & Edward

A MODERN REIMAGINING OF *JANE EYRE*

MELODIE EDWARDS

BERKLEY ROMANCE · NEW YORK

BERKLEY ROMANCE
Published by Berkley
An imprint of Penguin Random House LLC
penguinrandomhouse.com

Copyright © 2023 by Melodie Edwards
Readers Guide copyright © 2023 by Melodie Edwards

Library of Congress Cataloging-in-Publication Data

Names: Edwards, Melodie, author.
Title: Jane & Edward : a modern reimagining of Jane Eyre / Melodie
Edwards.
Other titles: Jane and Edward
Description: First edition. | New York : Berkley Romance, 2023.
Identifiers: LCCN 2022025640 (print) | LCCN 2022025641 (ebook) |
    ISBN 9780593440773 (trade paperback) | ISBN 9780593440780 (ebook)
Subjects: LCGFT: Romance fiction. | Novels.
Classification: LCC PR9199.4.E356 J36 2023 (print) | LCC
    PR9199.4.E356 (ebook) | DDC 813/.6—dc23/eng/20220531
LC record available at https://lccn.loc.gov/2022025640
LC ebook record available at https://lccn.loc.gov/2022025641

First Edition: March 2023

Printed in the United States of America
1st Printing

Book design by Elke Sigal

With thanks to Mum, who made the suggestion

Dear Reader,

Jane of *Jane Eyre* has always been one of my favorite heroines. She's self-aware, freethinking, competent, fiery and calm by turns, and a stronger character than any of those who wittingly or unwittingly abuse her in the book. When she declares, "there I plant my foot," the reader believes her.

And where would this fascinating heroine be without a setting ready to test that nature? Charlotte Brontë knew what she was doing with that looming Thornfield Hall and its craggy moors. I've been reading and rereading *Jane Eyre* for years, forever and always watching Jane navigate life at Thornfield. But when I went to work in Toronto's Financial District as a communications professional, and passed through several different law firms, for the first time, Jane came unglued from that gothic setting in my mind.

Here was a certain kind of environment with the same sense of strange hierarchy, secrets, labyrinthine corridors, awe-inspiring architecture, and unspoken rules. I saw it on the face of nearly every person, uninitiated in that environment, who walked into the lobby for the first time, goggling at the view and trying to make sense of their place in this thing. They reminded me of Jane Eyre walking into Thornfield. I started to see a modern Jane sitting in empty cubicles I passed, or nipping into the elevator, going higher and higher as if it was the battlements of Thornfield she liked to climb.

I told my mum this, and she suggested I turn the idea into a novel.

There are elements of the original *Jane Eyre* story that modern readers might find out of step with twenty-first-century sensibilities. Jane and Rochester are an imperfect love, and it was a difficult choice whether to carry forward their employer-employee relationship into a post-#MeToo world. Ultimately, I kept it—this is a prismatic relationship, problematic but not abusive or coercive, and its complications are an essential part of the difficult path Jane has to walk. Even in the original novel, Jane loves the man but not the situation they find themselves in. When she declares, "there I plant my foot," it is because her line in the sand has been crossed, and we cheer her on for her agency and for her strength of character in turning away from a golden path to tread an unappealing road simply because she believes it is the right one. One of the most satisfying things about *Jane Eyre*'s ending is that Jane *chooses* to reunite with Rochester, now from a position of equality and with wealth and experience on her side.

Reader, I hope you enjoy this story, no matter that the inspiration is nearly two hundred years old. I happen to think that a novel about the complicated emotional and intellectual life of a resilient woman is timeless.

Happy reading,

Melodie Edwards

Jane & Edward

Chapter 1

She hated burgers.

Hated the smell of them, the sight of them, the over-puffed buns and leaky meaty grease that dripped out of them, hated the sticky condiment bottles that shuffled from table to table to accompany them, and the ever-present customer complaints of overcooked/undercooked. As if there was some universal color wheel of patty pinks and browns that she should have memorized to the nth degree.

It's possible she liked burgers as a child, she mused waiting for order-up by the kitchen, but she really couldn't remember. She didn't often think of before or beyond this job, except for today. Even rarer for her to think back on her childhood.

Last day, last day, last day. Order up table six, check ready table nine. She pushed past the swinging doors into the dining room, a heavily laden tray in one hand, four burgers and a child-sized spaghetti bowl, and a sticky leather check folder in the other. She wove among the tables, a rictus smile of polite calm on her face, while her feet moved madly below. *I'm that* Jetsons *character with the wheels for feet. Whee!*

"Burger well-done for you, burger medium-rare for you,

burger just shy of well-done for you, and spaghetti." She plopped the last dish down in front of the booster seat.

"You sure this is medium-rare? I don't think medium-rare is this pink."

"I assure you the cook understood your request for medium-rare, but if you're dissatisfied with it I can take it back to the kitchen and bring you another. It'll take about fifteen minutes." She put on her best blank expression. A fifteen-minute wait deterred some customers, but only if they hadn't figured out that the delay was designed to frustrate their request.

"Well . . . I guess it's all right."

Blow me over with your enthusiasm. "I hope you enjoy your meal." *Choke on it.* "I'll be back shortly with a drink refill."

Left turn, right turn, and a check for the creep at table nine. *Last day, last day.*

"Here you are, sir. Cash or credit?" She rested a hand on the credit card machine in her apron pocket, but table nine's eyes strayed higher to fix on her chest. The uniform supply cupboard was always short of size smalls, and the baggy size large helped hide the constant sweat that came with the exertion of the job; between that and her barely developed figure, she wondered what exactly table nine thought he was ogling.

"Sir? Cash or credit?"

"Cash. I always pay for a meal in cash. If I put it on my card I've passed it before I've paid for it." He laughed.

Charming. "I'll be right back with your change." She reached for the money, but table nine took that opportunity to wrap his fingers around her wrist and tug her hand closer.

"I'll leave you a big tip."

Jane smiled queasily, hearing the buzzing white noise of

muted panic inside her head, as she did whenever a situation like this occurred. No matter how many times it occurred. She kept her expression carefully blank.

He released her wrist with a final leer, the grease of his fingertips leaving a burger-scented trail behind on her inner wrist like a swipe of sick perfume. She turned back to the kitchen, forcing her pace to stay the same as usual, surreptitiously rubbing her wrist against her apron's rough polyester.

It's my last day.

For six years Jane had religiously refused to contemplate a "last day." A "last day" would imply a next step, a plan, some other job, and she had none.

The restaurant was neither fancy dining nor greasy spoon but part of a respectable mid-tier chain that peppered the suburbs outside Toronto's city reach, suitable for family meals, date night, and rowdier things like sports games in the bar. Pay was low but tips were good, and the baggy polo shirt and apron were supplied free of charge. Dental was included, and the constant turnover of mostly teenage waiters meant there was always a ready supply of shifts. It was fine. Really. She could do a lot worse.

I could do a lot better.

But that was a thought to be pushed down. *I have nothing but a high school education. I have no real skills. I have no help. This is a good job for someone like me. There's dental.*

Her twenty-first birthday came and went, and her twenty-second, her twenty-third, her twenty-fourth: the mantra of acceptance scraped increasingly thin. The burger smell grew stronger; her feet felt more tired at the end of every shift. *I'm young; this is hardly backbreaking labor; suck it up.* But young wasn't permanent. She pictured herself at forty still staring down at those same tabletops, moving the same condiments from place to place, keeping her mind on her hands and her hands on the orders and ignoring the bleakness. That same inner voice that once hardened her to her fate now instead began to berate her, to harden her to the idea that this was not sustainable, and that no rescue would come, no improvement in sight, unless she did it herself.

The answer came from the most unlikely source during closing one night.

Fellow waitress Mandi had just returned home from university after dropping out for the second time. She'd moaned about pressure from professors, pressure from her studies, and now pressure from her parents and their insistence she work unless she returns to school. Any school.

Mandi's friend "Whatever," as Jane had mentally named her after hearing her use the word so repeatedly it was like a tic, was proposing a solution to Mandi's problem.

"Training college. Legal assistant. Legal secretary. Whatever."

"The hell do I wanna be a receptionist for?" Mandi pouted at her phone, minutely adjusting the tilt of her head for the fluorescent lights to capture the shine of her dexterously applied Sephora highlighter, and snapped a selfie. She examined the result critically while Whatever continued to stack chairs. She had stacked two tables to Jane's six.

"Legal assistant, it's like a lawyer's office person. It's like a brilliant plan. They'll back off 'cause you're in school, and 'sides, they won't care if you graduate—they'll, like, think maybe it'll make you want to be a lawyer or something, whatever," Whatever said.

Jane paused in her chair-stacking clatter, listening.

"But would I have to, like, *study*?"

"Tina's reject brother did it when he got back from rehab or whatever; that's how I know. Whatever, it's *barely* a year and mostly online, which means"—she paused as Mandi looked up, clearly waiting to lay out the ace card on her brilliant plan— "there's *hardly* any classes, and whatever, your parents can't complain when you're on your laptop! More time to work on your Insta, so when they think you're working on your career, you totally are, but, like, your actual career as an influencer."

Huh.

That night Jane googled the community college she'd heard them name and pored over their website. Whatever was onto something. A part-time program, mostly online, requiring nothing more than a GED and an application to get started. The tuition . . . would be a stretch, but it was doable. Completely doable.

Her one experience with a lawyer's office had been just after her father died. Jenson, Jenson and something. Three men in a family law office in a big building beside a plaza. There had been a middle-aged woman behind the desk who had smiled sadly at her and cooed like she was three instead of thirteen. Was that their legal assistant?

An hour down a Google wormhole and two episodes of the drama *Suits* later, and things felt a little clearer—except for the part where their NYC office was so obviously filmed in Toronto—but the rest of it sounded promising.

Legal assistant. A clean, quiet office. A specific skill set. Better pay. Burger-free.

Yes, this was a future. This was achievable.

The thought followed her around for six months. The condiments changed blindly under her hands, orders in, orders up, crappy tips and good tips, and a new kid's menu special fetchingly called Zucchini Spirelli that parents approved of and kids invariably left in a fat wet spiralized clump under the table.

Jane didn't blame them.

Six months to build up the bravery, alternatively chiding herself for being unsure and ridiculing her fear around what was really such a small step—wasn't it? It wasn't. It was an awful, sickening wrench to hand over the money, the largest purchase Jane had ever made, and another nausea-inducing case of nerves for the first day on campus for registration and orientation in a packed classroom.

It felt a bit like a joke. A cliché. A former foster kid and waitress looking for a better life.

If someone's reject brother can do it, so can I. Whatever.

And so she did.

That conversation between Mandi and Whatever had been nearly two years ago now. A year of school had since passed, neither slowly nor quickly, but with a steady stream of class assignments and burgers marking the days. And there'd been a steady drip of short-lived forgettable waitstaff at the restaurant. Mandi and Whatever were replaced by a cutesy blonde named Kirstie before being replaced by a surly Stanley, who stole everyone else's tips and was fired, and then eventually an acne-seared teenager named Rob who dropped everything he touched.

Jane didn't know it was possible to shatter industrial-sized plastic ketchup containers quite like that.

Graduation day for Jane had been two months ago. She skipped it in favor of working a double shift, but her diploma had come in the mail just the same. It was sitting on her kitchen table at home, a morning touchstone, a surety that soon she wouldn't need to deal with any more Mandis and table nines.

And now today *was her last day.*

"I need change for table nine. Rob! Can you take this back to the customer at table nine?" Jane swapped the two twenties for a five and loose change and flagged down the fumble-fingered teenager.

"Whuh? Why?"

"Creepy customer. Can you just drop this off for me?" She held the change-filled check folder out to him and tried to look matter-of-fact about it, certainly not like someone seeking a hero. She was not pleading with a seventeen-year-old to save her. Nope.

"Oh, uh, sure, I guess." He took the proffered folder and turned back to the seating area. His apron caught on the corner of the counter as he pivoted, the fabric tensing at the same time the folder slid through his fingers to the floor, coins pinging and rolling everywhere. With an almighty *riiiip,* his apron pocket split down the side, dropping its contents—three pens, a loose stick of gum, and five still-wrapped Band-Aids—onto the floor with the change.

"Shit."

He bent down, grossly misjudged the relative distance and spatial permanence of the objects around him, smacked his head on the marble countertop, and crumpled at Jane's feet.

Jane sighed.

"Marianne! We need a paramedic for Rob . . . again."

Last day.

Chapter 2

Marianne, Jane's manager, was grossly disappointed with the caliber of paramedic sent, as per usual.

"I mean, he looks like someone's dad, for eff's sake. Why do we never get the young, hot ones? I've *seen* them at the hospital. I *know* they're there! Oh, gross, that's blood . . ."

"Marianne, it's not like they're deliberately hiding hot paramedics from you . . ."

"Aren't they? Just because that one time when I *maybe* faked choking . . ."

"Oh, you're the choking girl." The friendly middle-aged man looked up from where he had affixed the last of the butterfly bandages to a dazed Rob. "Yeah, you're on a list, sweetheart."

"Hey, I don't judge your life. Next time they send help, I want visible back muscles, understood?"

"All right, son, you know the drill. Follow my finger . . ."

Rob's head wound dealt with, table nine handled, her polo shirt and apron hung up for good and locker cleaned out, Jane walked out the door for the last time with a trepidatious sense of freedom that felt as tantalizingly dangerous as it was fresh and new.

It was already dusk as she left the plaza. Daylight hours were shortening—Canadian winter soon on its way. But tonight, tonight the air was warm and still, a stubborn September holding on to its dregs, and with an uncharacteristic feeling of leisure, Jane passed her usual bus stop in favor of walking home.

Home was a one-bedroom apartment at the top of a three-story walk-up that Jane had moved into at eighteen with the help of the social worker who closed her file. The building was old and peeling, but the landlord was a Polish woman with a stare that made hardened criminals confess, and she vetted potential tenants like she was deciding whom to admit to an Ivy League, so Jane's neighbors were all quiet, keep-to-themselves types, which suited her fine. They always emptied the lint trap after using the coin-operated washing and drying machines in the basement and never had loud parties.

The neighborhood was called Port Credit, the borders loosely defined. It was part of a series of neighborhoods, once small villages in their own right, that dotted the perimeter of Lake Ontario. They had been swallowed up by the sprawling suburbia bleeding outward from Toronto decades earlier, and now were just names on a commuter train line heading west from the city. Twenty minutes down the road would take you to the more affluent neighborhood of Oakville, the teenagers of which referred to Jane's neighborhood as "Pot for Credit."

But "Pot for Credit" would soon be no more. A development boom was transforming the slightly shabby streets into a series of impressively faced town houses, yoga studios, even a nightclub where a boozer-infested bar once stood. Rents were starting to skyrocket, and Jane was grateful that Mrs. Zielinski had yet to sell up or raise her prices. Jane liked Port Credit; it had an easy-access transit terminal, a walkable grocery store, and though the newly refurbished harbor and pier only looked out on the lake and not an ocean—a lake that smelled like hot swamp in the summer and was too polluted to swim in—she liked it just the same. It was easy to pretend it was an ocean with the two-story red-and-white lighthouse standing nearby, though it only served to light the way to the Starbucks next door. Besides, it was her first permanent home since age thirteen. She was attached to it.

Pushing through her door with a happy sigh, Jane toed off her sneakers and dropped both bag and jacket on the floor in the hallway before heading toward the kitchen. Then immediately doubled back to pick them up and put them away. This wasn't summer vacation. No need to get delirious just because she'd permanently seen the back of Marianne, Rob, and the assorted burger gang. Hopefully.

She drifted back into the kitchen, cramped but meticulously tidy just like the rest of her place, and touched her fingertips lightly to the diploma that sat on the table in pride of place. Still real. Next went her phone beside it, placed exactly so like cutlery on a place setting. She queued up her voice mail and flipped it to speakerphone.

"Hello, Ms. Raine, this is April Kindree from the MD Associates legal staffing agency. It was a pleasure to meet you last week."

Some evenings Jane would listen to the message as background noise while she fixed herself dinner, a soothing chatter over grilled cheese. But tonight she stood listening, alert. The professional clipped tones of one of the agency's coordinators traveling through the room.

"We have an opening—perhaps unusual for someone just starting out in the profession, but your instructor gave a glowing reference, you seemed very focused in your interview with us, and their HR wasn't concerned with your lack of experience when we forwarded your résumé and proposed you for the placement, which was very . . . well, it's for a position with a law firm downtown . . ."

At first, Jane had mistakenly thought that this meant "downtown" Mississauga city center, a clump of tall buildings grouped around old city hall and a massive shopping center that stood as a focal point for their section of the suburban sprawl west of Toronto. But she now understood "downtown" meant downtown Toronto. The actual city.

"You'll find the exact details in an email sent this morning . . ."

There was an employment contract to sign. They needed her social insurance number. The starting salary would be—Jane still couldn't believe it—and would include full benefits after the first three months. Naturally, her continued employment with the firm would be subject to a satisfactory performance review after a six-month trial.

The emails from both the staffing agency and the firm's HR department confirming details were printed out and stacked neatly behind her diploma, indicating where to show up on her first day. There was even a congratulatory email from the college instructor who had kindly introduced her to the agency and provided the glowing reference.

"You look like you could use the help, and you're getting an A in my class, so . . ." Professor Grady had said with a smile at the time. "I've a friend who works at this agency. I always pass on good students to them."

Everything was set for Monday, her first day on the job.

Jane finished listening and tapped the phone twice to save the message again. It was three weeks old, and the phone kept prompting her to delete it. Rude. Old Androids were so heartless that way. But really, she should delete it.

She smoothed her hand over the diploma and hit play to hear it again.

Chapter 3

The dreamy quality of Friday night cracked and splintered the next morning. Grim reality wrapped a hand around her hope and held it down hard. Nothing could be allowed to go wrong. Which meant everything probably would.

I need to eliminate all the probabilities.

Saturday morning she printed spare copies of the emails indicating she was to be at 100 King Street West at 8:30 a.m. Monday morning, and stuffed them in two different sections of her handbag in case someone spilled coffee on her on the train and soaked one set. She memorized the train schedule and the platforms, Port Credit Eastbound to Union Station, Line 1.

That seemed insufficient.

Saturday afternoon she walked the short distance to the Port Credit GO station, rode the train to Union Station in Toronto, and after enjoying a brief coffee at the Starbucks inside the station's concourse level, turned around and rode straight home again, where she berated herself for not having gone all the way to the office itself and wasting the price of a train ticket on what was essentially an aborted practice run.

Sunday afternoon, she ironed her outfit for Monday again, after laying it across the bed and deciding the navy blouse and black pants looked sad and wilted, though she had pressed them only two days before. The pants were the same she wore for waitressing.

Stop spiraling. No one will know they're waitress pants. Except, yes, I'll know. I'll know they're sad waitress pants.

Distracted, it was too late when she finally noticed the delicately plumed smoke coming from the iron in her hand. Too much heat and pressure had melted a plastic button hopelessly into the fabric of the blouse.

After Jane decided lying to herself was a luxury she simply didn't have, she sat down in her bone-dry bathtub and cried.

"Shit. Shit! SHIT!"

But only for ten minutes.

Because in addition to lying to herself, crying for more than ten minutes when the shops shut at six was also a luxury she simply didn't have.

Multitask, Jane. Cry at the mall while you shop if you have to.

The mall was its own form of hellish stress. Those pants and that blouse were her only dress clothes. At the college they had given handouts with "helpful hints," but the only advice they offered about clothing was: "Be sure to dress professionally. Remember, conservative dress-casual is what is expected. Pay extra attention to personal hygiene."

Personal hygiene, so brush my teeth. Got it. Super helpful. Thanks, college.

Terms like "dress-casual" meant as much to Jane as beauty magazine terms like "understated elegance" and "date night–worthy heels." For girls who had bought new shoes for a date, gone on a date, or at least been asked out on a date, this term might mean something, but "dress-casual" for the girl who had been wearing the same jeans from the Salvation Army for three years . . .

Two buses and a transfer later, she found herself outside a massive mall complex. The first trip through was a disaster. The second gave her cold sweats. The third was an act of desperation. She fretted over store windows, where to go for her size, her age range, her sad, sad budget. The minutes were ticking by. Finally, she walked into Reitmans, only because she had seen ads on the bus for it; the models seemed annoyingly delighted with things as simple as breathing and smiling, but they looked clean-cut and professional, and their slogans were about being classy on a budget.

It was quiet and empty in the store, some Top 40 pop radio station playing faintly in the background. The two sales ladies, the only other occupants, glanced over wearily as she walked through but seemed happy to ignore her. Jane did a cursory sweep of the racks before grabbing an armful of what looked like office-worthy stuff and slipping into a changing room. People did this all the time; this was doable.

Dress pants utterly defeated her. None of the lengths were right, too long, and they had seams in weird places, gathers of extra fabric where the curves of her should be. Everything seemed built for a theoretical figure.

Whoever the woman is who actually fits these pants, I fucking hate her.

Abandoning the pants pile, Jane dug through the skirts. A black elastic-waist polyester number finally did the trick. It was nondescript, but it fit. She added a plain white blouse. There was another blouse in a soft blue that was a bit too big but looked decent tucked into the skirt. Then there was a black suit jacket. Jane slipped it on and off, and then on again, trying to decide. It seemed the thing to have, a jacket would be office-y and serious, but it was a mannish, heavy piece.

She checked the price tag and decided to leave it. A blazer would have to wait until a real paycheck arrived. Jane tried to indulge herself in thinking of that paycheck while the cash register flashing her outfit's total cost made her wince. It would be worth all this, to be paid a steady rate instead of by an hourly shift plus tips.

Like a domino effect, the new skirt would need proper dress shoes instead of the scuffed black oxfords she originally planned to hide beneath pants, but dress shoes felt like one learning curve too many today. A pair of plain black flats from Walmart did fine, and after trying to work out what kind of socks to wear with them, Jane found the pantyhose in the next aisle over. Buying the hose was the easiest part of the trip—she consulted the charts on the back of the packages with sizes according to approximate height and weight and took a guess at both.

Beyond relieved to be finished, Jane dragged her hard-won purchases home.

You're in over your head, Raine.

Chapter 4

You're in over your head, Raine.

100 King Street West towered above her.

Literally towered.

It was a monolithic giant of an office tower, a soaring behemoth clad in shining white Carrara marble that outstretched and outshone the shorter jet-black and gray office towers clustered near it as if it were an emperor.

The base of 100 King Street West seemed to monopolize the entire city block; massive marble columns with outcroppings covered the numerous entrances, which hugged either side of the corner of an intersection. It sheltered denizens of smartly clad smokers clustered near the sets of revolving doors, puffing and texting furiously. Some doors led to an equally cavernous white marble lobby with fleets of sleek elevators. Others connected to a glass annex emblazoned with the Bank of Montreal "BMO" logo, behind which sat rows of green velvety cubicles filled with bank workers. A digital marquee wrapped around one marble column, its bright blue screen flashing the logo in sharp clarity and scrolling stock market numbers, green or red arrows frantically indicating global economic performance for the benefit of anyone within a two-block radius. It was impossible to even glimpse what the other side of the building's ground floor might look like—it was too many blocks over, would take too much time to walk the distance, equivalent to several football fields, and see.

So that's the BMO tower.

A stranger had enlightened her to its name. Walking the few blocks north from Union Station, following the Google Maps app on her phone, Jane made her way to the Financial District. Tourists and everyday folk ambling from the station morphed instantly into sharp suits striding along at a brisk pace, creating a wave of charcoal gray, navy, and pinstripes. She stopped at the corner of King Street and Bay Street, feeling helpless and grateful when a lounging security guard at his post saw the look on her face and took pity.

"Lost?"

"Yes, I'm looking for 100 King Street West."

"Ah, the BMO tower." He pronounced it "beemoh" as one word, instead of enunciating the acronym.

"No, I'm looking for a law firm office."

He huffed his amusement. "BMO owns the tower. Most of the big banks own towers down here. The shorter black ones all belong to TD Bank." He pointed across the street at a cluster of four opaque black towers flanking each side of a courtyard, plus two farther away that Jane could just see the tops of. "That goldish mirrored one on the corner is RBC. One hundred King Street is owned by BMO, but it's officially called First Canadian Place. Bank owns the tower, but businesses rent the floors. Tons of them."

Craning her neck back, Jane conceded that that's how it

must be. A few floors each would still take up more room than the mall she'd spent Sunday in.

"First time on Bay Street?" he asked. Jane glanced doubtfully over at the sign demarking Bay Street at the corner.

He laughed again. "No, sweetheart, not the actual . . . King Street and Bay Street, heart of the city, center of wealth. UK has the Square Mile and Canary Wharf. And 'muricans"—he pronounced "Americans" the way some Canadians who disliked outsiders did, with an exaggerated, abbreviated drawl of the word—"'muricans have Wall Street. You heard of Wall Street? Right. So ours is called Bay Street. And that's where you are. And *that*"—he pointed across the street—"is the BMO tower. That's your stop. 100 King Street West."

Oh god.

In two minutes of conversation what little confidence the new skirt might have brought with it evaporated. A security guard knew more of the lingo than she did. A man *literally* on the outside of it all was more an insider than her. Jane found this darkly hilarious in her rising panic, and she grimaced to hold in the laugh while the revolving doors continued to swing blithely around, taunting her to go through them.

Her watch read 8:15. She slipped into an alcove near the door, pulled out her phone, and set a timer.

You can freak out for three minutes. Then you have to go in.

She pretended to text for the benefit of the nearby smokers. The subterfuge was completely unnecessary; the scrolling stock numbers, phones, and rapid consumption of cigarettes was their only interest. Jane, in her plain, cheap clothes with an old battered Android, could best be described as nondescript and held little interest for anyone. A small, slight figure, lightly freckled skin, muddy brown eyes, and hair indeterminately caught between brown and blond, though not unattractive, was unprepossessing when accompanied by a habitually reserved and guarded expression.

True to her own self-imposed deadline, at 8:18 Jane walked in the door. It took some trial and error to locate the correct elevator bank and a few more minutes to decide that suite 6300 could be reasonably interpreted as the sixty-third floor.

Stepping off the elevator onto the sixty-third floor did nothing to dissipate the earlier panic.

It was an immediate swaddling into a luxury that stifled, the likes of which she had never seen before. Floor and walls were polished white marble (*is everything in this building freaking marble?*); a claret-colored runner carpet marked the long path from the elevator bank to the receptionist's desk. The desk itself was chest height, a massive sweeping arc of marble, this time jet-black, at least the length and breadth of Jane's kitchen, with ROSEN, HAYTHE & THORNFIELD LLP in black lettering on the wall above it. Behind it lay an open waiting room, resplendent with studded leather chairs tranquilly arranged around low mahogany coffee tables, on top of which the *Times*, the *Wall Street Journal*, and several other international newspapers lay in minutely fanned offerings. A demure candelabra shone down on everything, the light bouncing off the glossy surfaces of marble and mahogany before being absorbed by the rich materials of carpet and couch.

Jane stood frozen in the elevator, stunned by the opulence. This was a mistake; this whole thing was a mistake. No way in hell did she belong working in a place like this, not in any position. Everything screamed old money and exclusion. This place probably had butlers. Did law firms have butlers? Was that a thing? Should she have watched *Downton Abbey* in preparation instead of *Suits*? The receptionist looked up, blond bouffant and tortoiseshell designer frames cocked quizzically to one side, regarding Jane. Someone in the waiting room coughed.

Jane gave in to her panic. The elevator doors slid closed on her gobsmacked face with a discreet *ding* and began the descent back down to earth.

The hesitance of the staffing agency made sense now, their slight air of confusion that Jane's sparse résumé had been acceptable to the firm's HR department.

"Most legal secretaries newly graduated from college start out with small stuff. Personal injury firms, ambulance chasers, small claims tax attorneys," Ms. Kindree had said in her email confirming the employment, still safely tucked in Jane's bag. "So this is a big opportunity. Good luck."

This didn't feel like luck. This felt like the opposite of luck. This felt like . . . well, fuck.

Jane's stomach sank. The UPS guy slouched across from her swung his jaw back and forth, dispelling pressure, and Jane understood why when she felt her ears pop from the elevator's swift loss of height.

His uniform polo shirt reminded Jane of her own polo, ditched only three days ago. She would need it back.

The thought snapped through her.

Back to what? *What?* she demanded of herself. Back to waitressing and lousy tips and always smelling like a burger? Forever? The UPS guy got off at the fifth floor, and in the sudden privacy, she stamped her foot and angry tears pricked her eyes. "If you can't even do the first day, you can't do anything," she hissed. The doors slid open at the ground level. She jabbed the button.

Up to the sixty-third floor. Again.

There were worse things than being laughed out of the room on the first day of the job. Probably.

The next hour passed in a dream. Jane was directed to sit in one of the studded leather chairs where she perched on the edge, until "Diane" from HR could "collect her," according to the tortoiseshell glasses.

Diane proved to be a woman no older than Jane, who spoke leisurely without checking her audience's reaction, explained little, and constantly scanned her phone and any reflective surfaces they happened to pass by for her optimal angle. Jane was irrepressibly reminded of Mandi and wondered if she had been left waiting to be collected because, like Mandi, someone had to remind Diane to perform the job she was paid to do.

"Right, so tour first, yeah? We have four floors—reception is on sixty-three, which is the main floor, sixty-two is the 'basement,' where the litigators sit, sixty-four is 'upstairs,' and sixty-five is called the 'attic.'"

A basement being sixty-two stories in midair seemed strange, but Jane simply nodded.

"Kitchenettes on every floor, help yourself, but the big kitchen is on sixty-three, and only kitchen staff are allowed in there." *Why does a law firm need kitchen staff?* "Accounting, marketing, and HR are on sixty-four; it's a half-staff floor.

Lawyers are everywhere else. Partners' offices have windows and ring the outside of each floor—stay out of their way; assistants sit in cubicles in the interior; and the hierarchy goes like this: senior partners, partners, junior partners, senior associates, associates, junior associates, law clerks, law students." Diane had raised her hand to indicate a level and then dropped it progressively lower with each title until it had descended from her eye level to her waist. Jane figured whatever came after law students must be mud. "All nonlegal staff come after that." *Figures.* "Two partners usually share one assistant, three junior partners to one assistant, and so on. If you're a junior associate, then you have to share an assistant with, like, five other junior associates."

Up and down they trotted, an endless labyrinth of desks and cubbies, kitchenettes and hidden closet rooms. Closed doors led to further halls with more offices. Diane swiped and blipped her key card repeatedly, moving between spaces with blind ease and efficiency, while blisters rubbed in Jane's new shoes as they walked for seemingly mile after mile.

"Annnnd . . . here we are back on sixty-three, lotta boardrooms here. And we'll just nab this one . . ." She led Jane inside and they sat, rather ridiculously Jane felt, at the head of the long, polished wood table that ran the length of the massive room, some twenty-odd empty leather office chairs situated on either side. It was like children playing at being grown-up while the adults were away.

"Right, so paperwork. These are maps of each floor, here's your temporary security pass, we'll get you a new one with your picture in a week or two, we need you to fill this out for payroll, and then I'm supposed to brief you on our accessibility policy, our workplace behavior and sexual harassment policy, our confidentiality policy, and our social media policy."

She plunked four heavy binders down in front of Jane with a kind of grim resignation.

"Buckle in. It's pretty dry."

"Social media policy?"

"And confidentiality. They kind of go hand in hand." Off Jane's polite look of interest she elaborated, "This isn't some divorce court law firm; these guys are big. One of the biggest and oldest on Bay Street. They do work for, like, *everyone*. Banks, conglomerates, billionaire tech companies. Y'know that Orella cosmetics company that was in the news 'cause, like, their product was supposedly giving people eye cancer and, like, all those people brought a class action suit?"

"Eye cancer?"

"Uh, I said *supposedly*. Or I guess, like, *allegedly*."

"This firm represented the class action?"

Diane sneered. "They represented Orella. It's a multi-million-dollar international company. The payout on the file was, like . . ." She rolled her eyes upward and flicked her hair over one shoulder. "Anyway, the firm made a huge donation to charity after, almost the whole payout, actually—it was in the news—so it's, like, all okay, but if you're a granola-eating, save-this-heritage-building kind of person, you can't be saying bad stuff about the firm on your Insta or whatever. And if you have, like, a banker boyfriend or something"—her eyes flicked over Jane's plain outfit and telegraphed that this was clearly a very hypothetical scenario—"you can't be telling him about stuff like the latest company merger we're dealing with; it'll be insider trading. You can't even take pictures around here unless there's no paperwork or computer screens in sight. So yeah, confidentiality."

Jane was tempted to return Diane's unspoken dismissal with a smart remark of her own about not spilling company secrets regarding ethically dubious class actions with a new employee *before* they had signed a confidentiality clause, instead of after, but she bit it back and instead turned her attention to the first of the massive binders.

Pretty dry proved to be an understatement.

Jane listened as dutifully as she could, but her head spun from the whirlwind tour, the strange terms and jargon Diane threw about, and the incongruous nature of so much of the information. She itched to jot things down to be able to look up their meanings later, but when she started to withdraw her notebook and pen from her handbag, Diane rolled her eyes and said there wasn't a quiz coming, and to just sign the form at the end saying HR had explained it and she understood and agreed to the terms.

What kind of law firm is asking me to sign legal documentation on the basis of this selfie stick explaining it to me?

The morning dragged on. After the binders ordeal, Jane was deposited in a room filled with computers while a young man from the tech department clicked through a demonstration of every software program she might possibly need. The only interesting item was the boardroom app, which finally explained the presence of kitchen staff: it was possible to order a full three-course meal to be served for clients, with selections from an on-site wine cellar.

Several more handouts were added to Jane's growing stack.

"You're probably gonna want to take notes on this," Whats-hisname (he had never introduced himself, only his purpose for being in the room with her for many consecutive hours) mumbled halfway through an explanation, and Jane tried not to flush and cursed internally as she pulled out her notebook and pen.

"Yeah, this place is brutal," Whatshisname supplied later, his eyes bugging slightly with emphasis. "They say a senior partner once told a pregnant woman that if she wanted work-life balance, there are other places to work."

"Isn't that against the workplace behavior policy I went through this morning?" *Am I working for Hell, Inc?*

"Oh, that, yeah, they put that policy in a few years ago. They really enforce it too; it's great. But when you work here, they own you. They're pretty up front about that. But if you can keep up, the pay and benefits are awesome."

Jane was beginning to wonder if all the employees had this same seesaw habit of going to pains to point out how despicable the firm was, and then dialing back and defending it in the next breath, without being troubled by the discrepancy. Perhaps the firm itself was morally ambiguous, and that's why it couldn't be explained to an outsider like herself.

Remember, Jane, justice and logic are often cold, heartless, and full of fallacy. Her father's voice rang in her head. *Consider the assassination of Julius Caesar. Caesar is a good man. But Caesar must be destroyed. Both these statements are true, and yet both cannot be true.*

Jane started, momentarily thrown. When was the last time she thought of her father?

By midafternoon, fatigue settled in. The monotonous drone

of Whatshisname ground on, his PowerPoint slides infinite. A low-level headache took up residence at the base of Jane's neck, throbbing in time with the blisters on her feet. She thought longingly of her tidy little apartment, the dented kettle bubbling away, with Netflix queued up on her laptop. Not this oppressive, sumptuous place where not an inch of her felt like it could relax.

"And so that's the app to order more office supplies, and they usually deliver them to your desk in a few hours. Moving on . . ."

At 5 p.m., like a metronome jerking to a sudden halt, lessons were declared over for the day, and Jane felt all the rushing relief of a penance come to an end. She said goodbye to Whatshisname, who responded with a spasm of facial features and a mumble, then wended her way through the labyrinth of halls, only getting lost twice, to the nearest elevator and the glorious prospect of home.

Chapter 5

At home, Jane fell asleep almost immediately after dinner, slept a solid ten hours, and arose to the nightmarish prospect of having to do it all again.

The marble columns glowered at her, the tortoiseshell designer eyeglasses clicked and typed away at her, Diane collected her, and then deposited her once again with Whatshisname who began his instructions on what to do in the event of a terrorist attack, a shooting, or a fire, and the déjà vu glitch in the matrix Jane was stuck in seemed to twitch on.

(And as far as she could tell, if the fire started anywhere between the ground and the sixty-second floor, they were basically screwed, so what was the point of this, really?)

"Any questions?" Whatshisname had finally reached the end of his Sisyphus-ian PowerPoint deck.

Jane shook her head.

"M'kay. So Diane is supposed to pick you up, take you to your workstation . . ."

"Hi, hi, I'm here! She all done?"

He blinked. "I've gone through everything on the checklist." Jane was unclear if this was a statement or a question, but Diane seemed inclined to take it as the former.

"Great. Was it super dull? It's always super dull. No worries, 'cause shit's about to get real. I'm taking you to your workstation, and then you'll probably get to meet your boss. I mean your actual boss is the supervisor of secretarial services, Shirley—she runs all the staff like you—but I mean you get to meet the lawyer you're working for. Mr. Rosen."

"Whoa," said previously deadpan Whatshisname reacting to something in her speech.

"Right?" Diane raised her eyebrows and smirked. Whatshisname looked back at Jane with nervous uncertainty, as if she suddenly possessed unheard-of powers she'd hitherto kept hidden for two days while trapped in this room.

Jane didn't ask. If people had something to tell you, they'd tell you; otherwise, you were just being baited. A certain type of customer would always sigh and look askance, waiting for their server to ask what's wrong before complaining about their meal, demurring at having it replaced before eventually giving in; essentially, the customer was making you ask for the chore. Six weeks into waitressing, Jane had learned not to ask.

So she didn't ask now, just gathered her things and dutifully followed her smirking host, up the brass railing staircase that corkscrewed through the center of each floor, connecting all four levels of the firm to the "attic" of sixty-five. Diane led her down a long corridor. The closer they got to wherever they were going, the more curious heads popped up from behind cubicles, tracking their path and destination. Diane sailed on with a performative indifference to the looks, a new kind of self-importance making her usual distracted manner dissi-pate. Jane received the impression of a priest proudly bringing her sacrifice before a god.

When they reached the second-to-last office door, an older woman sporting a complex blond chignon stepped into their path.

"Adele," Diane intoned coolly.

"Diane," the Adele woman replied, with a tone that was scrupulously polite, yet somehow coldly dismissive at the same time, which Jane found impressive.

"I'm just showing someone to their spot, as the HR repre-sentative."

"I doubt he's here today," Adele said cryptically, but moved on, disappearing around the curve of a cubicle.

"Nosy old bitch," Diane muttered, but the wind was out of her sails. She turned a corner and brought them to a dead end.

It was quiet here: one closed office door was to the right, a gold name plate beside it that read E. W. ROSEN in a no-nonsense font; to the left, across the corridor and facing di-rectly opposite, was a spacious cubicle fitted against the corner of the hall so that the high gray partitions seemed to stretch and blend into the walls behind it, as if a cave had bubbled out of the building itself.

"This is you," Diane said, with a dismissive wave of her hand, but her focus was fixed on the office door, and Jane de-tected a disappointed curiosity. Whoever Mr. Rosen was, and whatever Diane found so fascinating about him, the door re-mained shut and no light spilled out from the gap to the floor.

He wasn't in.

"So, like, if you need anything . . ." *Don't bother me.* Jane filled in the rest. She nodded. The corridor was quiet and cool, the sounds of the people and offices back around the corner muffled. With one last instruction, that Jane should occupy herself with the training programs on her desktop computer, Diane trotted back down the corridor and Jane was left alone.

Her cubicle was sparse. A long dark wood desk ran the length of one partition wall, and a black adjustable wheelie chair was tucked in beneath it. There was a standard metal filing cabinet, some drawers, a coat hook. Laid out on the desk in a neat stack were yellow ruled pads of paper, a box of new blue ink pens, and a sticky note with her computer password scrawled in Sharpie.

Gingerly, Jane sat down at her desk, smoothed her hands along the top, and for the first time in two days, smiled.

She checked the drawers and found paper clips, colored flags, highlighters, elastic bands, a used nail file, and what looked like a package of stale gum, the last two items presumably left by a previous occupant.

Jane had always had a secret affinity for office supplies: the smooth sheen of a fresh pad of paper, the glide of hand and pen across it as the ink flowed down in definitive marks, the authority of a weighty bull clip. She liked standing in the aisle at the Staples store, perusing the ballpoints, finding new organizers and paper sleeves, infinite ways to arrange, file, and label the paper matters of her life, the bills, taxes, pay stubs, the control of it. The contents of her desk at home were immaculate.

So she took a certain pleasure in staking her claim now—tidying, chucking things, scooping the paper clips back into their box, and finding a spot for her purse that was just so.

The computer she touched last, carefully booting it up. It was a brand-new model, and Jane blinked at the sharp clarity of the screen.

At 3 p.m., having run through all the training programs loaded onto her computer, and for lack of anything better to do, and with no mystery boss appearing or further instructions from HR, she consulted a map for the nearest kitchenette.

White mugs were in the cupboard, a vast array of coffee and tea flavors on the counter. Jane aborted her mission to make coffee at the sight of the dirty plates and cups stacked in the sink and instead tucked up her sleeves and prepared to wash up. She hated a dirty kitchen.

Suds had filled the sink when a tall brunette walked in and Jane froze, feeling embarrassed without knowing why. The brunette curled her lip. Brushing past Jane, she tapped an iPad affixed to the wall.

"If the kitchen's a mess, you use the app to alert the kitchen staff. They come clean it up. Office staff don't *clean*."

Jane put on her best blank expression and nodded. Carefully, she extracted her hands from the sink and resumed making coffee. She would not rush.

The brunette moved around her with equal care, selected a yogurt from the fridge, and left.

Well, fuck.

At 5 p.m., Jane declared her own day over and joined the thronged rush to Union Station. She ate, slept, rose, and returned to her cubicle once more. The E. W. Rosen door remained closed.

It didn't take long for the inactivity to chafe. She persuaded herself to leave her cubicle and do a brief lap of the floor. She observed a man in green methodically watering office plants, a woman in blue with a white smock trundling behind a cart with clean cups and saucers, and a man in brown delivering mail to each office and cubicle.

At 11 a.m., Jane circled back to the scene of the crime kitchenette once more.

And was brought up short.

I really need to find another kitchen.

Inside the kitchenette a man was . . . doing something to the expensive, gleaming silver coffee machine that Jane had immediately come to revere.

A near industrial-sized packet of Folgers grounds clenched tight in one hefty fist, the dark-suited man was whacking it repeatedly against the large machine as cups and plates rattled and Nespresso pods clattered to the floor.

"For fuck's sake. Coffee! Give me coffee!"

It beeped innocently back at him, and an error message blinked across the screen. The man paused and pulled back, as if affronted, then growled, eyes narrowed.

"Think you're R2-D2, do you? Don't you dare beep at me! I will destroy you and replace you with a real coffee machine."

The machine beeped again, as if questioning the threat.

He grunted and resumed his strikes, punctuating each blow with words.

"I will replace you." *Thwack.* "With an old-fashioned coffee machine." *Thwack.* "With a filter!" *Thwack.* "And a coffeepot!" *Thwack.* "And COFFEE in the coffeepot!" *Thwack. Thwack.*

Beeeep.

"I SAID DON'T BEEP AT ME!"

He paused the assault, red-faced and growling. Jane stood frozen in the entryway, one foot in and one foot out, undecided.

He turned and did a double take, suddenly aware of his audience. If she expected him to be embarrassed, he wasn't.

"Help or fuck off."

Years of waitressing kicked in. An irate man demanding coffee? She didn't even stop to think.

She shepherded him out of the way, flicked reset, jabbed the button for one cup, and selected "coffee, plain" from the menu. Grabbing a mug from the cupboard, and automatically adding a stir stick and napkin from the nearby containers and folding the latter into a neat square, she slid all deftly under the spout and hit brew before she even knew what she was about.

Shit.

People who belonged here waited to be served, and did not serve, unless it was a client or a partner.

Embarrassed, Jane stepped back from the machine. "There. It's brewing." He stared suspiciously at her and then moved forward to peer into the cup.

She comforted herself that though she had forgotten the rule of strict helplessness in the kitchen, he had too. He had been full throttle attacking the machine instead of calling it in, as per office etiquette, so he must be . . . Jane tried to puzzle it out. Not the plant man or the deliveryman, or their like. They didn't wear suits, and he was wearing an admittedly very rumpled suit and tie. Well, either way, she consoled herself, it wasn't worth worrying that he saw her fix the machine. Judging from his frenzied antics, he was clearly no one that belonged here. She forced herself to minutely relax.

"Why isn't there coffee yet?" he grumbled.

"A watched pot never boils," she told him flatly. "It will brew, just stop staring at it."

"Coffee doesn't know it's being watched."

"Coffee *machines* know to stop beeping because you tell them to?"

He glared.

Splat!

Coffee spewed everywhere, splashing his white shirt, suit jacket, and the formerly pristine kitchen counters. Having thus expressed its displeasure and achieved its revenge, the machine then gave a polite gurgle and placed a steady stream of beverage neatly into his cup.

"Goddammit!"

Jane couldn't help it. She laughed. And immediately stopped, belatedly moving to catch the sound into the palm of her hand. Too late.

"You little witch!" The stranger rounded on her. "You made it do this!"

"*I* did? You insulted it." She shook her head. This conversation was nonsensical.

A corner of his mouth twitched up in an almost-smile.

"My insults were deserved. But you were the last one to touch it."

"You're the one who was hitting it."

"It started it! It kept beeping at me!"

His splattered chest rumbled with exasperation, but he was grinning now, an unholy grin of delight. Jane stared back, amused against her will, and aghast.

The buzzing of his cell phone interrupted them.

He fished it out of his pocket to glance at the screen. "For fuck's sake. Well, I'd love to stay and finish this coffee date, but I'm needed elsewhere." Without once looking up from the screen, he abruptly turned and strode out of the break room, his departure as strange as everything else about this encounter.

"Don't you want your coffee?" Jane called after him.

"NO!"

Typical.

Jane noticed two things when she returned to her cubicle. One was that a tall, poised woman with curly black hair was waiting, hip propped against her desk like she owned it. Two was that the office door to Mr. E. W. Rosen was ajar. There was slight movement inside.

The woman swept Jane with a gaze that traveled swiftly from head to foot, assessing, and she smiled a small, friendly smile that still looked ill at ease. Jane stayed perfectly still under the scrutiny.

"Jane? I'm Beth Fahmey, the executive director of human resources."

"Nice to meet you."

"And you as well. I'm sorry I haven't had a chance to introduce myself before now. I hope Diane took care of you and welcomed you to the firm."

Welcomed me? Sure, let's call it that.

Jane gave a polite but wordless nod.

"Training went well, I hope. I know it can be a bit tedious, but it's all important information to have."

Jane nodded again. "The instructor was very thorough."

What does this woman want?

Her chic dove gray suit looked tailor-made, her manicure immaculate. She could have passed for one of the partners: unlikely to be concerned with one lowly legal secretary when the firm had over a hundred.

Beth continued to smile, and Jane smiled back. She knew better than to fill the silence. People who wanted to draw you out did that. Her social worker used to do that. Her reassuring smile had left Jane feeling similarly wary. For a teenager in the system, there was never good news coming.

Beth ended the stalemate. "You've been assigned to assist Mr. Rosen exclusively. Given his standing in the firm, and the demands of his workload, and consequently the demands of your workload, he will be the only firm partner you assist."

Jane nodded.

"You may find this to be a very . . . intense working relationship. He will need a lot of your time and focus."

She was clearly talking around the point, and Jane wished she'd just arrive at it already.

"Mr. Rosen has been traveling, but he's back in the office today, and I wanted to be the one to introduce you, to help smooth over the first meeting."

"Thank you," Jane replied. "Does . . . the director of HR usually do that?" It seemed a small task for the head of the department.

"Not usually, no, but I thought it might help, and you'll need all the help you can get."

So many questions about this looming shadow of her new boss, and finally, this seemed like an opening to get some real information. She just needed to be diplomatic, tactful.

"Are you saying he can be a bit difficult to work with?"

"He's a holy terror," was Beth's flat response.

Luck was such a scant thing in her life, really, she wondered why she bothered to be surprised anymore.

"We've hired dozens of seasoned, experienced, highly competent assistants. He's lost every single one."

Lost how *exactly?*

"Frankly, it's been exhausting and a drain on my staff's time," she went on. "So now we're trying a new approach. We outsourced to the agency and told them we wanted someone keen for the position, but without much experience, and maybe more willing to adapt to his ways."

The unsolved mystery of being hired with barely a résumé was suddenly solved, and Jane fervently wished it hadn't been.

"I'm simply being honest with you." Jane's neutral expression, so well honed, hadn't flinched, but Beth's tone turned defensive just the same. "I think it's only fair for you to be prepared. I can step in as HR and stop it from getting too bloody, but he . . . has very high standing in this firm, as I've said"—*No shit*, Jane thought, having made the connection, *his name is on everything, it's on the letterhead and the freakin' signage in the lobby*—"so you can appreciate my limitations.

Don't come running to my office for every little thing, but I'm here if you need real help." That didn't seem to require a response, so Jane made none. Beth continued to lean on her desk and surveyed her with the air of a farmer who was looking over a horse to buy but wasn't quite sure if it was up to the plow.

"Sometimes people from different walks of life . . ."

Just for a moment, a slight flicker, Jane's iron composure fled. But Beth never got to finish her sentence.

"SON OF A BITCH."

Jane jumped. Beth sighed.

"Speak of the devil . . ." Beth sighed again. She straightened her suit jacket and spine and clicked her heels across the hallway into Mr. E. W. Rosen's formerly uninhabited office, inclining her head for Jane to follow. Jane did so with a sinking stomach. It couldn't possibly be him. He didn't even look like a lawyer. The universe couldn't hate her that much, right? Wasn't orphanhood and foster care sufficient punishment in life?

Apparently not. For standing there in Mr. E. W. Rosen's office was the coffee-splattered hurricane from the break room. *Fuck.*

"Fahmey! Beth Fahmey! Just the woman I want to see. But you don't want to see me, do you?"

"Mr. Rosen . . ."

"No! Don't start with that calming crap! Don't take that clinical tone with me. I'm not a dog about to have my balls chopped off by the vet, petting me with one hand and the needle in the other. I want to know why, *why* have we replaced good old-fashioned coffee machines with fucking . . . whatever? Whose bright idea was that?"

"Sir, may I remind you that I'm the head of human resources. Coffee machines are not my purview."

"Fuck your purview! You're human resources. Coffee is a necessary resource for us, the humans!"

He finally noticed Jane.

"Who's this?"

"This is Jane Raine." Beth replied.

"Well she can piss off too."

His office was massive, an actual corner office, nearly the size of Jane's apartment, and a complete wreck. Two green upholstered settees were covered in books, papers, an umbrella with a bent spoke, and dry-cleaning bags. The massive mahogany desk he stood behind was likewise covered in miscellaneous items. The ornate red carpet that covered the floor was stained with coffee. There were scattered chairs. Only the two gigantic windows, looking out onto the tops of the glinting buildings of Bay Street and south to Lake Ontario glimmering in the sunlight beyond, were immaculately clean.

"No, wait, I know you." He peered closer at Jane, like it was taxing his memory and he hadn't just met her five minutes ago. "Come to finish the job have you? Pretending to serve me coffee by dousing me with it wasn't enough? Are you going to offer to trim my hair with an axe next?"

"Jane is your new assistant," Beth cut in, delicately choosing to ignore his incomprehensible ranting.

"My what?"

"Your new assistant."

He gave Jane an incredulous once-over. "She won't last the day."

"Well, you've burned through all the assistants in the city . . ."

"Every legal assistant in Toronto? Really?"

". . . so this is what's left. She's qualified and she's a full adult. Take it or leave it."

Take it or leave it? *It* being herself? Jane worked to keep her stony expression, but inside she fumed. They couldn't just drop her like shit off a shovel because this jerk didn't like the look of her. They had hired her with the promise of a six-month probation period, and besides, she was a human employee, not a potted plant to talk about and move around the office.

Mr. Rosen's thunderous expression, quick as lightning, slid into a crooked grin. He seemed to read her quiet rage.

"Offended, are we?"

Jane said nothing.

"Quiet, are we?"

She forced herself to maintain eye contact. *And now he's talking like Yoda.*

"Oh, annoyed, are we?" His quicksilver mood flipped over again, his growl softened to a purr. "But I see we're too smart to say anything. And too proud to cry. Well, where does that leave us?"

She blinked at him, and her heart beat double. When in doubt, stay silent.

"I said where does that leave us, Folgers?"

"Mr. Rosen . . ." Beth interjected.

"Well, now it's a mystery! I'll have to try this one out, just to solve it. She can stay. Thank you for your time, Ms. Fahmey. Do me a favor and see yourself out, back to your human resources cave. You, too, oh silent one. I've got things to do, and the first rule of working for me is I don't like to be pestered. If I need you, I'll shout."

He plopped himself down in his chair with a grunt. Coffee machines, stained shirts, and new assistants apparently instantly forgotten.

Jane didn't see Mr. Rosen again for the rest of that day. When she timidly crossed the hall back to his office at 5 p.m., just to see if he needed anything before she went home for the night, she found it empty, lights off and briefcase gone.

For someone who arrived everywhere by storm and noise, he sure was stealthy about his exits.

At home in her apartment, which always looked a little dingier after a day in that opulent office, Jane pondered the dilemma while she ate dinner. She stood at the sink, sandwich in hand, and stared at a bleached spot on her counter.

He was clearly unhinged.

Should she look for another job just in case? Go back to the agency and ask for another go round? Send out new applications for other assistant positions?

Should I at least wait and see what happens before bailing on the whole thing?

Exhausted from the day and unable to come up with a plan, she went to bed early. She would just have to take it day by day.

She tried to get some rest. Mostly, she stared at her bedroom ceiling.

Chapter 6

Life with Mr. Rosen back in the office was wild.

That next morning, Jane arrived early, wary but determined to be professional, only to find Mr. Rosen sitting on the floor in his office repeatedly throwing a tennis ball against the wall, like he was Steve McQueen in *The Great Escape*.

"Folgers! Look alive!" he called through the open door. "I have two different clients coming in today, so I'll need two different boardrooms, and client A can't bump into client B, and they'll be here back-to-back, so I'm depending on you to find a way to keep them apart." He gave the ball one last toss, only this time he failed to catch it and it smacked into a massive stack of papers on a chair, knocking them to the floor and into what looked like a puddle of spilled coffee, dyeing each page brown. He seemed unconcerned.

"Client A can't see client B." Jane put down her purse and grabbed a pad and pen to make a note, just as Mr. Rosen got up and wandered over to her desk, apparently having lost interest in his one-man tennis game now that he had successfully managed to further destroy his office.

"Ah, she speaks! Yes, you see one is a commercial real estate development company that's paying us to prove they did not defraud investors on their latest high-rise project as suggested by a certain newspaper whom they are now suing for libel, which is going to be fun because that journalist has been throwing around holier-than-thou declarations without proof for a while now and it's time someone made him sweat; and the other client is a very large charitable foundation for whom we are reviewing amendments on their deed of trust, completely pro bono of course because, hello, it's a charity, and their newest charitable crusade is preserving green spaces in the city and limiting the development of those god-awful high-rises that block out the sun, so you can see how this could get very messy. Very *West Side Story* but with less dancing and more court appearances."

Jane rubbed her brow and thought.

"On my first-day tour I saw a folding partition in one of the boardrooms that can be removed. If I ask the facilities staff, they could rearrange it to keep your clients to the south door, instead of the north. They would have to walk around to get to the elevator banks, but it would mean they can avoid . . ."

"Don't care, just do it."

Jane nodded and made another note.

"And what is client B's real name?"

He ignored her.

"Next, my dry cleaning. The last assistant might have taken it down to the parking garage and burned it in a dumpster fire, which is totally fair, but if she didn't, you'll find it at Sam & Sons across the street. Pick it up for me, would you?"

"And your dry-cleaning ticket?"

He raised an eyebrow.

"Right, dumpster fire. I'll . . . figure it out."

"Excellent. Third thing. Charities, unsurprisingly, like to drink. Get me some mimosas for the client B meeting."

Jane nodded, making a note to talk to the kitchen.

"And if you think it's as easy as just talking to the kitchen, you'll probably find out we don't have a liquor permit for drinks before 11 a.m., so you'll need to find some supplier, somewhere, that does have a liquor permit for drinks before 11 a.m., and can come in and serve, and that will probably piss off the kitchen, so good luck with that."

Jane looked up.

"Because the next thing I'm going to ask you to do is arrange a dinner for myself and two benchers from the law society who will be here at eight. I have five files closed for different clients, so you'll need to file those and send the hard copies down to the records room. Then there's a brief on my desk I need you to type up, and then circulate it to Ron Jensen and Mike Cormack—they're part of the securities law group. They sit down on sixty-two, and we need to request their comments on the brief, but I also don't want their comments on the brief because they're both idiots, so if they have any comments on the brief, don't give them to me. Know what you can do with them?"

"Dumpster fire?" Jane asked tentatively.

He laughed.

On and on it went. Jane's head spun, the folders on her desk piled up, her to-do list grew. She called the kitchen, phoned a restaurant called Bymark that was across the street and had a valid liquor license for all hours of the day, ran across the road to the dry cleaner and pleaded with them to return his order without the proper claim ticket, emailed the lawyers on sixty-two, panicked when they did indeed send back comments, agonized over interpreting Mr. Rosen's chicken scratch on his brief, googled likely-looking legal words that might be what he'd written down, and tried to compare the loops and dips of the letters as if they, too, had been handwritten.

The *Devil Wears Prada* movie had made this kind of abuse look a lot more glamorous and cute.

And Mr. Rosen wasn't a cold, imperious *Vogue* editor who glided in and out ignoring her while dressed in impeccable Prada. He liked to pop up and bellow, and seemed infinitely amused as he heaped his demands on her.

By three o'clock, a stress headache was creeping up behind her eyes. At this point it seemed inevitable that half the firm would hate her as she spread the pain of Mr. Rosen's demands. The other half seemed inclined to pity her.

The sixty-fourth floor, Jane discovered, had its own legal library with floor-to-ceiling metal bookshelves. The bookshelves were set in tracks and had massive wheels on each end so that by turning them, which took some strength, they would slide along the floor, stacking close or fanning out in an accordion move that conserved space. The books were all series volumes with spines that said things like *Tort Law, Saskatchewan 2005*. In the dusty quiet, Jane cranked one of the wheels to create a small gap between two bookshelves, slipped into it, and, hidden from sight, gave herself five minutes to breathe, and to cry.

Five minutes and no more.

Because at four o'clock Mr. Rosen had more clients coming in and Jane needed to ensure they didn't see each other. Which would be a freaking miracle.

"What? Oh, those jerks, no, they had to rain check. They'll probably come in next week. Did you move that whole partition yourself? Mail room lads wouldn't help you? Ha. Strong little thing, aren't you?"

Forget crying. Alone in her cubicle, Jane muffled her coat into her mouth and screamed.

Whap. Whap. Whap. He was back to playing with his tennis ball. There was a pause, then a crash.

"Folgers, you there?"

Another hour to go.

The next day brought a more pleasant kind of interruption.

"Bonjour!"

Jane looked up from her computer. The woman from before, the one who had conquered Diane on her second day, stood in the doorway of her cubicle. "So you are the new assistant. Oh, mon dieu, and so young! La pauvre. What were they thinking?"

Up close Jane could see she was in her late fifties, perhaps early sixties. She was about Jane's height but with a decidedly matronly figure. However, neither that nor her age had diminished an inch of her vanity or her beauty: from her bleached blond hair, styled in a complex chignon, to the elegant tailored blouse, jewelry, and sky-high heels, she looked every inch the magazine cover, or a retired Bond girl. Her accent sounded familiar to Jane, who remembered a visiting graduate student who worked for her father when she was ten or eleven. He had been studying at the Sorbonne but said he was raised in Marseille. He had given her some French lessons in his spare time, some of which she still remembered.

"Bonjour, madame. Je m'appelle Jane. Je suis la nouvelle assistante de Monsieur Rosen."

"Enchantée! Parlez-vous français?"

Jane held up her fingers in the universal "just a bit" gesture. The woman smiled and switched to English.

"Well, your accent is very good anyway! I am Adele. I work down the hall from you. I am Mr. Breck's assistant. I just wanted to welcome you to the office." Adele then proceeded to launch into her life story, how she was in fact from Marseille as Jane guessed, how she had come to Canada, married, had three children, all now grown-up, and had been working in the firm for Mr. Breck for the last fifteen years or so. All of her story was interspersed with bits of French and detailed descriptions of what outfits she had worn on certain significant days, such as the day she had met her husband, or the "simply sumptuous" silver maternity coat with cashmere lining she was wearing when she went into labor with her first child.

In return, she required very little information from Jane about herself. Adele seemed to have assessed her at a glance, and she clucked sympathetically for the girl who was alone in the world, inexperienced, and scared of her first real job.

"Did HR gossip about me?" Jane asked, trying not to sound suspicious. She instinctively liked Adele, although her complete lack of concern about restrictions on personal information should perhaps be a red flag. But anyone who pitted themselves against the Dianes of this world and came out on top deserved respect.

"Chérie, they go through so many assistants in this post, HR does not spend time to keep track of them anymore. No one will bother to gossip about you until they see that you last. And no one lasts."

Jane remembered her resolve and tried not to slump in defeat.

"I've been here a few days. I've seen what it's like. I can take it." Her tone was polite though wintry, but Adele merely looked pleased.

"Well, you seem determined. Perhaps that is something to work with. I hope very much that you do last. There are not many other assistants on this floor, and it's lonely to be without neighbors."

Leaving the topic of Mr. Rosen, Adele gave her a few helpful pointers about the office, such as which kitchenette was stocked better, who in IT actually knew how to fix a glitchy computer versus who would just tell you to turn it off and on again and then give up, and who in accounting processed travel expenses for the lawyers.

"And try to avoid the very tall man with a beard who works in the mail room." She made a series of strange hand gestures and weird facial grimaces, which Jane concluded to imply that the fellow in question was liable to be inappropriately hands-on. "But if anyone tries anything with you, go straight to HR. They are strict on their sexual harassment policy here."

Off Jane's no doubt incredulous look, Adele shook her head and said, "A workplace that is so demanding of employees, that has a stressful culture, must ensure that culture does not tip into something else altogether. It is a—what's the word in English—a dichotomy. Employees may want to tear their hair out, but they must still be safe."

What about safe from Mr. Rosen's roller coaster?

". . . and if you need anything else, I am right down the hall."

"Why, Folgers, are you making new friends?"

Mr. Rosen was back, arms crossed over his broad chest, dark head cocked to the side, leaning in the doorframe of his office.

"Monsieur Rosen." Adele greeted him.

"Madame Benoit." He bowed with a flourish, his lip curled sardonically. "Taking Folgers under your wing? Protecting her from the snakes and ladders? Or should that be snakes and lattes?"

"I am merely saying 'ello," she replied with dignity. "Welcoming her to the firm."

He grinned as if she had told a joke, then turned to Jane.

"Hope you didn't have plans this evening. Client coming in at eight; you'll stay late. Take notes on the meeting."

"Yes, sir."

"Yes, sir, no, sir, three bags full, sir. Isn't that how it goes, Folgers?"

My name is Jane. Jerk.

"Well, if you need me, I am right down the hall." Adele emphasized her last words to Jane and laid a warm hand on her arm.

Mr. Rosen watched her retreating chignon. "So, three hours to kill, but have I got a job for you! The time will just fly by . . ."

Jane spent the next three hours trawling through more of his chicken-scratch notes, to make amendments to something already typed. It was two hours before she realized the document she was editing was out-of-date, Mr. Rosen having created a new version on the document management system forty-five minutes ago.

At ten to eight, she heard him leave his office. Were the clients here? Was she supposed to go with him? Follow after? Why wouldn't he come and say so? She stayed put.

At five to eight Jane's phone rang, the evening reception shift—whoever replaced the tortoiseshell glasses when she went home—wanted to let her know that Mr. Rosen's guests had arrived.

"I think he's already en route. I'll come right down. Could you please show them into the boardroom?"

"Oh, never mind, Mr. Rosen is here." She hung up.

"Shit, shit, shit." She gathered up her notepad and pen, and walked, okay *ran*, the length of the hall and down the stairs to the boardroom. The evening receptionist—nearly identical to the tortoiseshell glasses except a little younger and brunette—looked up and gave her a worried glance. Mr. Rosen was standing at the door of the boardroom, arm spread wide and a pleasant expression on his face as he ushered three white-haired men in ahead of him.

Maybe she could slip in just before the door closed, ghost-like. It took courage to approach; she felt every lacking inch of her five-foot-one status. The men were tall, substantial; they moved leisurely, taking up space, voices low and booming as they greeted one another, like massive ships plowing powerfully through heavy waters.

Mr. Rosen entered the room last. Jane almost slipped in unseen behind him, but he suddenly turned—"Dinner. Tell the kitchen to serve now, or these rats will be here forever"—and shut the door in her face with a snap.

Jane jolted back, cheeks burning.

Twenty minutes later, a white-clothed kitchen trolley rumbled by quietly into the room, and Jane took the opportunity to finally slip in behind it. The men were laughing loudly, reclined back in their chairs around the boardroom table. The woman from the kitchen laid out the meal—clearly artisanal and expensive sandwiches with sides of salad—buffet style on the sideboard, along with imported beer and water, and juice in ornate pitchers. With a rumble like a herd of slow rhinos rousing themselves, they got to their feet and began to help themselves.

"Where have you been? I said I wanted you here to take notes," Mr. Rosen snapped at Jane as she hovered. "Sit there, the chair against the window. Notes on my desk Monday morning."

Jane obeyed. But not before one of the men caught sight of her.

"Hello, who's this, then?"

"New assistant, er . . ." Mr. Rosen clearly had no idea what her name was.

"Lucky man to have such a lovely one." He smiled genially at her, eyes twinkling behind his silver glasses, white hair standing in tufts. Jane smiled back. Then his eyes ran over her figure and lingered.

"Such a lovely . . . *blouse*." He smirked. His buddies sniggered.

Her smile froze; her heart started pounding rabbit-quick.

"Sagittarius," Mr. Rosen suddenly barked.

". . . What?"

"Sagittarius . . . my star sign. House of something, with a tendency toward . . . whatever. Sorry, I thought we were stating irrelevant things about one another. We must be, because I know you didn't just make that kind of remark to an employee in my firm."

The other two men froze, one with a forkful of salad comically halfway to his lips. Mr. Rosen stood calmly, hands in pockets, but his jaw was set, his eyes blazed. The air in the room had evaporated. Electricity crackled in its stead.

"Wha . . . no, no, of course not. You've misunderstood me. No harm meant." The older man smiled feebly at her but rapidly made his way to the other side of the room, sitting so there was a good ten feet of distance between them. With a face like thunder, Mr. Rosen watched him go, never for one second taking his eyes off him. Jane quietly took her seat.

"So let's talk about next year's benchers election . . ."

The moment passed.

Jane took notes with her full concentration. After about an hour, Mr. Rosen, who had been pacing the room, picked up a wrapped sandwich from the sideboard and dropped it unceremoniously in her lap.

"Eat."

At ten o'clock, the meeting was finally done. Jane had five pages of notes, only half of which she understood. It was too late to decipher tonight; she'd have to come in Saturday morning to get it done for Monday. Her eyes itched. The air in the boardroom felt stale and breathless, heavy with men's cologne.

The city lights shimmered through the window, neon and artificially bright. With the trains running more infrequently at this hour, she'd be lucky to make it home before midnight. She stayed seated in her chair as the men, shown out by Mr. Rosen, finally left.

"Here." A paper stack—like a checkbook—was dropped in her lap. Mr. Rosen was back. She looked confused.

"It's a book of taxi payment vouchers. You fill one out, give it to the cab driver. It'll be charged to the firm account."

This didn't resolve her confusion.

"It's late. Traveling home alone late at night, it's not . . . Just take the vouchers."

"I don't live in the city. I live in Port Credit. That's nearly . . ."

"Then it's some taxi driver's lucky night. Or you can use Uber if you prefer and expense it. You're here late because of work; you get home safely. Don't argue with me, just take it."

Jane tore one slip of paper away and handed back the rest.

"Thank you, Mr. Rosen."

"Keep them. Use them. You'll be here late often enough. I don't want to hear that you took public transit home."

Chapter 7

On Monday and Tuesday, the following week, Mr. Rosen more or less ignored Jane. He spent mornings down the street at another law firm, trying to mediate something before it went to court. In the afternoons he was feverishly drafting things in his office. He had stopped calling her "Folgers" but now he wasn't calling her anything at all. He dropped stacks of typing for Jane to do and communicated mostly through grunts. He asked her to get him burgers, and to type faster, and said little else.

Jane wondered specifically what it was he'd done to make the last assistant start that dumpster fire.

Despite typing and inputting amendments to something the equivalent of a book in length, Jane couldn't determine more than that there was a pension fund involved, and something called AML, which stood for anti-money-laundering.

By Wednesday, whatever it was that had so deeply absorbed him was resolved, and a new whirlwind commenced.

School had left Jane feeling rather unqualified for the mind-boggling experience of working for Mr. Rosen. On one hand, she was well prepared for the ordinary duties of a legal assistant, which were more or less easier to master than her tasks at the restaurant. On the other hand, Beth Fahmey wasn't lying when she called Mr. Rosen a holy terror. As her "day by day" plan progressed, Jane felt helpless to try to separate her ordinary tasks from her "wild-ass boss" tasks.

For example, her class on taking minutes at meetings had taught her to quickly and carefully pick out the salient talking points from the general discussion and carefully record them for future reference. Pleasantries and small talk that usually preceded and ended a meeting could be omitted. But when your boss lost his temper with opposing counsel and called him "a thundering moron who couldn't find his ass with both hands let alone write a legal brief," and the opposing counsel and client stormed out, Jane found herself at a loss for how to make appropriate notes for that.

Meeting unexpectedly adjourned?

She had taken a course in her second semester that thoroughly covered corresponding on behalf of your boss: how to politely respond to a junior partner versus a senior partner in another firm or your own firm, how to petition a judge for an early adjournment, how to decline or accept a speaking engagement from a law school, and the most diplomatic language to gently remind a client of unpaid fees. Her course did *not* cover how to write apology notes to the firm's junior lawyers, senior lawyers, opposing counsel, and sometimes even clients that Mr. Rosen made cry on a regular basis. This task was made more difficult by the fact that Mr. Rosen, when questioned, seemed utterly unaware of what he had done to cause the crying.

"I'm supposed to be giving work to young lawyers like you who need experience! And teaching them when they make a mistake! So if I ask you for some research on shareholder rights from the Blue Mountain case, and you give me crap, I shouldn't say its crap? Opposing counsel is going to eat you for lunch one day—is that what you want? I'm doing you a favor! Oh, what, you're going to cry now? Really? Come back here!"

Mr. Rosen wishes to sincerely apologize for expressing himself so vehemently this morning, and to explain that the quality of the legal education you receive at our firm is always foremost in his thoughts . . .

Jane had been taught how to properly complete paper-work: how to file an appeal, proof a motion, format a reply to a court order. She knew what to do when being asked to take care of (yet another) contempt of court notice or warning. But when Mr. Rosen demanded a memorandum on the evils of modern coffee makers to be sent to building services?

Item 1. They are liable to cease working without explanation and receive a thrashing in return.
Item 2. They are liable to spew coffee without warning.
Item 3. ~~I am working for a bona fide caveman . . . It causes my boss to have ridiculous tantrums . . .~~

At first she wondered how he kept his job. However, even with her limited education, she could soon see that underneath his eccentricities and temper there was a blazing intellect even the most senior and talented of the partners respected and envied. There was a perpetual parade of them dropping round their little corridor, asking him for a favor, for five minutes of his time, to consult on a knotty point of law. Opposing counsel groaned when they saw him coming. Clients, if they could stand him, fought over him, leaving aggressive phone messages for Jane to transcribe. Many doubted if he was sane, but no one doubted he was brilliant. The pension fund case he had been working on soon popped up in the news, and although Jane couldn't quite follow what had happened, she knew what the terms "landmark" and "precedent-setting" signified.

If she could keep that in mind, she decided, it might be possible to bear with his impatience a little better. If his brain operated at light speed, everyone else must seem very slow to him, and ordinary things—like polite manners—simply weren't on his radar. She remembered her father, the brilliant academic, always lost in his own thoughts, lost in his own world. He was the opposite of Mr. Rosen, slow and calm and gentle, passively accepting of the world around him, but he, too, had a certain disregard for the mundane necessities of life. Like remembering to turn off the coffee maker in the morning or misplacing the student exams he was supposed to mark. Forgetting to make a will or choose a legal guardian for his only child. Just the little things.

"Raine! I need you to write another apology note . . ."

After two weeks of working with him, Jane felt she was getting a better grasp of Mr. Rosen and made another important discovery. He wasn't *actually* cruel, per se. Not in the ways she'd come to associate with real cruelty. He was spoiled, demanding, and harsh. He had no filter on his mouth. He worked relentlessly and expected everyone else to do the same. He was generally careless about people and their feelings. But she might be able to do this job. Beth had described him as a terror. He was more like a tornado. At least he'd started using her real name . . . sort of. That was some kind of progress, right?

"Raine! I need you to hunt down a fire extinguisher, quick as you can. Don't stand there and stare at me! Run! I set some papers on fire in my garbage can. Why? Because she's not the only one who can make a dumpster fire . . ."

After three weeks, Jane had made up her mind.

No one had lasted at this job—well, fuck it. She would.

He could fire her if he wanted to, but there would be no quitting. Of course, receiving her first paycheck had made a big difference in her resolve. She kept checking the balance on her bank app on her phone. Whatever he threw at her, a glance at those steadily increasing numbers kept her working.

But strangely enough, it was more than the money; there was just something about the challenge. No one had lasted at this job? No one had been motivated like she was. He wanted to rant and rave that her work was substandard? Fine by her. No different than a customer ranting and raving that their food was cold. He wanted to storm around the office, arguing with himself at the top of his lungs? He had nothing on foster parent number four, who screamed profanities at the least provocation. He wanted the same document rewritten ten times? She would rewrite it twenty times, without a word of complaint. She had worked damn hard to get here. He wasn't driving her away so easily.

On the outside, she was nothing but quiet compliance. Inside, she was gritting her teeth.

At first, he seemed to hardly notice her, except to bark

orders and then find fault with her work. After six weeks of near silence on Jane's part, speaking only when necessary and completing each task to the best of her ability, it was as if he finally became aware of her existence. Instead of storming past bellowing his demands, he would come to her desk to give orders and then wait, bouncing on the balls of his feet, as if gearing for a fight, then deflate, stumped, when he received nothing more than a "yes, sir" each time. He took to staring curiously, as if she were some strange animal at the zoo. Jane kept her eyes trained on the computer screen, trying not to blush under such blatant scrutiny.

One day he finally came out with it: "You're not afraid of me."

Surprised, Jane looked up at him in confusion. "No. Why should I be afraid of you?"

He smirked. "Most people are."

Well, that was true. Jane had never actually *feared* him. Not exactly. Wariness, trepidation, annoyance, anger, nervousness, and many other things, he (and the rest of this strange Bay Street ecosystem she had wandered into) made her feel all of it, but not fear. True fear, she had decided somewhere around week four, was finding yourself orphaned at thirteen. Fear was having your apartment broken into. Fear was unemployment and falling short on rent. A deranged boss was something she could either manage, or not. "You know most people are extremely wary of me, right?"

"Yes, sir." Pointless to deny it. After a pause, he kept prodding.

"Aren't you afraid I'll fire you?"

"Don't you fire most of your assistants?"

"I *lose* most of my assistants."

"What does that mean?"

"I'm a very intimidating person, y'know." He sounded almost petulant.

"Yes, sir."

"Well, what about my yelling?"

"It's not pleasant, but it's just noise."

"Aha!" He crowed happily. "You despise me. I knew it!"

She nearly bit her tongue off as his rapid-fire back-and-forth finally caught her off guard and forced an honest answer. She had a feeling that was his favorite lawyer trick.

How bad was it to tell your boss he was just noise? But Mr. Rosen was pleased.

"So I'm nothing but noise? Not flattering to a man's ego, but I mentally shake hands with you for your answer. Not one in a thousand would have answered me like that, and I should know: I've had at least that many assistants." He chuckled. "They act like they're working in a war zone and I'm the live grenade."

No way to answer that.

"Well, Raine, you might just be my most enduring assistant yet. You're certainly the most useful."

"Useful?"

"I heard about you and the printer save." At Jane's horrified expression, Mr. Rosen burst into laughter.

How the hell does he know about that?

It had happened a week ago. An important client (but weren't they all important? It seemed to depend on Mr. Rosen's mood

61

each day.) was coming to sign off on the final papers of the financial restructuring of his company. Mr. Rosen gave her only ten minutes' warning of his arrival and asked her to print some papers and bring them to the conference room lightning quick. Neither her cubicle nor Mr. Rosen's office had a printer.

The firm prided itself on their "corporate and environmental responsibility" and went as near to paperless as they could a few years ago. Things were done whenever possible on computer screens, tablets, smartphones, PowerPoint presentations, and LED projectors. Personal printers were unnecessary. The only real paperwork was contracts and signings such as this, so an entire wing of one floor was devoted to four massive laser printers, three photocopiers, and a scanner with a round-the-clock "paper production" staff of two running the machines. Despite the cutting-edge, quiet technology, the cumulative effect of several printers working at once could be deafening. On this particular day, three printers were already occupied running off documents, and the last was malfunctioning.

The gum-popping technician leered at her and estimated, "'Bout half an hour—*pop*—It's just a paper jam, but I gotta help finish this job first—*pop*—an' then change my shirt—*pop*—'cuz when I open up one of these suckers, it'll get ink on me. Sorry."

Must be new to the firm, then; otherwise, Mr. Rosen's name would have scared him into a quick "yes, ma'am." Instead, he sauntered to the other end of the hall where the deafening noise of the working machines mercifully drowned out his *pop*s.

Jane waited until his back was turned.

A quick examination of the broken printer showed where the paper trays stood in the front, and where the casing opened up in the back. In a pinch she had fixed deep fryers, coffee machines, and once a persistent smoke alarm. This was doable. So many of the tasks at the firm were pretty doable, except there was always a person whose specific job it was to do that particular task, and they were often busy, absent, incompetent, overworked, or convinced your project was a make-work one that should be fobbed off on someone else, until you mentioned Mr. Rosen's name. The learned helplessness that everyone exhibited here—that she panicked over on the day she made Mr. Rosen's coffee—it was a faux pas to ignore those rules, but it was a real pain in the ass sometimes to comply with them.

Jane grabbed a clear plastic bag from an industrial-sized recycling bin that stood nearby, ripped three neat holes in it for her head and arms, and pulled it over herself like a smock. Clothing protected, she crawled around to the back of the machine, pried open the casing, and, with a splattering of ink, managed to clear the jam. Exactly eight minutes later, there were four clean printed copies laid out on a boardroom table. No one had been the wiser. Except apparently . . .

"Who told . . . How did you even know about that?" Here's hoping he only knew that she fixed the printer, and not the part about wearing homemade bag protection to do it.

Mr. Rosen grinned. "Aha! Finally I get a reaction out of you!" Jane's face flamed. "You're not scared of me—that's fine, I don't want you to be. But don't be thinking you're oh so clever, either, and above it all with your quiet 'yes, sir, no, sir.' Man up, Raine. Sorry, woman up, I should say. Tell me to piss off if you want, but I hate tiptoeing around each other."

That was him tiptoeing? Are you serious? "Mr. Rosen, most bosses don't let their subordinates tell them to . . . to piss off."

"Most assistants don't wear garbage bags and get their hands dirty to fix a printer when the printer guy is standing right there." His eyes sparkled. "I look forward to seeing more of your excellent work in the future, Raine." Hands in his pockets, he sauntered back to his office, whistling.

Jane dropped her head into her hands and, for what felt like the umpteenth time since she'd met him, groaned.

Thank god for Adele.

Her early offer of being "right down the hall" if Jane needed anything proved to be as good as her word. The first time Jane approached her for help finding a file number, she was promptly given both the file number and an invitation to go out for lunch.

"Sweetheart, you can leave the office for lunch! It's allowed, mon dieu! There is a deli down in the PATH."

The PATH, as Jane had discovered, was an ornate and labyrinthine underground walkway that ran nearly the length of the downtown core, from Union Station in the city's south, to Nathan Phillips Square and beyond, but the majority of it was concentrated under the towers of Bay Street, the floors and ceilings of the tunnels changing from marble to red tile or jet-black to reflect the building it stood under. The halls were wide and ceilings tall, room enough for the hundreds of thousands of Bay Street workers down there every day, moving in such a dense wave that it was nicknamed "salmoning." It was stocked with multiple food courts, shops, restaurants, shoe shines, tailors, barbers, nail salons, and more. To Jane, it was like the wonderful city of Oz, a whole separate world teeming with life under the Toronto streets. In the winter, some people walked directly from Union Station to their office via the PATH, not once having to step outside. Jane had never been able to venture down there without becoming hopelessly lost. She once heard Mr. Rosen refer to it as "purgatory" and he'd had her write a memo proposing that unlikely interns be set loose in it as a way of disposing of them permanently. She bit back that he was no Swift to be making "a modest proposal." Except she didn't say it out loud. Obviously.

"I like Druxy's. We can go there for a chat."

But Adele didn't chat. Or at least she didn't spew information at Jane, as she had done at their first meeting. Instead, she sat back in one of the metal chairs, twirling her fork around in her pasta salad and examining Jane thoughtfully.

"There is more to you than meets the eye," she finally declared. "I did not think you would last so long. They don't hire many young women for jobs like ours, you know why?"

Jane shook her head.

"One: the women flirt with the men, both the young and the old. Bad for wives, bad for business, and bad for HR when it goes wrong, and it always go wrong. Two: because it takes an experienced woman to manage men like these ones. Every morning, Mr. Breck asks me to bring him strong coffee. Every morning, I bring him decaf. Fifteen years the decaf, bien sûr, he still thinks he drinks strong coffee like a young man. He boasts about it. One time I get sick, the temp doesn't know, and brings him regular coffee. He was climbing the walls! Then he crashed."

She clucked her tongue at the hapless, absent temp. "They are smart, powerful men, but a man is a man. Thank goodness we have more female partners now; they have some sense. It may seem old-fashioned to a modern thing like you, but this end of Bay Street is the old boys' club. Traditions, exclusivity, old blood. It doesn't change."

Jane nodded thoughtfully. The firm had a clear caste system: lawyers were lords of the manor; everyone else was a servant, albeit a well-paid one with good health benefits. Among the lawyers, everyone knew everyone from way back; they were on the rowing team in university, their kids went to private school together, their wives or husbands were all sorority sisters, fraternity brothers—highly accomplished, beautiful, often lawyers or doctors themselves. They knew which forks to use for which dish and the correct things to say at a polo match. Then her mind turned to her boss. Messy, eccentric, blunt.

"Adele, how does Mr. Rosen . . ." She stopped, her thoughts turning slow circles in her mind, unsure of what she was asking.

Adele seemed to catch the unformed question. "Mr. Rosen's grandfather founded the firm. His son, Mr. Rosen's father, became the cleverest, richest, crustiest, oldest moneybags of them all. But he was also a very cruel, harsh man. Your Mr. Rosen, he inherited the brains, the good name, and when his father died, the firm as well."

So that explains why he has so much power.

"But he is not his father's son. And I think . . . I think somehow his father broke him." Adele offered the word "broke" as if it encompassed many things, none of which Jane understood.

"Broke how?"

"Eh, I do not know. Nothing too sinister, only he is not what he once was. He used to come round the office when he was young, bright young puppy he was, following in his father's footsteps. And he does not seem to want that world anymore."

Jane felt herself getting frustrated. Was it possible to be more vague?

Adele shrugged, as if aware of this failing herself. "I only know what I see, and what I overhear . . ." She shrugged again rather than finish her sentence. "But your Mr. Rosen"—Jane chafed at the "your"; she didn't buy into Adele's antiquated philosophy that he was hers to manage—"your Mr. Rosen did a lot of good when he took over the firm. Charity donations, better benefits for employees, more hiring of female lawyers, more lenient about maternity leaves. Work placements for new immigrants. The firm has over five hundred employees; it is an enormous responsibility. People don't talk about those things, because he is a scary man."

Jane smiled at that, remembering how he had gleefully told her people were scared of him. Adele caught her smile and raised her eyebrows in question.

"He knows he's scary. I think he's actually proud of it. And he says I'm not scared of him, and that's good. That I should . . . stand up to him, I guess? Or speak my mind at least. Not hold back my personality." Adele looked impressed. "But I don't know," Jane rushed on, confessing the doubts that had been on her mind since that conversation. "I mean, what if he just said that to be nice, or to try to make me feel comfortable, and what if I do speak my mind and I overstep? I'm not scared of getting fired, but if this is some sort of trap to fire me . . ." Jane cut herself off, wholly unused to sharing so much.

"Chérie, listen to yourself!" Adele said kindly. "Mr. Rosen, being nice? Mon dieu, he doesn't *fire* anyone; they walk out! Life is too short to deal with a madman. They leave and he lets people assume the worst. If you have lasted this long, it is because you are doing well. *If he wants you to speak, then speak!* Who knows what goes on in his head? Maybe he is bored."

Jane thought about some of the other waiters she knew at the restaurant, who liked to kill time by chitchatting with customers on slow days. She supposed it was plausible, but . . .

Adele turned her attention to her mostly neglected salad, picking up her fork and resuming eating. Not until she had finished most of it, delicately piling the olives to one side, was she ready to converse again. "So, let me tell you about my daughter Charlotte's wedding. She had the most beautiful wedding dress, cream, with this exquisite lace. I'll show you the photos on my phone—where is it . . ."

Adele prattled on through the rest of lunch, and Jane mulled over the advice she had been given, picking at her sandwich. *If he wants you to speak, then speak!* Never before had she been invited to speak her mind. Not since her father died. So maybe she could relax her silence just a little bit. Why shouldn't she speak her mind? Mr. Rosen certainly wasn't afraid to speak his.

The next time she heard the telltale *whap* of his tennis ball hitting the wall, instead of just ignoring it or waiting for the inevitable crash, she strode into his office and—with the reflexes born of many years of waitressing—snatched the ball out of midair. Sitting on the floor, Mr. Rosen stared at her dumbly, his arm still raised from the throw.

"I paid your gym membership last week."

He blinked at the non sequitur.

"What?"

"Your corporate gym membership. I paid it along with some other expenses."

"Okay . . ." He drew out the syllable.

"I figured you must want some exercise." She dropped the ball so that it bounced once and then rolled gently to his feet. He grinned sharply.

"Passive-aggressive much?"

"You told me to speak my mind. Feel free to reverse that policy anytime." She kept her face blank and her demeanor calm—she had an instinct that that annoyed him—and returned to her seat.

Thirty minutes later she heard him slam a drawer shut, knock over his lamp, curse at it roundly, and storm out into the corridor.

"Fucking quarterly partners meeting . . ." He blew past her, but not before dropping an object on her desk with a thump.

It was the tennis ball, nearly cut in half, with two X's for eyes and a tongue lolling out drawn on with permanent marker. Her email inbox dinged with an incoming message from Mr. Rosen.

Raine—1, Rosen—0.

Jane smiled.

. . .

October blew into November. Jane indulged herself and bought a vibrant red rug for her bedroom floor, the pop of color brightening her mood every morning as she curled her toes in the lush, long pile in delight.

But she stressed about her cold-weather clothing—a warm sweater and ballet flats were okay for now, but what about when the real cold hit? Already, some of the other women were beginning to show up in smart peacoats and sleek high-heeled leather boots. Jane's blue puffy parka that was starting to leak downy feathers and practical secondhand brown UGGs weren't going to cut it. Some of the mature female secretaries dressed sensibly instead of fashionably, but there seemed to be an unspoken rule that their settled status and long tenure with the firm afforded them this luxury.

Oh well, barring any early snowstorms, she maybe had a few more weeks to figure it out, but she knew counting on Canadian weather to behave was always a dangerous thing.

An invitation to the company holiday party had arrived in her inbox the week before, and that, too, was causing her stress. Would this learning curve never end?

Learning to work with Mr. Rosen carried on. His handwriting was becoming a little easier to decipher. She jumped a little less when he bellowed. With discretion, she allowed herself a few more rejoinders to his constant talking, but still often fell back on the usual "yes, sir, no, sir" as a safe bet when his ramblings turned nonsensical, as they often did. His quicksilver mood changes were certainly still something to get the hang of. Still, she was surprised to find herself offering up an anecdote—the most she'd ever spoken to him—one night when she oddly ended up bandaging his hand.

Mr. Rosen was the very definition of a bull in a china shop. He was big and broad, and his large, sweeping motions and bellowing shouts seemed perpetually out of place to Jane in the cool, sleek quiet of the office with its trim corridors and modern tech, or in the old-world opulence of the lobby and other client-facing areas. When he lost his temper, broken furniture was sometimes the result, and Jane's tidy nature reluctantly learned to live with the dented filing cabinets, pulled-out drawers, and keyboard letters made useless from being repeatedly and aggressively punched.

But the sound of broken glass one night was new, as was Mr. Rosen's pained yelp, instead of his usual growl.

Jane had been halfway out the door, so to speak, with one arm in her sweater and her bag packed up. He had been in a foul mood all day, darker and more acidic than usual. In a rare instance, opposing counsel had gotten the upper hand on him with a last-minute reference to a twenty-odd-year-old tax fraud supposedly committed by one of the two merging companies that the firm had been hired to represent. Even Jane could hear the glee in the voice of the other firm's counsel as they laid down their ace card.

In high dudgeon, Mr. Rosen had slammed down the receiver on the conference call that afternoon, and finding that it did nothing to disconnect the speakerphone they had been using the whole time, swept the entire thing off his desk with his arm. Jane, taking notes in a corner of his office, flinched minutely but continued jotting down a memorandum of the call. The junior partner sitting directly across from Mr. Rosen had been less sanguine.

"The due diligence only went back ten years. We didn't think twenty was . . ."

"You didn't think, full stop. Do you have any idea how amateur this looks? Really? Just get out. GET OUT." The younger man scrambled for the door. "Now I've got this FUCKING mess to deal with. Client's going to go BALLISTIC when he finds out. Goddamn embarrassing . . . you too. Out. *Now.*" He spat the last words at Jane, who quickly followed the junior partner out the door.

That had been hours ago. Jane saw the client's name flash briefly on the display of her telephone around seven, but the indicator for the second line blinked on, showing that Mr. Rosen had picked up immediately. She was glad not to have to be on that call. Now it was just after eight. No one had asked her to stick around, but Jane felt a sort of compulsion to see the car crash of a day through.

That's when the actual crash sounded.

"Mr. Rosen?" She stood at the threshold to his office.

"Damn it all to hell . . ." His voice sounded weaker than usual—in pain, almost watery. It gave Jane the courage to push open the door.

"Mr. Rosen?" He sat splayed on the floor, the remains of his ugly ceramic desk lamp beside him, the pieces of the base strewn ominously about in large, upturned, jagged chunks. He cradled one hand in the other, the former bleeding freely from a gash across his palm. Jane sucked in a breath at the sight of the blood.

"Thought you went home. Lamp broke," he muttered petulantly.

Jane mentally counted to five and then went and retrieved the first aid kit stored in the cupboard under the sink in the nearest kitchenette. When she returned, Mr. Rosen hadn't moved.

"Watch your feet!" he said suddenly as she picked her way through the debris in her thin ballet flats. He swept his leg across the carpet, clearing a small path for her and creating small snags from the ceramic in his trouser leg.

"I'm perfectly fine," he grumbled preemptively, as she sat down and opened the kit.

"Of course you are. Wounds are very fashionable this season, aren't they?" It was a feeble attempt at a joke, but Jane was somehow less intimidated of him and more sure of herself in this moment than she had ever been in his presence before. She was indelibly reminded of the fabled lion with a thorn in his paw, hurt and sulking.

"Let me see, please." Wordlessly, he thrust out his hand, refusing to look at her.

The gash was more ugly than deep. Jane briefly left and then returned with a damp washcloth to wipe the blood away. She dabbed at it with a disinfectant wipe from the kit, then set about sorting through the jumbled pile of bandages, looking for an appropriate size. Somehow, she managed to do it all without touching him skin to skin and keeping a fair arm's length of distance between them.

"This isn't part of your job description," he said.

"I know."

"You don't have to be nice to me. I'm not nice to you."

This didn't seem to merit a reply.

"You had a really crappy first week working for me. I know; I made sure of it."

"So you were responsible for that man in the boardroom being rude? And you *weren't* responsible for making sure I got home safely?" Jane asked sarcastically. He scowled.

"Your threshold for decent treatment is pretty low."

Jane shrugged. "Maybe. I'm not bad at patching up injuries. Why waste the skills?"

"Moonlighting as a nurse?"

"No. Abilities born of necessity . . . and a clumsy colleague named Rob."

By the time she had finished telling him about Rob's many mishaps and Marianne's ongoing feud with the paramedic dispatcher, he was howling with laughter and the palpable awkwardness in the air had dissipated.

"She sounds hellish. And she was a manager?"

"She wasn't that bad. And I think he was probably joking about the hospital having a list."

"He wasn't. Hospitals keep all kinds of lists. Possible drug use, low-income areas." He paused. "Injuries that may be domestic abuse." He rubbed his thumb over his newly bandaged palm as he said the last bit, his head ducked, and an inexplicable pang went through Jane, like she'd just inadvertently seen something private. His eyes flickered.

"Anyway." He hauled himself to his feet with a groan. "Big fuss about nothing. Just embarrassed in front of the client, that's all."

"You don't usually care what clients think."

He looked at her sharply for a moment, and Jane was taken aback by the boldness of her own observation of him.

"I don't like it when they think I'm stupid, when I'm not."

Jane nodded. His considerably large intellectual pride.

"My father would have had plenty to say about a screwup like this. And now old Lamp's taken the brunt of it. Poor fragile slob." He addressed this to the pieces on the ground.

"I'll order you another one."

"But Lamp's been with me since my law school days. Nicked him from a professor's office."

"Have you . . . personified your lamp? And named him Lamp?" asked Jane, who sensed the capital L in his words and remembered that first day when Mr. Rosen had addressed his complaints directly to the coffee machine. "Did you get emotionally attached to the object you yourself personified?" It was so quizzical to her own no-nonsense nature, that emission of whimsicality and emotion into the world.

He made one of his curious facial expressions, something resembling an embarrassed grimace covered over with defiance. "Lamp's been with me longer than any assistant," he scoffed.

Sensing this had been too many vulnerabilities for him in one night, Jane blanked her face back into the wallpaper assistant. "I'll take care of it in the morning." She tidied up the remains of her impromptu hospital, disposing of the bandage wrappers and clicking shut the kit. "Good night, Mr. Rosen."

"Good night."

Jane already knew, though she tried to persuade herself otherwise, that she'd be coming in early tomorrow and trying to mend Lamp.

Chapter 8

It felt like a turning point between them. He ignored Jane for three days, as she expected he would. Any display of humanness from him seemed to send him scurrying to his corner to recover. She wasn't offended; she was starting to anticipate his patterns. When he reemerged from this self-imposed hiatus, his gruffness was just as gruff, but something felt like it had relaxed just a fraction between them.

Jane pulled back her focus from his orders, the fallout on her workload of his tics and peculiarities, his specific character traits and how they clashed with the way the firm saw him—only Adele seemed to be in the know that he didn't actually fire every assistant—and began to puzzle him out as a whole man.

He was medium height, leaning toward tall. Broad shouldered and well-built, he gave off the appearance of being naturally burly and imposing rather than aesthetically sculpted by a gym rat's vanity. *He was probably always first pick for football teams*, Jane thought. A thought that was reaffirmed when she saw the controlled strength in his movements. He pulled a heavy metal chair out from the table and picked up a water glass with the exact same ease.

His age was more difficult to guess. The set of his jaw and broad, stern forehead said "man," but when Jane dropped her papers and he caught her embarrassed blush, his bright laughter still said "boy." His suits were the best Armani, but he wore them carelessly with shirtsleeves rolled up and the jacket flung to the corner of his office every morning when he stormed through the door like a paratrooper, bellowing Jane's name and damning the traffic in the same breath. His dark hair was perpetually rumpled, and an omnipresent five-o'clock shadow darkened his jaw. The state of his tie was a lost cause.

Jane had noticed the pristine appearance of the other lawyers, how their assistants would fret over the slightest crease in their suit before a big meeting, or surreptitiously hand them a comb as they walked to a boardroom. Hour-turnaround dry cleaners and tailors that came directly to the office for fittings were on everyone's speed dial. Feeling that perhaps she was falling down in this regard, Jane had tried ever so delicately to suggest . . .

"*DAMN* my tie!"

. . . and had never tried again.

An hour later he had stomped into her cubicle. "It's ridiculous: a man has to wear what is essentially a hangman's noose around his neck just because he works in an office! I don't like to feel choked, and if you feel the need to talk to me about my clothing, I'm going to return the favor and talk to you about why you wear the same three blouses and one damn skirt! Don't we pay you enough?"

A week after this, Jane was informed by HR that due to her exceptional performance so far, as detailed by her early performance appraisal conducted by Mr. Rosen, she would be moving up the pay scale ahead of schedule, and her annual salary would be—*effective immediately*—increased to . . .

"You didn't actually do a performance appraisal, did you?" Jane stated flatly, showing him the letter. He barely spared it a glance before turning back to the papers on his desk.

"I don't have time to go around appraising people and filling out bullshit forms. We don't pay you enough. The other assistants have nice, neat bosses with tidy ties and *GQ* haircuts, and you have to put up with me. You're probably the laughingstock of the watercooler. You should get paid more for it."

Knowing a thank-you would only irritate him, Jane simply walked back across the hall.

"Buy yourself some new clothes!" he shouted after her.

With her new income, she wasn't rich by any means, but it was more money than she'd ever imagined earning. She could move to a nicer apartment, get some new furniture, maybe a . . . but no.

Three months into this steady job had not been time enough to eradicate the pinch of fear that accompanied Jane's finances. She doubted any amount of money ever would.

She had a habit of calculating positives and negatives in advance: if X number of paychecks came in and she was able to save this much, then in six months' time she might have in savings . . . and then before the feeling of that possible future figure could buoy her up, she'd always flip to the inverse: if rent is raised, or the window air conditioner goes out and needs to be replaced, if she loses her job and the rent piles up, etc., until she was sufficiently cautioned into renewing her devotion to self-imposed austere budgeting. She was her own better angel and worst devil, perpetually scaring herself straight.

So no, she wouldn't go all out. The next paycheck still brought with it a measure of relief, and for Jane those deposits in her account twice a month were like magic. Mr. Rosen was temperamental, and this job could still end in disaster. Never mind that, secretly, she sometimes thought he might be getting sort of . . . well, *fond* of her. Dorky as that word was, nothing else fit. Lately, he seemed to almost smile when she came into his office every morning, and when he mocked her there was more teasing tone to it than actual bite.

Jane shook her head to clear her thoughts. That was ridiculous; he had just gotten used to her, that's all—or maybe she had gotten used to him, so his outbursts and swearing and storming around didn't bother her anymore. Not because he had softened toward her. She was essentially just a secretary with a fancy title. He was a preeminent lawyer.

So no, she would hoard this money and tuck it away into savings, in case she ever needed it. But surely she could use just a *little* bit to have some fun with. After all, she did need more clothes . . .

"Adele, would you like to go shopping?" That was okay to ask a coworker, right?

Adele made a curious noise of excitement and clapped her hands. "Oh, mon dieu! But of course, you need my help! You cannot keep wearing those 'orrible big blouses and baggy skirt. You could be so charmante. Not like I was when I was young, you are very . . . well . . . ! But in your *own* way you could be attractive. There is something, eh . . . romantique about you, like a painting. A waif with voluminous hair. We can work with that."

This was more enthusiasm than Jane had counted on.

Apparently, going on their lunch break would not be enough time, so Thursday after work found Jane not at a suburban mall this time but among the sleek, upscale shops of the Toronto Eaton Centre, flustered and exhausted as Adele dragged her from shop to shop, shoving her into fitting rooms with armfuls of clothing, pushing and pulling her into different dresses and tops, turning her this way and that, accompanied with critical remarks in French. If Jane had any shyness about her body, there was simply no tolerance for it.

"Chérie, I am a woman, too, and an old one at that. We are not competitors, I am not a man, and there is no need to hide from me." She ordered the saleswomen around with a dismissive wave of her hand, clucking at their poor taste. For a woman who spent her professional life answering the demands of powerful people, she certainly enjoyed having the shoe on the other foot, Jane thought.

Any protests were, of course, completely futile:

"It's too clingy!"

"You are skinny; clingy is only a problem when you show too much. You 'ave nothing to show but your collarbones, and we can work with that!"

"But Adele I don't wear makeup! It's too expensive to buy all the time, and I don't know how to put it on . . ."

"You're too . . . just a little rosy color for your lips, and your eyelashes are too fair for your complexion; you look like . . . This is painless to learn, just a little mascara and lipstick, very natural!"

Eventually, she just gave herself over to Adele's whirlwind. She wasn't fully comfortable, but she could appreciate that Adele was, in fact, painstakingly tailoring every choice to suit her, and not just picking what was fashionable. Warm, dark tones to contrast against her coloring, soft fabrics, feminine cuts ("you are too shy to look power-hungry in suits; it will make you look younger than you are, and like you are trying too hard"), everything fairly affordable, and durable to last more than one season.

Finally at an end, she tried to thank Adele for all her efforts, only to be cut off.

"This sort of project is what I live for! You are a nice girl and you need some help; you struggle like a pup in the jungle! Just don't tell the others I helped you. Let them think it was all on your own. Besides," she added as they said goodbye, "with that boss of yours, at least one of you should look professional!"

Jane waited until Monday to try out her new wardrobe. She chose a soft green woolly wrap dress, the ties nipping in at her slender waist ("Chérie," Adele had said, "when you are all waist and no hips, you *must* learn to work with that!"), and paired it with low-heeled black pumps. She did her minimalist makeup as instructed, wiping off the lipstick and reapplying it twice as her nerves got the better of her, fretting that it was too much. For the first time she decided to leave her hair down. She realized she liked how the light brown strands lying against her shoulders contrasted against the green of her dress. It was the first moment of feminine vanity she had ever experienced, and it surprised her, the little burst of pleasure it caused.

At work she tried not to blink too much around her mascara and concentrated on staying steady in her heels. This would take some getting used to. And the good-looking young man who had smiled flirtatiously at her on the train this morning? Well, if incidents like that were going to become a recurring thing, that would take some getting used to as well.

"Goddamn that goddamned traffic! Why in the bloody hell do they drive like they're in . . . RAINE!" She heard the *thwump* of his suit jacket hitting the floor and the *bang* of his office door bouncing off the wall after being swung open with too much force.

Heart rapidly beating in her chest, Jane picked up her notepad and walked across the hall into Mr. Rosen's office. She tried to remember Adele's advice: shoulders back, chin up, no shrinking in on yourself. She had every right to look how she wanted, or to change her look, or to do whatever she liked. It had nothing to do with him, and he probably wouldn't even notice. So there.

He was already seated behind his desk, buried in his papers, and hadn't noticed her come in.

"RAINE!"

"I'm right here, Mr. Rosen," she said calmly.

"Oh." He glanced up before looking back down at his papers. And then his head shot up again.

She had never seen Mr. Rosen surprised before, but she guessed this was pretty close to it. He stared stupidly while Jane fought not to blush and cover herself with her notepad.

There was a long, awkward pause. The seconds ticked by.

"Did you want to go over your schedule for this morning, sir?"

Finally seeming to snap to, he exhaled noisily and yanked at his tie.

"I . . . Yes. Of course I do. Don't ask stupid questions."

Jane said nothing in reply but sat down and began to go

through his lineup for the day, while Mr. Rosen sat hunched in his chair, shoulders tense, and kept his gaze firmly fixed on his desk.

". . . and a conference call with Mr. Lang. Please try to remember the time difference to China and keep your temper if he's a little groggy."

"Fine."

"That's it for today, sir." Jane rose from her seat to leave.

"Y'know I've offered to call him at 2 a.m. *my* time, so he can be fully awake for a change."

"Your temper is actually worse when you're tired, if that's possible," Jane reminded him dryly. "Last time you did a 2 a.m. call you nearly started a war with that company in France."

"They're French." He sulked. "Obviously, they overreacted. Look at all their revolutions."

"They had *one* revolution."

"And invented the guillotine while they were at it. Don't tell me that's not over the top."

Ignoring him, she turned to go.

"You got new clothes." He still wasn't looking at her but was staring at the pen he was fiddling with on his desk.

"Well . . ." Jane hesitated, and then unable to resist, she fired out: "I figured at least one of us should look professional."

The bark of his laughter followed her back to her desk.

It was nearing the end of the day, and Jane was desperately looking forward to going home. No matter how low and sensible the heels of her pumps, the arches of her feet still ached. She wanted to wash her mascara off and be able to rub her tired eyes freely. Adele assured her that after a few weeks in her new look she wouldn't notice these small discomforts, and even if she did, suffering for beauty was expected and understood by all women as part of their great feminine inheritance and acceptance into the divine sisterhood that was their womanly allure. Remembering Adele's great kindness toward her prevented Jane from rolling her eyes at this pronouncement, but she laughed to herself thinking about what Mr. Rosen's comment on it would be.

She just fervently hoped that Mr. Rosen didn't need her to stay late this evening. Her nice squashy couch and fluffy slippers were calling to her, and with just one more hour to go . . .

"Hey, Jane." Cristian from IT had just rounded the corner, a plethora of cables looped casually around his neck like Mardi Gras beads.

Wait, was it Cristian or Christopher? "Hi . . . there," Jane replied.

She still couldn't remember half the names of the people in this massive place. Christopher/Cristian had fixed her computer once or twice, and she could just about recall that he was several years younger than herself and a computer science graduate student on a co-op contract with the firm. He was also very good-looking—she'd once witnessed a trio of assistants mock fanning themselves and giggling to one another after he had sauntered by. There had followed a mortifying ten minutes trying to explain to Adele, whose English comprehension sometimes eluded her on double entendres, what their hard drive and RAM joke had meant.

"Real quick, just need to check a cord on your PC, routine

upgrade, doing all the cubicles on this floor," Christopher/
Cristian said.

"Oh, sure." Jane wheeled herself and her chair away from
her desk and stood up, inadvertently revealing her new look
once again.

It was obvious the appeal of her transformation was not
lost on Christopher/Cristian.

He leaned up against her cubicle partition, suddenly in no
hurry to check the cable, and subtly flexed his biceps. From the
practiced manner of his preening, Jane surmised that, yes, he
did in fact know how attractive he was.

"So, how's work going?"

"Uh, it's fine," Jane replied.

"Awesome. So I got the new iPhone last week, dual-camera
system, bionic chip."

Jane blinked. "Congratulations?"

"Yeah, it's pretty sweet. What kind of phone are you on?"
He gave a coy head tilt.

"Um, it's a phone? It makes calls."

"Cool, cool. Wanna skive off early and go have a drink?"

"What?"

"C'mon"—he gestured down the hall—"just leave early.
We'll go for a drink, end the workday. There's a nice little
pub . . ."

"I . . . I can't," said Jane, a little thrown. "I have another
hour of work."

"What, for that old bear? He never tracks what us low-end
get up to. Does he even notice you're here?"

It was lightly meant, but Jane jerked back, stung.

"Yes, he . . ." She could not say why she was hurt and uncomfortable but was saved further confusion when a deep voice rumbled in both their ears.

"I do, in fact, notice when the person who is here to assist me is no longer here. Shocking, I know. My powers of observation are second to none."

Christopher/Cristian and Jane both froze. Mr. Rosen continued on blithely. "Actually, when I say second to none, I mean second only to one, because last week Jane spotted a typo in a document that no less than six lawyers had reviewed and declared perfect. I might just fire them all. Just for the fun of it. What do you think, Alec?"

Alec! That's his name. Wow, I wasn't even close.

Alec gulped.

It had the earmarking of one of Mr. Rosen's epic scenes. Jane braced. Instead, though, Mr. Rosen seemed to take stock of the fear on Alec's face and restrained himself. He sighed and gestured to the cords Alec was still sporting. "Better get back to that. Everyone's job at this firm is important, and they should do it well."

The younger man nodded as frantically as his remaining dignity would allow and quickly fled the scene, clearly deciding he didn't need to update Jane's technology right then. Mr. Rosen sighed again. "I'd like to kick him down the stairs just for making me feel like an old Luddite."

Jane said, "I'm impressed you know his name."

Mr. Rosen laughed in reply. "He's the only one in IT brave enough to take my calls. The rest of them screen me to voice mail and then probably draw straws. He's one of the co-op students, right? It's a pilot program we started—taking in more than just students of law these days, got to modernize . . . although I draw the line at modernizing the coffee makers."

"Yes, yes, the coffee makers I know," Jane reminded him. "You made me write a memo." He laughed at her disgruntled expression and moved to return to his desk.

"Oh, wait, I have a message for you. A Mr. Steppenwolfe called, asked you to ring him back. I can't believe there's actually someone out there named 'Steppenwolfe.' It sounds like . . ." Jane cut off as soon as she looked up.

Mr. Rosen's relaxed demeanor had suddenly disappeared; he was tense, jaw clenched.

"It was a California number," he said lowly.

"Umm . . ." Jane consulted the number on her sticky pad and did a quick Google search. "Yes, Malibu area code," she confirmed, though he hadn't posed it as a question.

"They leave a message?"

"No, just the name and a number, and a request for you to call them back at your earliest convenience. Is everything okay?"

"Everything's fine." He breathed deeply. "Why don't you go home? You've had a long day, three back-to-back meetings, dealing with roving IT characters . . ." He smiled weakly. "If you catch up with Alec you could probably still have that date."

"What? Why? So he can tell me more about his bionic phone chip?" Jane said, irked at this encouragement.

"No, I . . . I just meant I shouldn't have interrupted. I was out of line and I had no right."

She stared. She was used to his rapid-fire mood changes, but this wasn't that. This was something else. She might have almost called it fear and guilt, but he covered it up so fast. "I mean it Raine; it's nothing. Go home." He meant it kindly, but the order was unmistakable.

"Yes, sir."

On the train ride home, Jane googled Steppenwolfe and the phone number he'd given. Nothing very alarming turned up: it was a law firm based in California, but with additional offices in Tokyo, London, and New York. Their website was sleek, with a minimalist white background and artistic photography of interior offices silhouetted against their respective skylines. Jane had thought the Rosen firm website was the epitome of sleek, but next to this, their stock photos and constrained tone and font looked positively dowdy. She wondered if the marketing team knew about firm websites like this. Was it possible to feel defensive on behalf of a firm she'd . . . silly, after only three months.

At home, she put it out of her mind. Time to take advantage of being home before eight, for once.

While still doubling down on resistance to any extravagances her newfound wealth might engender, after a long debate with herself, she'd conceded that painting the walls of her bedroom might be allowable. That bright red rug was putting to shame the brownish-white walls that'd she lived with since moving in. Last weekend, she had binge-watched YouTube home-decorating and how-to-paint videos and blogs, followed by a trip to the hardware store, where she'd carefully selected a cheap quality of sunny yellow paint, along with rollers, tape, drop cloths, and liners. Then there was a detour down another aisle where they kept various industrial-level tubes of glue; pieces of Lamp were still collected in a cardboard box hidden under her desk.

Tonight, she wanted to finish taping the baseboards and ceiling. By the upcoming weekend, maybe she could drag her bed and lone dresser to the center of the room and begin to actually paint. She ate a sandwich over the kitchen sink, eyeing the bleach stain on the counter from her first foray into cleaning many years ago, and hoped it wasn't an ominous sign of the success of this new project to come.

Why would he freak out over a California lawyer?

Chapter 9

The next morning, Mr. Rosen seemed back to his usual self.

That is to say, he swore and knocked over a stack of books when Jane informed him he'd missed a partners meeting.

But other than that he seemed fine. No mention of the mysterious phone call from yesterday or why it had upset him so much.

Trying not to feel nosy, Jane looked up the number again on her desk phone history. If Mr. Rosen called him back last night after she left, he would have had to dial long-distance. Charges for long-distance numbers had to be coded so that the expense could be charged to the appropriate file or client, or, if it was a personal call, to the partner's expense account. Jane kept an Excel sheet of just such codes, to reconcile with accounting at the end of every month.

She pulled the timekeeper app that tracked Mr. Rosen's outgoing phone calls and checked: he had dialed the California number at eight o'clock last night—so 5 p.m. their local time. The code associated with it was entered as BW 5232-8. Huh. She didn't know that one.

She consulted her Excel sheet. The code was there, in black and white, but where a descriptor should be, it was blank.

Curiouser and curiouser.

She pulled up the document management system that contained every Word document, email, memorandum, or Excel file related to a lawyer's work with a complicated and labyrinthine system of organization. The other assistants called it by its acronym, DM. Mr. Rosen called it "our evil overlord."

Jane typed in her assistant pass code that gave her access to Mr. Rosen's files, and keyed into the search bar BW 5232-8.

And . . . came up blank. *What?* No, not entirely blank; she clicked the message box.

This file has been restricted by order of E. W. Rosen.

Jane sat back in her chair, stumped. No corner of Mr. Rosen's work had been barred to her, not since October when she'd passed some invisible test of his and was declared worthy. Well, worthy-ish.

It seemed bizarre that he'd lock this down. It wasn't unheard of to hit restriction lines in DM. So many lawyers in the firm working on so many things, sometimes there was overlap between cases and clients, two teams working on something that the other wasn't legally allowed to see. In cases like that, restrictions were laid down in both DM and the records, any meetings in boardrooms had to be at opposite ends of the hall with locks on the doors should papers be laid out, and the receptionist became a traffic cop, ensuring no one encountered the other going to and fro with the clients. The lawyers called it an "ethical wall" and were regularly inspected on it by the powers that be.

But Jane knew every case Mr. Rosen was on, and he had none that merited such a wall. What was so private that no one could see it? So important it involved him tangling in DM where he had always steadfastly refused to go?

"Raine!" She jumped at his voice and quickly closed the browser down. Why did she feel guilty? She could just ask him.

"Raine," he bellowed as he crossed from his office to her desk. "Are you hungry for lunch? Gerry is in the city today. I thought we could have lunch at the National Club."

Gerry was Professor Gerald Graham, a semiretired law professor who still occasionally lectured at Osgoode Hall Law School, a few subway stops north from Bay Street. He sometimes consulted for the firm, but his relationship with Mr. Rosen ran much deeper than that. He called Mr. Rosen "Eddy," had known him since he was a boy, and treated him with an almost paternal kindness. He didn't seem the least perturbed by any of his outbursts, although there were certainly far fewer when Gerry was around; Mr. Rosen seemed happier, a little calmer, smiling warm and friendly, and basking in Gerry's approval when he praised him.

Jane secretly adored him. He always wore a bow tie and waistcoat, and his manners were as gentle and antiquated as his clothing might suggest. They were introduced when Jane was administrating at another droning meeting. Gerry had pulled out her chair for her to begin with, and then later glared at a young junior associate who had carelessly tossed his brief across the table for Jane to collect when the meeting concluded. Professor Graham was such in the legal community that that glare was sufficient to wring a sheepish apology and a more considered handing over of documents from everyone else.

The few times he had been in the office, he had stopped to chat and ask about her day. So many clients and partners seemed to regard her as if she were no more sentient than a filing cabinet. He always called her "my dear," which Diane from HR overheard once and remarked on later in the elevator that day as "old-world sexist bullshit." Jane had shot back that kindness was kindness and politically correct language could hide an unkind person just the same. Diane had sniffed and turned back to her phone.

To hear that Gerry was coming today was a treat.

"You want me to book you lunch at the National Club?"

"No, I want you to join us for lunch at the National Club. But also, yes, could you make the reservation too?"

That pulled her up short.

"Why am I invited? Is it a work-related meeting?"

Mr. Rosen smiled at her like she was being precious. "Sure, let's say that. Bring your pad and pen. But also, Gerry likes you, and it'll be nice to have lunch without subjecting him to just me and my ranting the whole time. Do us both a favor and vary the conversation a little. Besides, you've never been inside the National Club. Do you know women were only allowed to become members after 1992?"

"That doesn't make me want to go."

He laughed. "You'll love it. It's super historical. Let's do one thirty."

"Mr. Rosen . . ." Delighted as Jane was to be invited to lunch with Gerry (surely the idea was just one of Mr. Rosen's random impulsive moods; not many assistants were allowed to partake of meetings like this, although Adele, from her long-standing tenure with Mr. Breck, was sometimes treated with something approaching equality by both him and his clients), Jane was still stuck on the mystery of code BW 5232-8. "Mr. Rosen, what client is BW 5232-8?"

The smile died on his face, though he recovered it in the next instant.

"What's this now? BMW?"

"BW 5232-8. It's in your timekeeper app and on DM, but there's no descriptor and I can't get access to anything to do with it. Is it for a client?"

"Madam Raine, not everything needs your magic touch of perfect organization. That's private. Leave BW 5232-8 alone, all right? It doesn't concern you."

"So I'm 'Madam Raine' now, am I?" Jane said dryly, immediately sensing she needed to back off, despite his friendly tone.

"Ms. Raine, then. Ms. Jane Raine. Hey, did you know your name rhymes?"

"Really? I'd never noticed."

"All right, Madam Sarcasm, what's the full handle, then? Middle name?"

"Why do you need my middle name?"

"I'm mischievous and charming."

"Annoying and nosy." He grinned. And Jane could tell he was pleased to have redirected the conversation. "Go away. I have a reservation to make. Or I'll tell Professor Graham you've been misbehaving."

"Nah, no need. He already likes you better than me." He

seemed pleased at that fact, and walked away whistling, hands in his pockets.

The National Club, of which Mr. Rosen was a vetted and approved member, appeared out of nowhere, wedged between two soaring modern buildings, like something time forgot. Jane was unescapably reminded of Diagon Alley, when Harry Potter's magical ancient wizarding buildings mysteriously rose up in modern-day London.

It was no more than four stories tall, a redbrick and white columned Georgian building, with recessed, white-trimmed windows, and a flight of stone steps flanked by short wrought iron gates leading to the front door.

Once inside, Jane immediately relaxed. She had been expecting marble-lined opulence, like the firm decor, or sleek and chic modernity, like some of the other lunch places Mr. Rosen frequented, which she'd seen when she'd googled pictures online. The restaurant Canoe, for instance, was lodged in the penthouse of a nearby tower, with sweeping, magnificent views of Lake Ontario from every table and upscale minimalist decor.

But the National Club was cozy, cramped. Sure, it retained some grandeur, but it was from a different era, one that had long begun to fade.

The front room had a massive fireplace, roaring in the November chill. Burgundy leather upholstered armchairs, dotted with scratched brass studs, stood scattered around, the surfaces old and cracking. A dark wood bar ran the length of one side of the room, and there was a low table nearby, laid out with things for tea. The walls were wood panels, and a thin, patterned red carpet lay underfoot. The windows facing the street were foggy and warped, bisected by lead piping in diamond panes. Somewhere nearby a clock ticked, and the receptionist, who was ensconced in what was really no more than a cubby, a bite out of the front hall, smiled at Mr. Rosen and Jane in a friendly way.

"Professor Graham is already here. Go right on up."

Mr. Rosen held out a hand for Jane to precede him up the wide wooden staircase that lazily curled through the building. Jane was reminded of her father's old building on campus where he lectured, a grand relic of the 1800s, made soft and shabby by centuries of students, though the impressive bones remained.

"They've been in this building since 1896," Mr. Rosen murmured to her as they ascended the stairs, confirming Jane's impression. It made her feel comfortable but a little homesick, in a way she didn't want to examine too closely.

The small bistro-style dining room was on the fourth floor, and Jane was beginning to wobble from climbing stairs in her heels by the time they got there. An old elevator was available down on the first floor, but it, too, looked more like a relic than something Jane was comfortable riding in.

Professor Graham was sitting at a table, completely at ease, reading a newspaper. He smiled his genial smile at them and rose to pull out Jane's chair.

"Hello, hello, my dear, what a treat. The young man over there was just telling me that they have a lovely salmon special today."

He sat down again and patted the back of Mr. Rosen's hand in a fatherly manner. "Keeping busy?"

"Always."

"Good boy. Now, how about that salmon? No, I'm not asking you, Eddy. I know you'll eat anything pulled out of the sea."

Lunch passed enjoyably. Very enjoyably. Which was a surprise: Jane had been waiting, expecting some business to be discussed that she would need to pull out her notes for, and when that didn't manifest, she worried she'd be an awkward interloper, a third wheel with no business being there and no part in the conversation, but instead the conversation moved smoothly. Professor Graham with his Victorian manners was more than considerate and kind; he was an expert in so many subjects, and an excellent storyteller, and he kept Jane laughing with stories of his students. He also asked her some gentle questions about herself—Jane wasn't sure if that was mere manners to give her a chance to speak; it seemed as if he was genuinely trying to get to know her, but why?—and just as gently backed off when she showed the least discomfort at giving answers.

"Fort Knox, this one." Mr. Rosen rolled his eyes. "Doesn't give away anything. I'm still working on getting her full name."

"For a man that regularly brawls and threatens and says and does things that would get you canceled on Twitter, discretion in your assistant is probably much to be valued," Professor Graham said dryly.

"Gerry, you know what cancel culture is? Good god, man, are you and your ancient bones on Twitter?"

Over dessert of angel cake with custard and Ontario strawberries, Mr. Rosen stepped away to take a phone call. Cell phone conversations were only permitted in designated areas of the club.

Professor Graham leaned back in his chair and turned his twinkling eyes on Jane with an air of beneficent shrewdness.

"I hope he's not working you too hard."

Jane smiled softly and shook her head.

"And life in the firm, the other employees? Everyone playing nice on the playground? I remember what it was like; before I became a professor I worked in one of those firms; in fact, I worked in your firm."

"You worked at Rosen, Haythe & Thornfield?"

"Yes, I did, when I was a younger man. I realized it wasn't for me, went into teaching. I was there for a good ten years, though. I used to be friends with Eddy's father. I've known Eddy since he was a boy."

This was fascinating. And explained so much of their relationship. Then Jane remembered what Adele had said, about Mr. Rosen's father not being a good man.

"He doesn't talk about his father." She was baiting him, like Mr. Rosen did to people, she realized, and Gerry seemed to know that but played along.

"No. He wouldn't. I stayed in touch with Eddy and his mother—both his parents have passed away now—but my friendship with his father died soon after it had begun. He was not a good man."

Jane was inexplicably reminded of the pang that had gone through her the night Lamp broke, when Mr. Rosen spoke of hospitals and domestic abuse. It was nothing, just a feeling; it had no basis in facts, and she couldn't ask that of this man, it was so grossly personal . . .

Professor Graham's eyes were flicking back and forth over her face, as if he were reading lines in a book. His expression was uncharacteristically serious.

"Eddy was a lovely lad, clever as they come, and his mother was a nice lady. They used to live a few blocks down from me and my wife in Rosedale."

Rosedale was an old-money but understated neighborhood in the north of Toronto.

"He'd come over sometimes after school, or hang out at the office waiting for his dad, when he got a little older. After my wife and I moved away, and Eddy was in university, we kept in touch." He sighed. "I don't know what their home life was like, Jane. I don't want to assume the worst of a man I've shaken hands with, but I worked with Julian Rosen in the office, and after a few years, it was enough. Eddy's nothing like him, you know. He's a good man."

"Why are you telling me all of this?" Jane asked. "I mean, I appreciate it, but I'm just his assistant."

He smiled. "I love the boy, but he does go about things backward."

What?

"So that's over and done with!" Mr. Rosen had come back, and no further conversation was possible. "Did I miss dessert?"

It was raining gently when they said their goodbyes, and Jane frowned, thinking about her mascara.

"C'mon, we'll take the PATH," Mr. Rosen said.

"It connects to this building too? Where? I haven't seen it."

"Of course you haven't. It's a very big secret, and also you're terrible at the PATH. Seriously, every time you say you're going down there I worry we'll never see you again and I'll have to send out a search party."

Jane scowled and he laughed. They took a staircase down into the lower levels of the building, past some meeting rooms and lavatories, and then several more steps down into a long, empty corridor with wood-paneled walls and a red carpet. At the end of this very long corridor was a heavy wood door, and from it they emerged, blinking, into the modern glare of the busy PATH. Jane turned back around, half expecting the door to vanish. It was still there, but so discreetly tucked behind a pillar, its aged wood frame an anomaly with its surroundings, just as the façade of the club up on the street level had been.

Freaking Diagon Alley. Jane smiled. Mr. Rosen was right; she did like the National Club.

On the walk back to the office, Mr. Rosen resumed their conversation in trying to guess her middle name.

"Eleanor? No. Something weird and celebrity-crazed like Apple? Applonia?"

"Is that even a name?"

"You'd be surprised what people name their kids, in the quest to be unique."

The tortoiseshell designer glasses paused in her interminable typing when they walked in together and eyed them with surprise. Jane wasn't sure why. Two partners passing on the stairs paused their conversation as well, when Jane and Mr. Rosen walked by, Mr. Rosen still gently ribbing her. A sliver of self-consciousness slid up Jane's spine. She didn't know what they'd done to cause the looks, but she felt sure something unpleasant would come of it.

T wo days later, something unpleasant did crop up, but it wasn't from the other firm members.

"I googled you, y'know," Mr. Rosen said one morning, as they sat in his office while Jane proofed a memo. He looked sly. It was his "I've been clever and you're about to find out why" face. She'd seen this face a lot during boardroom smackdowns with opposing counsel.

"What?"

"I googled you. Jane Raine. Found your father's obit. 'Professor Joseph Raine, dies prematurely of heart failure. Leaves behind one daughter, Jane Raine, age 13.'"

Jane stared at him, unmoving.

"Why didn't you tell me your father was Professor Raine?" He continued cheerfully, as if this were some common conversational detail that she'd carelessly omitted. "My god, your old man was famous. Brilliant and famous. Everyone studies his books. You're a smart woman, clearly got some of his brainpower, who knows how much—you're so quiet sometimes I have trouble reading you—so what are you doing taking crap from me for a living?"

He smiled encouragingly, but his smile quickly faded. To her utter mortification, Jane realized tears were stinging her eyes. *Oh god, now, NOW is when I have a breakdown? No.*

Her lips trembled. She would not cry. Absolutely, positively would not cry. She managed a watery glare, but unable to sustain it, turned on her heel and, as calmly as possible, fled to her desk.

In the semiprivacy of her cubicle, she took deep calming breaths. Focus on the present, focus on the job. Mr. Rosen's emails were piling up. They needed to be cleaned out.

Jane worked diligently at her task for over an hour, refusing to let her mind slide into any other thoughts. Mr. Rosen quietly left for a meeting (which she didn't remind him about attending, because she'd had about enough of him for one morning, thank you, and so was rather surprised that he remembered to go at all) and then quietly returned to his office. He didn't disturb her once.

It was late afternoon when she started to feel edgy. They had spent the day avoiding, frozen, not in their usual flow of bellowing and nagging. It was starting to unnerve her. Just as she decided that she couldn't take it anymore, that she would have to give in and be the first to crack, he finally approached.

He knocked softly on the cubicle wall (this was a first. He never knocked . . . like, *anywhere*. Jane was 90 percent certain the firm gossip of him bursting into a bathroom stall to keep ranting at a partner about tort law was totally true) before sitting down in the chair opposite her. She was still angry at him, still embarrassed at her own reaction, and so kept her eyes trained on the desk. He waited patiently. *I could refuse to make eye contact all day, buddy.*

"Raine."

Dammit.

She looked up and was struck by the expression on his face. It was one she'd never seen on him before. Remorse. Shame.

Contrition. As if he'd unwittingly lashed out and kicked a puppy and had only now realized it. Which Jane considered ironic, because the women at reception had a long-running joke that he could and probably did kick puppies in his spare time.

"Raine, I . . ." He hesitated, wet his lips, and tried again. "Raine. I'm sorry." Never had he seemed so unsure of himself. "That was unspeakably rude of me, and incredibly insensitive. I can't believe I made light of your father's death. That I degraded the work you do here. That's exactly the kind of privileged rich kid behavior I've always hated, and then I went and did it." He took a shallow breath and plowed on. "You . . . are a great assistant. The best. Who else but you could have put up with me for this long?" His attempt at a grin became a grimace as the humor fell flat. "I had no right to pry into your background, or to treat your personal information so disrespectfully. And I'm . . . I'm sorry."

Finished, he waited for her response, but Jane stayed silent. Moved by his apology, shocked to have received one, she battled the urge to forgive him. But oh, it was hard. He looked like a lost little boy. "Jane, you know I'm an asshat, right? And *I* know I'm an asshat, who doesn't deserve to be forgiven . . . but will you please forgive me anyway?"

He was so sincere.

"You are an . . . asshat," Jane said at last and watched him wince, "but I forgive you."

He exhaled with relief and gave her a hesitant smile.

Jane briskly shuffled the papers on her desk to give herself a distraction and break the increasing intimacy of the moment. "We're good. So you can go back to your office now." Best not to let him off the hook too easy. And she needed time to process . . . well, this.

He nodded at her dismissal and rose to leave.

"Why were you googling me anyway?" she asked, unable to stop herself.

He smiled ruefully. "I told you: I have trouble reading you. You're a mystery. I wanted to know who you were, where you'd come from, what you'd been up to before you showed up here one day to throw coffee at me and become my proper yet witty assistant . . ."

"I didn't *throw* coffee at you; you broke the machine . . ."

". . . I was curious. But next time I'll wait for the information to come from you. I have to earn your good opinion, so you'll trust me with it. I'd prefer that method to Google anyway."

He walked back across the hall, leaving Jane to think about that last statement.

Chapter 10

That night at home, in her sunny yellow bedroom with her plush red rug, Jane sat and thought about things she hadn't thought of in years.

Jane Raine's standard for living had been simply "survive" for so long it was sometimes a struggle to remember a time before.

But there had been a time before.

Professor Joseph Raine had been a distinguished academic. People liked to say he had produced one daughter and many books and couldn't tell the difference between them. He loved his daughter, but he approached parenting like he did his academic pursuits: with affection, complete absorption, even brilliance, but only a scatterbrained mindfulness of reality. So little Jane lived in the university just the same as the books, and her adored and adoring father homeschooled her.

And then Professor Raine died. So quick and so quiet, it was like breathing in and neglecting to breathe out. And the real world came for Jane.

The faculty whispered that Dean Richards might have preferred a more prolonged and lasting illness. Nothing painful, but enough time to get affairs in order. As it was, there was no will, no appointed executor, no money beyond a small saved sum from the immediate sales of his last book (that Jane had used mostly for first and last month's rent deposit at age eighteen), and no instructions whatsoever about guardianship of his child. As dean, and the person most closely acquainted with Raine's affairs, he was executor of the mess.

Jane remembered standing in his personal study located in the east wing of the university's main building after the funeral. It was a dark oak-paneled room, circular in shape, and the richness of the walls, the heavily laden bookcases, and the sweeping bay window could almost overpower the sight of the cracked linoleum floor. The dean had rubbed his bald head as he regarded her, and longingly eyed his scotch.

He explained to Jane that her father had been a great man, that his brilliant mind and brilliant work had to be preserved, immortalized. In the wake of his death they needed to look after his legacy. He made it sound like they were in this together, her and him. But Jane found the rest of that meeting had curious little to do with her, more like he was talking to himself, a list of what needed to be done. Her father had had a similar self-conversing habit. The first concern was precisely which bench on the main quad should be dedicated to Professor Raine's memory. Next, who would arrange to have hardcover copies of his books placed in a position of honor in the main library. Thirdly, who could lay claim to Raine's papers? Lastly, and perhaps this should have come first, what to do with Jane?

Jane's mother had died soon after Jane was born, and Jane was the professor's only souvenir from that one brief foray into the outside world that had brought him a wife. No relatives would be likely to step forward. There were no friends but his colleagues who taught alongside him, and they either had their own children, or they were old and solitary and in need of care themselves. Certainly not fit to take on a young girl of thirteen. That's what Dean Richards told her when he became aware of her presence in his office again.

There was an apologetic bend to this last bit of explanation, but still, he carried the air of a man simply being reasonable, and surely she would understand the necessity of his decision. He hunched over as he spoke, trying to bring himself to eye level with a girl too tall to be a child but still several inches short of an adult. "I'm sorry, Jane," was how he finished. And that was how Jane Raine found out she was to be uprooted from the university and replanted into foster care.

Everyone had agreed it was awful, but quicker still, everyone agreed there was nothing to be done, and they solaced themselves with finger sandwiches and comparing notes on dear old Raine's last lecture as they mingled at the wake. At the funeral itself, everyone hugged Jane and no one would look at her, while the lady who ran the home fussed with a rapid-fire whisper into her ear.

"Now, sweetheart, we have to be a big girl and put on a brave face. You say 'thank you' to everyone who gives you condolences, and be sure to stand next to the coffin—the head of the coffin, not where his feet . . . What? Well if it's a closed casket, it's not my fault if you can't tell which end is which. Just stand to the side that has more flowers, I guess—until we're ready to start the service. Don't wrinkle your nose at the flowers; they're from people who cared for your daddy, and they also, ah . . . well, never mind that; just don't wrinkle your nose like that, and don't tug at your dress. Just because it's black doesn't mean it won't show wrinkles. Okay, now, chin up, be sure to shake Professor Patrick's hand—good grief couldn't he find a decent tie? That one's just—shake his hand like an adult. We want Daddy to be proud of us now, don't we?"

First encounters with the world outside campus were not promising, and nothing that followed disproved those misgivings. In later years, in those rare instances when Jane thought about her time in care, she would tell herself it wasn't that bad, that other kids in the system had it far worse. That she wasn't molested or beaten or abused. Technically, she didn't starve, although she can't remember ever being *full*; the foster-kid diet seemed to consist mainly of mac and cheese out of the box. Some of the foster parents were genuinely good people: retired teachers, Samaritans, or religious couples. A lot of them were not.

Sometimes sharper memories rushed in. How there was never enough of anything, never enough shampoo or soap, so her hair was never quite clean, clothes were never quite clean; wearing the same grungy thing to school day after day. Never enough winter gear, so she was always cold and pinched until spring came. Never enough money for school trips, for trips to the movies, for an ice cream with friends, if it was possible to make any friends when everyone at school could spot a foster kid a mile off.

The homes themselves blurred together, with too many kids, yelling and crying, someone with the flu, someone being carted off to a new home. Dingy walls and grubby furniture, and bedrooms shared with other girls who smoked cigarettes and weed and tried to sneak boys in at night and frightened Jane. The carpets were always some off-shade pink or green turned brownish, and footsteps sounded crunchy with all that was stuck to their surface, chips, bits of Pop-Tarts, and stale toast crumbs. The bathroom and kitchen counters were gunky, and Jane's strongest memory was the smell of something over-ripe with fast-food grease that seemed to permeate nearly every home.

For years she felt a part of the grunge with greasy hair and baggy clothes, food stains on her jeans, sticky skin, and smelling overripe like the house. She remembered having dirty fingernails and gray-tinged skin with bags under her eyes . . . a sixteen-year-old going on fifty, a slimy half-drowned-looking thing. She kept her mouth shut, her eyes on the ground, sat in the back of the class, and slunk from school to work to home. "Quiet" read the social worker's notes, "compliant" and "slightly disengaged but nothing to cause alarm. Schoolwork is acceptable, maintains a part-time job."

Jane couldn't recall if she was "compliant" or not; all she could remember is feeling ugly and humiliated, unwilling to make friends with any of the other foster kids. She didn't want to be one of them. She'd rather be invisible.

Grief had transformed to a kind of numbness and an inherent practical instinct to survive.

Those first few months in foster care, Jane raged inside herself. *How could Dad have been so naive, so stupid to keep me coddled and insulated and so safe for thirteen years, and then to just die and leave me with nothing? Did he think he would live forever, that he never had to plan for me? Was I some kind of pet? Like when people move homes and they're going into some condo that doesn't allow animals, so they just leave the cat outside on moving day, and then after they're gone it wanders around the neighborhood and joins the other strays. How could my father—how could any of them—leave me without protection?* She tortured herself for months wondering, if she had been five, and not thirteen, if she had been a child and not a ripening teenager, would she still have been discarded?

The cheapness and misery she was taught stuck with her like a curse. She hoarded her little bit of money with something like panic at the thought of spending it. Two years out of foster care and living on her own, she still couldn't allow herself enough food or shampoo or soap, still existing as that gray, greasy thing that looked like it had crawled out of the sewer. She went back and forth to work and did nothing else. In her little apartment, she couldn't adjust to the quiet and isolation after those houses full of kids, so she sat up half the night terrified and listening for noises, and went to work drained every morning. Things went on like this for some time. It was as if surviving foster care had exhausted her, and she needed time to recover.

But I did recover, Jane thought, and tried to feel pride at the meager accomplishment.

She got used to living alone; she bought better locks and learned to sleep through the night. She cleaned up—first the apartment, then herself. She started a routine of giving her place a good scrubbing every week and found it gave her a sense of calm and control. She learned to care if her clothes had food stains and if they fit somewhat properly. She cut her hair shorter, cleaned her nails, ironed her shirts. It was an uphill battle, hard to get back into those habits. What most people take for normal behaviors, like showering on a regular basis, she needed to relearn. There was still that huge white stain on one side of the kitchen counter from the bleach experiment. Her first attempts at cooking a healthy meal had almost ended with the fire extinguisher. And she had firmly, and decisively, shut the door on those bad memories. Her efforts paid off, and eventually, Jane began to resemble something like she remembered herself to be. Or should have been. Something more recognizable.

So, who was she now?

She sat in her sunny yellow bedroom and got no sleep that night.

For two days after the incident, Mr. Rosen was, Jane came to realize, on his best behavior. There was no yelling, no door slamming, no throwing of pens or paperwork, and minimal swearing. He went to meetings on time, and without reminder. He didn't make a single person cry, and Jane did not have to write any apology notes. He did not verbally or physically attack the coffee machine. On the third day of this strangeness, Isla, one of the assistants from down the hall who sat next to Adele, and whom Jane was now on friendly terms with, grabbed her arm when they were alone in the elevator and asked what drug she had been slipping into Mr. Rosen's coffee.

"What?"

"Seriously, we've all been talking about doing it for years, but we couldn't figure out the logistics. Is it in the coffee itself, like a liquid sedative? Or is it like a pill you grind up and put in the bottom of his cup?"

"I'm not drugging him!"

"Okay, I get it. Plausible deniability." She winked as they exited the elevator together into the office.

Jane rolled her eyes and stormed off to her desk. She waited until 9:00 a.m. when Mr. Rosen strolled in, calmly bid her good morning, and seated himself in his office. Enough was enough. She walked across the hall and smacked her notepad with his morning schedule down on his desk.

"Whatever you're doing, stop it. Right now."

"Doing what?"

"Don't play innocent. This! This . . . being nice and polite and normal. It's freaking me out."

"I can't be polite?"

"People think I'm drugging you!" He snorted at that. "I'm serious! I just got asked if I'm using pills or liquid tranquilizers!"

He sighed with exasperation. "I wasn't . . . I'm just trying to . . . When I misbehave, I know you get more work. I'm trying to give you less of a hard time. That's all."

"Well stop!" Jane exclaimed. "I don't like it!"

"You don't?" he asked, genuinely perplexed.

Jane paused as the truth of her words hit. She didn't like it. Sure, the job had been easier for the past three days, but it was also . . . boring. The day dragged on with only the monotone of administrative duties to fill her time. It was like the restaurant all over again. The dulling sensation of repeating the same tasks over and over again, before going home to a lifeless, quiet apartment. The chaos Mr. Rosen created had been stressful to deal with at first, but then it had become exciting. Life had become colorful.

More than that, *he* was colorful. She had never met anyone who so adamantly did not give a damn what other people thought. It was liberating. He was noisy and messy and energetic. It was lively and invigorating and fun. He was blunt like a baseball bat to the head, but he was honest, open; you knew where you stood with him always, and you could be honest and say what you thought in turn. He was stubborn to the point of ridiculous. It was frustrating, but reassuring. He was constantly talking to inanimate objects: his desk, his old nemesis the coffee maker, and Lamp (still being mourned by him, unaware of a slow reconstruction process happening under Jane's desk. She was hoping to give it to him for Christmas). It was endearing and it made her laugh. He was a smart-ass . . . well, so was she, she had discovered. She liked their banter.

"Mr. Rosen, you and 'normal' have never really been on speaking terms. And I've gotten used to it, so let's just keep it that way, all right?"

A small, crooked smile stretched across his face. "You're actually okay with me . . . as is?" he asked. There was something strangely hopeful in his voice.

"Just . . . whatever, dial down the Stepford behavior, okay?"

The smile became a full-blown grin, his look suddenly as mischievous as ever. "I knew you liked me."

Jane rolled her eyes but couldn't help smiling. "I tolerate you, Mr. Rosen. Don't get carried away."

"I think you mean: 'Why, Mr. Rosen, you are positively delightful as your natural self, and I adore you.' Why, thank you, Jane. I am rather adorable, aren't I?"

"Are you bantering with yourself?" she asked, amused.

"Impressive, isn't it?"

She shook her head, exasperated, and went back to her desk. Within twenty minutes he was bellowing about jammed staplers. Alone in her cubicle, she smiled.

A week or so later, they were going over his travel arrangements—a trip to Montreal in December—when Jane decided to burst the remaining tension and let the whole episode go.

"I was put in foster care."

"What?" He looked up from his iPhone.

"After my father died. There was no will, we had no relations, Mum died when I was a baby, and all Dad's friends were old, retired, geriatric professors. No one wanted a thirteen-year-old girl. Famous Dr. Raine's offspring or not. So the court put me in foster care. Several different ones, actually. You kind of get moved around if no one comes to collect you." She tried to say all this matter-of-factly. She didn't want to sound like a sob story. He might start acting normal again out of pity.

"Foster care," he repeated. There was no reading his tone.

"I mean, it wasn't like a Dickensian workhouse; it just wasn't pleasant. I don't like to talk about it." She took a breath. "Anyway, now you know."

His face was contemplative but guarded, giving nothing away. "Well, that's a shitty thing to have happened to you. And after foster care?"

She explained to him the after-care transitioning that was offered once she aged out of the system, her job as a waitress, and then her own foray into school.

"No family whatsoever?"

Jane simply shook her head.

"Friends? A boyfriend?" Jane merely blinked at him. "Jane, you may say it's not a Dickensian novel, but you're sounding a little like Oliver Twist to me." Her attention snagged on her name and she didn't answer. It was the first time he'd called her just Jane. "Well, who watches your cat when you're away?"

"I don't have a cat." And I don't have anywhere *away* to go, she silently added. Mr. Rosen swore quietly under his breath and rubbed the back of his neck. "You're not going to start being nice again, are you?" she asked with trepidation. "Because we discussed that. I don't like it."

"No, I couldn't keep that up much longer, even if I tried. And now I know what you've . . . I get that you're probably used to rougher treatment than I give you. I wondered why you never flinched, when others run crying from the room."

"Well . . ." Jane wanted this conversation over. "Enjoy your evening. You're taking a potential client to the symphony, and I've booked dinner at Reds. It's a nice night, so you can probably walk." She turned to leave.

"Y'know, in the end of *Oliver Twist*, the orphaned child gets a family."

"I've read the book," she replied.

"Oliver gets a happy ending."

Jane paused in his doorway. "It's fiction, Mr. Rosen. And I'm not a child anymore."

Chapter 11

So it's just you and him alone in that little hallway all day while he makes ridiculous demands?"

"I didn't mean to make it sound that bad."

"Uh, it sounds like a hostage situation."

A surprise phone call one Saturday morning had turned out to be her old boss, Marianne, who was asking if Jane wanted to pick up some shifts over the Christmas holidays.

"Just some weekends, maybe Boxing Day," she said. "Everyone I've got on staff now is shit. And they're all asking for holiday time off. You could have some extra cash in your pocket, even if your fancy new job pays well."

A large part of Jane shuddered at the thought of that rasp of polyester polo shirt settling across her back once more. She'd moved forward, and it was hard-won territory; turning back felt wrong on so many levels.

On the other hand, the lure of extra cash never lost its appeal. She looked around at the ongoing paint job in her kitchen. The sunny yellow bedroom had turned out so well, she was now slowly turning her kitchen mint green, with white trim.

There was a matching green plate set at Ikea; she could gift it to herself for Christmas and not even mind the expense if she had the extra cash. In fact, it wasn't even expensive, so she could probably afford it out of the tips that came in, and instead, she could spend the money on a short holiday, now that she was in possession of a three-week paid vacation. Maybe she could take the Via Rail train down to Ottawa in February, see the Winterlude festival for the first time, or go a little farther in August to Montreal, spend a hot week in the summer walking along the St. Lawrence River.

As she looked at the cheerful green paint on the wall and thought of her hypothetical vacation and the upcoming firm holiday party, she felt life was manageable and good. Mr. Rosen might well call her Oliver Twist, but she had these simple pleasures now, and it would be enough. She would not be brought down by revisiting her past. The feeling of goodwill overflowed in her, extending to even Marianne, whom she had formerly been ambivalent about.

That or I'm high on paint fumes. Better open a window.

"It's not a hostage situation. If anything, that would make him the hostage. Yesterday, I didn't let him leave his office until he'd signed all his expense reports for the week. It was a total tantrum." She tucked the phone between her shoulder and ear and struggled to throw up the window sash.

"Uh, okay. Is he at least hot?"

The question brought her up short, and she would blame that on the reason she caught her finger in the window track and swore.

"He's not . . . not attractive, I guess. I mean, he's my boss."

But the question went spinning through her mind, like there was more to it than Marianne's usual rapacious appetite for attractive men.

"Ugh, if you have to spend all that time with him, he should at least be an eight."

And they *were* spending a lot of time together, Jane mused. Lately, Mr. Rosen had adopted a new habit of sometimes ordering enough food for two. Whenever Jane decided to eat at her desk, rather than brave the lunchroom, Mr. Rosen suddenly found himself "starving" and sent her scurrying out to pick up a lunch order from one local place or another, the fragrant bags she brought back always full to bursting with food.

"Guess my eyes were bigger than my stomach. Even a man my size can't eat all this," he said the first time, arms spread wide to indicate the bounty of takeout containers on his desk. There was enough food for four people comfortably. When Jane merely blinked at him, he yanked a second chair over to his desk with a grunt. "Sit down. Eat."

She felt awkward, not sure if she should serve herself, mindful of taking too much despite the huge quantities, and cringing at the mess. She glanced over, hoping to take cues from him, but Mr. Rosen simply tucked into the food with gusto, ignoring her completely. So she did the same and nearly moaned at the flavors. It was absolutely delicious. Roast beef sandwiches with gravy, the meat piled high and still hot, with a rich smoky flavor, on a fresh kaiser roll. There were smaller containers of fries, onion rings, coleslaw, potato salad, and dill pickles. Infinitely better than anything she had tasted at her own restaurant. She stuffed herself to the brim, choosing to ignore Mr. Rosen's wry smile.

It happened a dozen more times after that, the invitation

always confined to that barked order. "Sit. Eat." There were croque monsieur sandwiches from a French restaurant one day, steak-and-mushroom pies the next. Two weeks later, there was seafood pasta with scallops, shrimp, and mussels imported from the Maritime Provinces. It delighted Mr. Rosen when she confessed to never having eaten a mussel before, and he burst out with his sudden laugh when she scrunched up her face at the first taste.

"Anything else you won't eat?" he inquired with a good-natured grin, watching her put the remaining mussels aside.

"Burgers," Jane told him.

"Why?"

"I was a waitress, remember? We served a lot of burgers. I got sick of them."

"Where did you waitress?"

"Chain place in the suburbs. You wouldn't know it."

"For how long?"

"Long enough to hate burgers."

He left it at that.

He ordered no burgers, but the roast beef—her favorite—made several reappearances. It was just as tasty each time, and Mr. Rosen seemed equally enamored of it, tearing into his sandwich with an almost visceral relish, licking the gravy off his fingers afterward.

And Jane did her best not to watch.

These thoughts of impromptu private lunches with Mr. Rosen were abruptly halted by the cold blast of icy winter air suddenly swirling in from the window Jane had finally shuddered open. That, and the realization that Marianne was still on the phone.

"Look, Marianne, I'll let you know about the holiday shifts. Thanks for thinking of me though."

They said their goodbyes and hung up, and Jane resumed her painting, making steady, even strokes that soothed, as stained brownish white became lines of green. It was turning out even better than she hoped. As she rolled paint, she thought.

The firm holiday party was next week, December 15. Already tinsel and colored lights, mini potted fake Christmas trees, plastic menorahs, and the electric black, red, and green candles of Kwanzaa were all around the office and people's workstations. The reception area was kept bare, and only a few white, feathered wreaths that were meant to "symbolize peace and hope," according to HR, were allowed, as the client-centric area was intentionally kept a "nondenominational" zone.

The towers of Bay Street and the PATH underground had no such compunctions, and the lobbies that Jane passed every day were now resplendent with towering fir trees, hanging garlands, lights, and wreaths. The shabby dollar-store decorations that Marianne had put up in the restaurant each year were nothing compared to the expensive, tasteful, and professionally arranged displays of Toronto's Financial District. Last week, there had even been professional carolers and a string quartet down in the PATH. Jane thought the whole effect was beyond magical.

Her dress for the party was neatly hanging in her closet, a simple green shift that she often wore to the office on days an important client was coming in, one of the nicest pieces she had bought with Adele. For a touch of flash, she would add low-heeled gold pumps she'd bought online. Hopefully, green and gold would be festive enough.

The party would be the last she'd see of Mr. Rosen for a while. He was journeying to Montreal directly afterward to spend the holidays with some old law school friends from his days at McGill University. The firm had a small regional office in the city to specifically cater to their French-language clients, and Mr. Rosen planned to spend a few weeks there to work with the newly appointed regional managing partner. The previous one had died unexpectedly last month.

"Just keeled over right there on his yoga mat. Total five-star heart attack," Diane confided to a small audience in the elevator last week. "The instructor had to stop mid-namaste to call the ambulance."

"How do you get a heart attack during *yoga*?" asked a skeptical young man from accounting, who was promptly glared at by Diane's usual followers.

"Uh, duh, because he had a heart condition. The doctor told him he needed less stress and more exercise, and you know what Phillippe was like." Diane always spoke about senior management as if she was on intimate terms with them all and was privy to their habits, when she actually picked up her information by listening at Beth Fahmey's closed door. "He was so extra, he did the treadmill, the weights, a couple laps in the pool, all in one afternoon, and then went right to yoga. Exercise plus stress relief, he figured. Boom. But instead it was like, boom, dead. They carried him out on a covered stretcher, just like in the movies. They did the same for Mr. Rosen's father. The stretcher, I mean, not the yoga. He was more the usual route, just keeled over right at his desk."

Jane wrinkled her nose as she remembered the conversation while she painted. She didn't like to think of that. Didn't like to think of how her own father had unexpectedly died, and that she and Mr. Rosen had that in common. Whatever his faults, at least her father had been kind and loved her well, if not wisely.

Another coat on the far wall will cover that water stain, and then I think I'm done.

Maybe she would pick out a color for her bathroom next.

*D*ecember 15 dawned bright and snowy. Jane felt a frisson of excitement. On the train, she kept careful hold of the garment bag that held her dress and the large tote that held her shoes. Adele told her it was customary to change in the ladies' room at four o'clock; those who could afford the more expensive downtown gyms would repair to their changing rooms to use the amenities of makeup mirrors and hair straighteners, and many more female employees would be spending their lunch hour at the nail salons and blow-dry bars down in the PATH. All the staff seemed excited.

Except Mr. Rosen, apparently.

"What's in the garment bag?" He poked at it curiously when he came over to her desk.

"It's the holiday party this evening. The *firm* holiday party," she elaborated off his blank look.

"Oh, that. Suppose I have to go."

"It's a party. It's meant to be fun, not a chore."

He smiled at her. "When you've been through as many as I have, the fun kind of leaks out of it. At least we stopped doing those long formal dinners with everyone bringing their significant others. God, that was dull."

"You ended up insulting a lot of people, didn't you?" Jane

said, having seen him in enough settings now to know that when Mr. Rosen got bored, he said things, and when he said things, invariably people got offended.

"Right in one. Cocktail party, stay on your feet, stay on the move. Much better way to go."

She laughed. "Those of us wearing high heels might disagree."

"Go barefoot, like the little match girl. Hey, that's what you should be next Halloween."

Jane laughed again, the tension between them over her sad past no longer present. She preferred laughing about it and liked Mr. Rosen's dark jokes.

Once he had wandered back to his office, she checked the cardboard copy box under her desk that contained reconstructed Lamp. She had been informed that traditionally, assistants did not get partners gifts unless it was a simple card. This had been established to alleviate the pressure and onus of gift-giving between those with vastly smaller income levels and the wealthy partners.

But Jane didn't think Mr. Rosen cared much about receiving holiday cards, and instead she planned to present him with his old friend Lamp, now good as new. Well, almost. It listed slightly to one side when stood upright. But it didn't cost anything beyond the price of a tube of glue, so she hoped she wasn't breaking any rules.

She really hoped he liked the resurrection of Lamp.

When Jane walked through the hallway at three o'clock, work seemed to be tapering off in favor of people chatting and visiting one another's desks, in order to compare notes on who brought which dress and which shoes they'd be wearing. For the first time, Jane really clocked how overwhelmingly female the support staff of the firm was, and how overwhelmingly male the lawyers, and particularly the partners, were.

By four o'clock, more and more women started disappearing to the ladies' room, where a line was beginning to form and where raucous laughter and the overwhelming scent of hair spray wafted out each time the door opened.

Jane waited her turn, and then locked herself into a cubicle stall to quickly slip into her dress and heels. The mirror was smudged over with the various remnants of too many women's makeup, but Jane found a clean corner to touch up her lipstick and slip in a pair of earrings. She let down her hair from the low ponytail she still habitually wore on the nape of her neck, and walked out before Brenda from the next floor, who had been eyeing her simple apparel beadily, could make any remarks. Adele was kind, but so many of the other "matrons" (as Adele called them) were not, and they often, under the guise of being self-declared "motherly," made remarks on Jane's physical person that she could have lived without. There had been remarks on the flatness of her figure, the bushiness of her hair, the beaten-up state of her handbag. After Adele's fashion intervention, those remarks had flipped into cautionary warnings on being attention-seeking.

She slipped back to her cubicle. Mr. Rosen was already gone, presumably to oversee and welcome everyone, and his office was dark.

So she'd be walking into the party alone. *Totally fine.*

"Chérie!"

Not alone. She turned and beamed at Adele, who was resplendent in a shimmery dress of silver, her blond hair glossy and makeup dark. *If Bond girls were allowed to age naturally but gracefully, that's what they'd look like.*

"Chérie, come with me. The party started fifteen minutes ago. It is the perfect time to go." She linked arms with Jane.

The venue was called the Design Exchange; it was an old building, art deco motifs inside, and in a former life it had housed the Toronto Stock Exchange from 1937 to 1983. Now it was enjoying a second life as a high-concept event space, and as Adele pointed out, it was mercifully connected to most of Bay Street through the PATH, making it possible for the ladies to walk over in their dresses and heels without venturing into the pelting snow outside that would have necessitated practical boots and mascara touch-ups upon arrival.

The party was already in full swing in a massive, open two-story room that was once the actual trading floor of the stock exchange. Purple lights lit up the dim space, and two bars flanked either side, with food stations scattered around a dance floor. A photo booth and clustered casual seating arrangements were underneath a flight of stairs that led to a balustrade overlooking the main area. A dais stood at the far end, and on it Beth Fahmey was welcoming everyone and reading through a page of reminders about things like taxi vouchers and safe practices for getting home. Mr. Rosen was nowhere to be seen.

"Come," Adele said, "you meet no one stuck in that hallway. I will introduce you to some young men from accounting."

"Uh, Adele, that's really okay . . ."

Adele's good intentions were futile: with the end of Beth's speech, the music cranked back up, and between that and the buzz of voices, the introductions to the eligible young men were inaudible. They were unable to do more than mime hellos and gesture that they would fetch her a drink before disappearing into the queue at the bar.

"Very different from the sit-down dinners the firm used to do. More fun, modern," Adele shouted in her ear.

Jane dutifully followed her around for more pantomime introductions, and even waved at her own growing number of acquaintances from her four months at the firm. She ventured off at some point to sample the food tables—duck and goat cheese canapés, mini quiche, bite-sized lobster rolls, shrimp cocktails, and even small containers of traditional poutine to "show we're a proud Canadian firm," the man ahead of her in line laughingly explained. "And for any of our partners who flew in from the Montreal office." She blindly circulated, munching on her spoils, admiring the dresses of the other women and feeling that though her outfit was undoubtedly plain, it still had respectably made the mark. She congratulated herself on the last-minute addition of the gold sparkly shoes, which she felt were mostly responsible for helping her pass muster.

At half past eight, the crowd quieted for the law students to perform a skit, apparently something of a hazing tradition to embarrass oneself before partners they hoped would eventually hire them. It was a dance routine mocking some recent film Jane didn't know, so she missed most of the jokes, but she was impressed by how game some of the students were, and cringed for those one or two who looked thoroughly mortified by their predicament. Jane realized with a start that they were mostly her age. They seemed so much younger in their exuberant glee.

At nine, Mr. Rosen took the stage. He was so commanding, his sharp, sure movements quieting the crowd with ease, his dark, blazing looks striking under the dim lights. He spoke briefly of the firm's success and its long history, and he expressed the best wishes on behalf of the partners to every member of the firm and their families during the holidays.

"Each and every one of you are vital to this firm. I know it doesn't often feel that way, and maybe not everyone gets the daily thanks they deserve, but from the mail room"—here there were cheers from the mail room staff—"to the kitchen"—more cheers—"to the assistants, HR, marketing, accounting, the tech team, and the receptionists"—he paused a moment as each of the respective cheers died down—"each of you are necessary to the well-being of the firm. This year, we've had eleven babies born to staff; we've had three happy retirement parties; we've seen John from accounting back at work fully recovered from his cancer, thank god; three newcomers to Canada among the staff got their permanent citizenship status—don't worry, pictures of their ceremony are going out in next month's newsletter; and ancient Ed from the litigators is back from his hip surgery. The man has been here forever— you'd think he'd take a break—but Ed, we know you'll be back in the courtroom and on the ski slopes in no time and putting all us younger men to shame."

An older man with a cane, wearing a dark suit, standing toward the front of the crowd, roared with laughter and held up his glass in cheers.

"What I'm trying to articulate is that a company only exists because of the community within it. The gold watch and twenty-five years' service idea might be out of fashion these days, but not here; here what matters is this: that I believe that so long as you work here, for however long or short a time, do your job well and you are owed care from the firm. It's a harsh road, Bay Street, and we deal with some pretty tough customers, myself probably the worst of all"—here there was some uncomfortable laughter—"but it's the holidays, so drink and be merry. Enjoy the open bar. Whoops, don't enjoy it too much, 'cause I see Beth Fahmey glaring at me. That's it. I'm out."

He hopped off the stage while people were still in the middle of their cheers to toast the end of his speech, and they wheeled around awkwardly to track his progress from the stage, unsure if the entertainment was over.

Jane clapped politely along with everyone else.

"He's a good man, Mr. Rosen." Adele nodded at her side conspiratorially, as if Mr. Rosen's speech had confirmed what she long suspected and met with her approval. "He's making this a good firm. It just takes time to turn the *Titanic*."

"What was the firm like before?"

"You are too young to have lived in the eighties . . ."

"I've seen the movie *Wall Street*, if that helps. The original, not the sequel."

Adele laughed, her face a little rosy with wine. "Well, Mr. Rosen Sr., he did not leave the eighties business culture behind, not even in the 2000s. Profits first, profits foremost, profits only. But it was not just that. It was, je ne sais how to describe it . . . the firm had to be known as first-class, front of the plane, always. Private lounges, scotch and handshake agreements for the right kind of people. Donations only to the right kinds of charities. No one blinked if an expensive escort was brought to dinner, but mon dieu, don't bring any lawyer who didn't go to the right law school! And the rest of us"—she waved a hand at the partygoers—"all those groups your Mr. Rosen named, just . . . eh."

Jane thought on this as Adele cried out, "Chérie!" and trotted off to talk to yet another person as if they were a long-lost relative instead of someone she saw with mild indifference every day. Apparently, holidays and wine were a very warming combination.

"What did you think of my speech?" Like the old adage *speak of the devil*, Mr. Rosen appeared at her elbow. He was wearing the same dark suit he wore earlier that day, and Jane should have known that the customary frippery of changing for a party would be beyond him, but the suit was slightly less rumpled than usual and apparently he had conceded the addition of a dark blue tie that often only appeared for clients. He stood stalwart and strong next to Jane, who was starting to feel oppressed by the ever-shifting close swirl of the crowd, none of which she could see over or past at her meager height, even with the addition of the gold heels. She was suddenly glad for his grounding presence. They both looked out at the crowd.

"It was a very nice speech."

"And that's a very bland compliment."

"Well, it wasn't 'Friends, Romans, countrymen, lend me your ears' energy, but for a company holiday party, it was pretty resonating."

He grinned. "Caesar's burial? That's your go-to speech tier?"

"Why, what's yours?"

"We shall fight on the beaches . . ."

"Of course." Jane turned back to face the crowd with a laugh. "Dogged, conquering obstinacy, that's you."

"Subtle, deceivingly compliant oratory, that's you. And Brutus is an honorable man, yes, Mr. Rosen, of course, Mr. Rosen. And then giving me a look that lets me know you'd like to stick me with a letter opener for how I try your patience."

"Don't be silly. No one has letter openers anymore."

"I have one on my desk. Silver and engraved. It was a gift from someone for something or other."

"What do you use it for?"

"I don't."

"What's engraved on it?"

"No idea."

Jane laughed again. "Well, probably neither speech would suit Ed with the hip replacement for an audience, so I guess it's good you said what you did."

"Want to dance?"

The question was so unexpected and abrupt that Jane jerked her head around in an ungainly spastic motion to stare at him, but his face was impassive as he continued to survey the crowd and he gave no indication that he'd said anything unusual or that Jane had responded alarmingly.

"Um." She faltered. "Okay."

Without a word, he placed a light hand on the small of her back and ushered her toward the small dance floor where a DJ had just set up. A little over a dozen or so of the younger employees from various departments were enthusiastically jumping around to a thumping hit by Rihanna, but they gave way as an old Frank Sinatra tune followed, and a number of mismatched couples took their place for an old-fashioned glide around the floor. Jane spotted Adele nearby, dancing gracefully with the head of the tech department.

Jane snapped to, suddenly confronted with Mr. Rosen, here on the dance floor in front of her, expecting them to dance. She felt a nervous urge to laugh. And maybe to hyperventilate. She prayed her palms weren't sweating.

Mr. Rosen was perfectly calm, which made Jane feel like her out-of-control reaction exposed feelings of being terribly miscast for this scene. But he was uncharacteristically serious. He slid one large hand around her waist and gently clasped her much smaller hand with the other. His palm was rough and warm. Flailing for how to position herself—she couldn't quite reach his shoulder—she rested her free hand as lightly as possible on his upper arm, just nearing his shoulder. A respectable amount of space remained between them.

Still, he must have felt her stiffen, and he drew back slightly for a moment.

"We don't have to dance if you're not comfortable. Really."

"I'm fine," Jane said, and hoped the loud music covered her voice's quaver.

He nodded, serious expression still in place, and swayed them lightly to the music.

Jane was glad to see that, far from the romantic clinging together of bodies that had typified high school dances, which were her only experience of couple dancing, the bodies here kept a polite level of disengagement, more like how people might dance with in-laws at a wedding: friendly and not quite stiff, as helped by the wine, but still with a level that would allow them to look each other in the eye at the office Monday morning. The jaunty, old-fashioned tempo of the Frank Sinatra ballad helped in that regard, it was more quaint than romantic.

Yet eye contact for Jane remained impossible, and instead she stared directly in front of her at the subtle diamond pattern of his navy-blue tie.

"It used to be tradition, back in the day, for partners to dance with their assistants every year at the holiday party."

Jane nodded receipt of this factoid, but did feel comforted that there might be a sort of precedence for this, in the eyes of the firm.

There was another long pause, and then . . . "Are you enjoying the party?"

This made her look up.

"Really? We do small talk now?"

He shrugged and grinned. "Thought I'd give it a try."

Jane smiled and shook her head, but felt a little easier now that he was being himself again.

"So I leave for Montreal tomorrow . . ."

Jane nodded. She had booked his tickets, after all.

". . . will you miss me when I'm gone?"

Jane rolled her eyes at his teasing tone but bit back a noise of surprise when he took the opportunity to pull her slightly closer. To anyone looking on they would still be just this side of a respectable distance apart, but it didn't feel respectable when Jane was hyperaware suddenly of the physical presence of him. She'd always known he was an imposing man, but from her usual vantage point on the other side of his desk, it was an entirely different experience.

Now he overwhelmed her.

The breadth of his shoulders that blocked her view of anything else, the anchor of his hand on her waist, and the solid way he stood, a rooted tree that couldn't be knocked down, made her feel . . . she didn't know. Only that she did feel, and it didn't help that his dark eyes were steadily searching her face. All she knew was that it felt frightening, but that she could never feel frightened of him, and that fact alone was a novel one in her solitary life.

The last bars of the song came to an end, and Jane pulled back, feeling almost dazed, her heart beating fast. The next tune blared on, a Top 40 dance hit, and the discord jarred her to her senses. "Thank you for the dance," she said carefully. People were flooding the dance floor, becoming a mass of fast-moving bodies that seemed to blur everything around her.

"It was my pleasure," he replied.

He leaned down.

Her eyes fluttered closed as Mr. Rosen's warm mouth brushed her cheek in a gentle kiss. His stubble rasped against her, and she shivered as he lingered for a moment, the slightest sensation of his breath in her ear as he whispered to her lowly.

"I'll see you in the new year, Jane Raine."

He stepped back and let her go.

The women's bathroom was nearly as packed as the one back at the office had been when it was taken over as a dressing room earlier in the day. Women were rolling and unrolling bunched-up pantyhose, swiping under their eyes with wadded-up toilet paper for renegade mascara, minutely adjusting their hair, and reapplying lipstick. The harsh overhead lights felt deeply unflattering after the dim, soft lighting of the ballroom, and Jane turned away from scrutinizing her own reflection as the others were doing.

When a stall became available, she locked herself in, sat on the closed toilet seat, and breathed. She just needed five minutes to regain her equilibrium.

Five minutes, and then you go back out there. You're a grown woman; it was just a dance.

There was a shriek of laughter and a burst of noise, as what sounded like three very giggly girls burst into the bathroom, in the wake of which many other women finished up their primping and left.

"Oh my god, oh my god, oh my god. I'm *sooo* fucked. Fucking *love* an open bar!"

"Uh, obvs!"

"Whoa, Evie, you don't look so good. Better use the . . ."

A cubicle door two down from Jane's swung open, and there followed the unmistakable sound of retching. The other girls burst into muffled giggles.

"Hey, can I borrow your cover-up? Can you see that zit right here?"

"It's barely noticeable. Chill."

Jane thought she recognized the voices of Diane and possibly one of her cronies who worked in marketing.

"Mmm, are we going partying after this? Lame office party ends in an hour."

"I'm out; you guys are on your own. I have to hang around and make sure everyone leaves safely or Beth will have my ass, and after that I'm totally gonna hook up with Alec."

"Hot Alec from IT? Didn't you already try that like a bajillion times already?"

"Shut up, I tried, like, *once*, and whatever, I just need him to stop rhapsodizing about Python programming for a fucking second to make a move."

There was quiet for a few moments apart from the moaning of their sick companion.

"Hey, did you see Jane Raine dancing with Mr. Rosen?"

"Oh my god, I totally called it; she's sleeping with him."

"Oh my god, really?"

"Please, the girl has, like, no résumé, and suddenly she's the only assistant that doesn't leave? Following him around to every meeting like a puppy at his heels, the immediate salary raise, the new clothes? They're so obvious. She's an idiot. He'll dump her when he's done; she's just a piece on the side to break the boredom, I'm sure of it. Evie, are you done heaving your fucking guts out yet? Jesus."

"Yeah, mop yourself up, the bar is going to close soon." A flush sounded, the cubicle door creaked open, someone gargled and then groaned. There was more giggling and phone beeps, and then with the bang of the door they were gone.

Jane had a sudden headache and pressed her hands into her temples. Her heart felt like it was beating in her throat. So that's people were saying about her.

It's just Diane and her friends, she tried to reason with herself. *But Diane works in HR, and if that's what she's saying . . .*

Jane let out a long exhale. She felt exhausted and hurt. Her feet were sore, her skin too hot, her eyes were stinging as she struggled not to cry. The party was effectively over for her, and now the simple act of getting home felt like too much, and she still needed to collect her coat and things from the office first. She gave herself a few minutes, to ensure Diane and her friends were long gone, and to get her feelings somewhat back under control, knowing she would have to encounter many people on her way out.

She splashed some water on her face and stared down her reflection, schooling it back into neutrality.

Back at her cubicle, she kicked off her gold shoes and pulled out the practical boots from under her desk. Climbing into them made her sigh in relief, as did the quiet of the darkened office. She balled up the dress pants and blouse she'd worn that day and shoved them into the garment bag, for once not caring about wrinkles. Her foot bumped against the cardboard copy box underneath her desk, the one that contained the resurrected Lamp.

She pulled it out and set it on her desk, pondering what to do with it. She had dithered over when best to give her gift to Mr. Rosen and in the end had lost her nerve and decided to leave Lamp on his desk as a surprise for when he returned from Montreal. Now the whole project felt ridiculously stupid.

"Jane, you still here?"

There was just no escaping Mr. Rosen tonight. He rounded the partition wall, tie and shirt collar undone, his coat in hand, and looking surprised to see her.

"Is that . . . ?" He'd spotted Lamp, and his face broke into such an expression of delight that Jane almost couldn't find it in herself to regret it. Almost. She cursed Diane for spoiling the exact scenario she'd been hoping for when she first played nursemaid to Lamp.

"Merry Christmas, or I guess it should be Happy Hanukkah? You seemed pretty down about his demise, so . . ." Jane's plan of staging Lamp's return evaporated.

"You fixed him, you wonderful human! Best gift ever." He stepped toward Jane as if to give her a hug, and she immediately flattened herself against the flimsy wall. He froze.

"Sorry, I'm sorry," Jane said automatically, not entirely sure what she was apologizing for, but feeling mortified for her reaction and the flash of hurt on his face.

He cleared his throat and looked away, trying to regain composure. "No, *I'm* sorry. I . . . It was the dance, wasn't it? I made you uncomfortable . . . Shit. Jane, you can always say no to me, you know that, right?" His tone was a little desperate. "I promise, there will never be repercussions for saying no. The last thing I'd ever want is for this to feel like an unsafe space for you . . ."

"No, it's not that. It's not you. I enjoyed the dance, the dance was lovely and Lamp is for you, and I do feel safe here, I just . . ." She didn't know what she was saying, only hearing the desperate cry of *fix it! fix it!* playing on a loop in her head. He still wouldn't look at her and was playing idly with things from her desk.

"They think I'm sleeping with you."

Mr. Rosen had scooped up a handful of paper clips. At Jane's sudden statement he fumbled and dropped every last one. He didn't look at her but remained calmly staring where they fell, as if they were runes he could divine and had tossed them on purpose.

"Did you hear me? Mr. Rosen, I said . . ."

"I heard you." There was a long pause. When he finally turned, his gaze slid over her and rested instead on some fixed point over her right shoulder.

"Well?"

"Well what? I think if we were sleeping together, one of us might have noticed."

Jane stared at him incredulously. "That's not the point!"

Spinning on her heel, she strode out of the cubicle into the hallway, needing space.

"Jane! I'm sorry!" As always these days, he was hot on her heels. "I'm sorry they think . . ."

"Not here!" she hissed, aware that though the floor was seemingly deserted, the thin walls offered no privacy for this kind of conversation.

"Then come back to my office and let's talk about this."

"Us in your office with a closed door is the *last* thing we need!" Jane was beside herself. She strode back into her cubicle, picked up Lamp, put it down again, unable to focus.

"What can I do?"

"It's your firm! Make them stop."

"I can punish whoever said it to you—obviously someone's said it to you—but even I can't completely stamp out gossip, scary as I am. You can't silence all the whispers people say and think about you. I learned a long time ago to make peace with that." He was being honest with her, and Jane breathed deeply in and out, and tried to adopt a more reasonable frame of mind.

"Okay, I get that, but . . . doesn't it bother you?"

"Does it bother me that they disrespect you like that? Yes.

Absolutely, yes. It makes me enraged. But I can't fix it, and if I tried, I'd only make things worse for you. I've never had an assistant last this long, and now one finally does and she also happens to be bright and beautiful, of course they're going to assume . . . And after all the people I've yelled at and driven mad, if I try to protect and defend this one woman? They'll only think that confirms it. It kills me to say it, but my involvement will fan the flames."

Damn it, he was right. If the owner of the firm got involved in petty gossip, when he never even learned his assistants' names before, it would only look like he was trying to stamp out the truth.

"Damn you and your strategic lawyer brain."

He smiled a little bitterly at that. "I'm sorry you have to face this down. It's unfair and misogynistic. I had hoped that by bringing more female partners into the firm, among other advantages, it might break up the locker room talk. Guess it was naive." He looked so genuinely downtrodden she wanted to reassure him.

"It was a good idea. It's still progress."

He nodded, but his usual energy was gone as he started to shuffle back to his office. "Jane, you should complain to HR. If *I* get involved it looks suspicious, but you have every right to file a grievance on your own behalf. If they don't take care of it properly, then I can have a word with Beth and put the fear of god into her for failing firm standards in general." Jane didn't have the heart to tell him that the rumor originated from HR in the first place. "And if you'd like to be transferred to another partner, or if you'd like me to keep my distance from you, then just say the word."

Jane sighed and shook her head. "I'm sorry I ruined this gift giving, and the last night before your trip."

He stepped cautiously toward her again.

"You didn't ruin anything. You rebuilding Lamp is the best gift I've ever received. But getting you assigned as my assistant comes pretty close."

Jane smiled weakly at him.

He picked up Lamp from the box reverently, cradling it like a child with a favorite plush toy, then paused one last time, and his gaze skittered back over her shoulder again. "People will eventually find out how smart you are and know you're here because you're good at your work. So does it matter if they think I have the hots for you?"

It isn't about whether you want me; it's about the fact that the gossips think I'm sleeping with you to stay employed. "You're my boss," was all she could offer.

"Right. Inappropriate." He nodded to himself. "Don't let them get you down. Have a very merry Christmas, Jane." He headed back into his office, placing Lamp on his desk with care.

It wasn't fixed, not by a long shot. She couldn't leave it like this.

"Mr. Rosen," she called. He crossed the hall again to her cubicle, looking hopeful.

It took so much bravery, like stepping off that elevator on her first day at the firm. The dim public hallway suddenly felt intensely private. She stepped forward and, stretching up on her tiptoes, wrapped her arms over his broad shoulders in an awkward hug. His open palms immediately came to her waist to steady her balance, and she felt rather than heard his soft exhale under her hands. She gave his shoulders a little tug so that he'd lean down a bit, and she brushed a kiss on his cheek, just as he'd done earlier, her pulse thundering all the while.

"I don't want distance, and I don't want a transfer. Getting assigned to you was a pretty awesome gift for me as well."

Because it was important for him to hear, even if she herself could barely hear it over the sound of blood pounding in her ears.

He pulled back a little, his dark eyes serious, searching her face to verify her words, and Jane forced herself to maintain eye contact, keep her guard down, and stay in his personal space. This close, she could see the slight hint of green in his irises, and just the beginnings of a few threads of silver at his right temple.

"Jane," he started, leaning into her again, and then he jumped back when an explosive guffaw of laughter echoed from somewhere down the corridor. A few revelers were returning to their work spaces to pick up bags and coats.

Mr. Rosen rubbed the back of his neck ruefully, his face a little flushed. "Get home safe, Jane." He turned toward his office. "I'll see you when I return from Montreal."

It was only much later that Jane realized he'd called her beautiful.

Chapter 12

Jane felt unsettled in the days after the party, that moment in the hallway playing on a loop in her mind. What might have happened if they hadn't been interrupted? She thought she knew but . . . had she been imagining things? Surely she could never matter to him the way he did to her; so what if he'd kissed her? It was a friendly peck on the cheek. But here her logic wobbled, the memory of the dimly lit corridor rushing in, the breathless pause, and the way he'd lingered . . .

But no, that way lay madness. She couldn't afford to entertain thoughts like that.

Seeking a distraction, and unable to resist the lure of extra cash, she took Marianne up on her offer and worked some shifts over the holidays. And when that wasn't sufficient, she spent her spare time painting her bathroom a warm copper color. It didn't turn out quite as well as the other rooms, but her green dinner plates had been delivered, and when she laid them out in her green kitchen, it looked so nice, she could view the bathroom with equanimity and decide her decorating attempts were going okay.

On Christmas Day she slept in until noon, and that evening she tucked into a rotisserie chicken she'd bought the night before from the grocery store, and a mini chocolate cake for dessert. She lit the solitary string of Christmas lights she'd purchased from the dollar store and wound them around her bedposts and piled all her blankets in a cozy heap on the bed. She burrowed in, with a hot cup of tea, and admired the warm pocket of glow created by her yellow walls and twinkling lights.

At midnight she went to sleep, thinking this was the best Christmas she'd had in some time.

January 2 of the new year dawned bright and bitter cold. Ice on the tracks had delayed the trains, so she ended up being twenty minutes late to work, but there was no Mr. Rosen today, and so no reason to rush. His office was quiet and empty.

By the second week of January, a square envelope had arrived from Montreal, addressed to her. Inside was a postcard featuring the Notre-Dame Basilica, and on the back was a simple message in block letters:

DID YOU USE MY LETTER OPENER TO OPEN THIS?
NO? TOO BAD.

Three days later, she received another, this time with the Montreal Museum of Fine Arts depicted on the front. On the back he'd scribbled a game of hangman, a stick figure already half-formed and nearly hung, wearing a top hat and bow tie, with a few letters filled in. It only took Jane ten minutes before she emailed him the answer:

GUARD MY STAPLER.

He immediately wrote back:

CORRECT. NOW DO AS THE HANGMAN SAYS!

Alone in her cubicle, Jane laughed.

His stay in Montreal stretched on, but items continued to be delivered to her desk: a carefully wrapped small bottle of maple sugar from a famous sugar shack in rural Quebec, a few more postcards with half-sketched games of tic-tac-toe or doodles, and on Valentine's Day she received a brochure for a Montreal boutique that created elaborate Swarovski-adorned light fixtures. He had scrawled a note on it with Sharpie marker in his usual block letters:

SHOULD WE GET LAMP A GIRLFRIEND?

Oh god, she really missed him. It'd been two months. It was all she could do to talk herself back from this feelings cliff, but if she didn't, she was absolutely going to make an ass of herself the next time she saw him, which would be soon, because the week after that Valentine's Day message, she received two important emails. One was a warning about an upcoming fire drill. This became important only after googling the number of steps from the sixty-fifth floor to the ground. She made a note in her calendar to wear flats that day. And a few practice runs using the stairs of her apartment building might be a good idea.

The other email was a two-word missive from Mr. Rosen. It simply said:

COMING HOME.

Jane arrived early the next morning, fervently persuading herself that she wasn't early for a reason or wearing one of her prettier work dresses for a reason.

Oh god, who am I kidding? He's back!

But when she raced to her corridor on the sixty-fifth floor, she stopped short.

Mr. Rosen was there, and Jane's heart gave a lurch, for he was so much better looking than she had remembered him in his short absence. His rumbling voice filled and soothed her.

But beside him stood a stunning, statuesque blonde in a creamy white, perfectly tailored suit.

She was lightly gripping Mr. Rosen's forearm as she threw back her silky blond mane and laughed becomingly, and Jane's stomach dropped like she'd missed a step walking down a flight of stairs.

There was another person there, a woman of about forty, with a short gray bob. She looked professional but had a fatigued air about her, like she'd rather be somewhere else. "Is this your assistant?" she asked.

Mr. Rosen's gaze landed on Jane and his face lit up. He eagerly took half a step forward before seeming to remember himself, coughed awkwardly into his fist, and turned to introduce his companions instead. "Jane, this is Isabelle and Clémence from the Montreal office. They'll be staying with us for a bit."

"Allô," Clémence, the older of the two women, said politely. She spoke with a thick French accent, and it had that slight twang native to Quebec's Eastern Townships.

"My assistant back at my office will be handling my affairs remotely. I'm sure I won't have much need for her." Isabelle's voice was dulcet, her accent just the barest trace over the English words and bearing the fluty tones of a true Montrealer. Jane decided she preferred the France-French accent of Adele.

"Good," Mr. Rosen said decisively, making direct eye contact with Jane and grinning. "I don't like to share her." Isabelle glanced contemptuously at Jane as if she very much doubted any assistant could possess such value.

"Now, your offices are downstairs with our tech law team. C'mon, I'll show you the way." He ushered them ahead down the hall and then at the last second pivoted to wrap a hand around Jane's elbow. "Don't run off anywhere, okay? I haven't seen you in fucking weeks. I just gotta get these two settled in first."

He strode off down the hall after them, the warmth of his grip still lingering, but all Jane could see was the coy look Isabelle tilted up at him as they walked away.

Clémence pulled away from the trio before they made it to the end of the hall, returning to where Jane sat. "Excusez-moi," she said, retrieving a file folder she had left lying on the edge of Jane's desk. She looked back down the hallway to where Mr. Rosen and Isabelle had already left without her and sighed. "And now I 'ave to watch them flirt all day, and sit with tech lawyers who will talk loudly about blockchain while I am trying to work." She sighed again, gave Jane a rueful smile, and trudged off after them.

Jane sat down at her computer, all the enthusiasm from earlier gone and dread creeping in.

Jealousy was such a bitch.

There was a resistance for a grand total of five minutes before looking Isabelle up on the firm website.

Born in Montreal but an alumna of the prestigious Havergal College school for girls in North Toronto. Completed an undergraduate degree at Queen's University in Kingston, followed by a law degree at McGill. She had once been a contender for a spot on the Canadian Olympic team for rowing. A further Google search gave Jane a full spread of images of Isabelle, long, lean, and athletic, rowing in the Kingston harbor. Images of Isabelle in a Dior cocktail dress at a charity gala, looking like Grace Kelly. Images of Isabelle presiding over a university moot, commanding yet demure in her sleek power suit.

A good party, a little wine, and sure, why not make eyes at your assistant. But in the cold light of day, there was a beautiful Isabelle waiting instead. What was a lowly, plain secretary next to that?

Jane took herself out to lunch before Mr. Rosen got back.

Chapter 13

The reason for the Montreal invasion, Jane later learned, was that Isabelle, Clémence, and Mr. Rosen were working on the legal logistics of an upscale American luxury retailer looking to set up shop in Canada, including taking over a massive seven-story lot in the Eaton Centre, and Clémence and Isabelle were the firm's experts on commercial real estate law.

Or perhaps it was more accurate to say Clémence was the expert. Jane had looked her up online as well—she'd been a reporter, and an impressive one, on the economics beat for some years before going to law school more recently, where she'd graduated summa cum laude. She seemed to always be elbows deep in folders and law books, rattling off facts and figures to Mr. Rosen in her thick accent. Isabelle seemed to spend a lot of time on the phone with her assistant in Montreal talking about getting references for a "Women in Law" award nomination.

Mr. Rosen was incredibly busy, like he had been on the money-laundering case when she first started working for him, and Jane used that to her advantage to make their interactions scarce for the next day or so without him unduly noticing.

Somehow, though, she couldn't shake the impression that as distracted as he was, he was perpetually clocking her movements, always looking for her in a room. But Jane also couldn't shake from her vision the perfection that was Isabelle, and Isabelle's obvious (to Jane, at least) interest in Mr. Rosen.

And she could barely suppress her own responses to him, tinged as they now were with a burning territorialism. She wanted to shove him away when he grinned at her, throw something at him, then inexplicably felt weak and listless when confronted with the breadth of his shoulders, the strong line of his jaw. It made her want to whine and say the world was unfair.

And she wanted to smack herself for it.

And then smack Isabelle when she laughed her throaty laugh and picked invisible lint off his jacket shoulder.

She supposed Isabelle was the reason for Mr. Rosen's newfound collegiality and openness with the Montreal lawyers. (Mr. Rosen had once famously addressed a law school graduating class with the opening line: "Lawyers. Check your back for a knife. If it's not there, know that they're planning the next attempt." He was not invited to give speeches anymore.)

Her suspicions were confirmed when she surprisingly ended up chatting with Clémence one afternoon. Isabelle and Mr. Rosen had gone for lunch with the clients while Clémence had stayed behind, and, feeling bad for the overworked woman, Jane had brought her a sandwich and a coffee.

"Thank you, you're very kind," the older woman said, unwrapping the sandwich. "I hope he treats you better than his other assistants."

"We get on all right," Jane said vaguely, and then feeling

emboldened by the woman's friendly and frank demeanor, she added: "Maybe he's turning over a new leaf. I've never seen him get along so well with colleagues before."

Clémence snorted into her coffee. "Nothing collegial about it; that's all about Isabelle. They've been dancing around each other since Christmas. Everyone in the Montreal office was gossiping about it. There *was* a rumor he was with some woman here in Toronto but . . ." She shrugged and then caught the look on Jane's face. "I wouldn't worry about it. Isabelle hates Toronto. She'll talk him into moving to Montreal in no time," she said kindly, misunderstanding Jane's distress. "You won't have to deal with them both. You'll get reassigned to another partner."

"You don't like either of them very much, do you?" Jane asked, although considering Mr. Rosen and Isabelle were out for lunch, wining and dining clients, and Clémence was currently sitting in a veritable tornado of paperwork eating a cold sandwich, perhaps the question answered itself.

Clémence leaned back in her chair and seemed to give the question some thought before she answered. "I like the work I do, and I know I am good at it, but I 'ave never cared for the sales aspect of dealing with clients, the lunches and that whole routine." She grimaced. "And I 'ave never liked the politics that comes with being a partner, fighting for recognition, for promotion. In a perfect world, I think your work would speak for itself. But in this world, people who speak up, sometimes people who did not even *do* the work, are often the ones who get the credit."

Jane had a sneaking feeling she knew who on the team was not doing the work but was certainly getting into position to enjoy the credit.

"That's just the way of the world, I guess," Jane said.

●

Clémence looked at her in surprise. "No, it doesn't have to be. I used to be a journalist. I knew how to advocate for others. Now I must simply learn to advocate for myself. It is a skill set, just like any other."

Jane blinked in surprise at the easy way Clémence turned defeatism on its head. Then a thought occurred.

"Y'know, if you ever needed something to back up your claims, I mean of who worked on what and when, you might consider the timekeeper app."

Clémence cocked her head in confusion. "Every partner has that app. It tracks our work for billable hours and goes to accounting; our assistants take care of it."

"Yes," Jane agreed, "I take care of Mr. Rosen's at the end of each month. Did you know it *automatically* tracks everything you do, every document you touch and every phone call you make? And that *every* partner has one installed in their system? And that if you are all working on the same project, you'll all have the same code associated with it?"

Jane saw the moment the light bulb went off. Clémence grinned.

Their conversation ended soon after that, Clémence digging back into her work with renewed relish while Jane sat at her desk, satisfaction at helping Clémence quickly ebbing as her mind returned to the first part of their conversation. Isabelle and Mr. Rosen moving to Montreal together. It made her feel numb.

Don't punch above your weight, she told herself. *It's time for a reality check. Start small, no more lunches together. Give it a few weeks, and you'll realize you miss the roast beef more than him.*

Bleakly, she contemplated the lies people tell themselves.

. . .

The next day was the first chance to put her new austerity measures to the test. She was halfway out of her chair before the aroma hit. Roast beef day.

"Jane!"

She grudgingly turned and walked into his office.

Laid out on his desk was the usual roast beef feast. Reception must have sent it up. But Mr. Rosen was pulling on his jacket and heading for the door Jane had just entered from, looking regretful.

"Listen, I ordered the roast beef, but I just got a call and I'm needed downstairs, so it's all yours if you want it. I'll probably be gone a while, but can we talk as soon as I get back?"

Jane stood blinking with a kind of smothered indignant fury. It was so much harder and so much less satisfying to snub someone if they weren't even asking to sit with you.

She was just framing a response—something quickly fibbed about lunch with Adele and a shame that all that roast beef would go to waste, and why didn't he take it down to *Izzy's* if he was going to be there over the lunch hour anyway—when any potential repartee was interrupted by the arrival of a very tall, very thin, sandy-colored man.

Sandy-colored was Jane's immediate impression because he sported sun-kissed skin and sun-kissed dark blond hair so that the whole effect was one of a monotone dark beige. He smiled in a friendly way, though there was something a little reedy about it, as if his being there suddenly in Mr. Rosen's office was of no concern to anyone.

Mr. Rosen, Jane noticed immediately, had gone white, and was now, by some visible effort, pulling himself together.

"Steven!" he cried and stepped forward to heartily grasp his hand in a shake. Steven winced a little under the firm grip but looked enthused by this warm greeting, and a micro tension in his posture relaxed.

"Edward. I hope you don't mind, I'm a little early. It's been ages."

"For fuck's sake of course not! But how did you get past reception? No one's allowed beyond the boardroom floor without a security pass or accompanied by a firm member." There was a well-concealed hint of annoyance in the question that Jane doubted anyone else would spot.

"I just . . ." Steven waved his hand in a vague gesture. "I was at reception, said I was an old friend, and this young woman from HR was walking by. She brought me here."

Diane, most likely. One of these days her desire to stir the pot and poke into everyone's business was going to get her fired. She'd probably tried to interrogate the man as she escorted him.

"Not much has changed." He looked around at the roast beef sandwiches, at Lamp with its hairline cracks, and at the mess of books and papers on the floor that, despite Jane's best efforts to tidy, always seemed to reappear.

"You know me, like a dog that would starve if you moved his food bowl half an inch," Mr. Rosen joked. "But I do have a new assistant. Steven, this is Jane. Jane, this is Steven Steppenwolfe."

They shook hands, Jane suddenly on the alert. Was this file BW 5232-8?

"Nice to meet you. But I see I'm interrupting lunch . . ."

"Nah, just a midmorning snack for me, but now I've gone off it. Listen, why don't we go out for proper grub? I know a great steak house . . . Oh, I forgot, you'll want your California style bowl of roasted quinoa sadness. Well, okay, I know a place that'll do both—steak and fountain of youth in a bowl. My treat. We can talk about your investment—I assume that's what you're here to check up on, but I just need a minute with Jane, confidential client business, you understand."

With a firm hand on his shoulder, he propelled Steppenwolfe through the door, and clapped it firmly shut behind him.

"Just be a moment!"

The air seemed to desert his body all at once, and he sagged and rested his head against the closed door, eyes firmly shut. "He's early."

"Mr. Rosen?" Jane queried timidly. He turned tired eyes on her.

"I'm fantasizing about running away, just right now. Maybe to warm Italy. Just buy a one-way airline ticket and start life anew. What do you think of that?"

Grasping for a reasonable reply to this bizarre non sequitur, Jane latched on to the concrete.

"How's your Italian?"

"Terrible. I've just about got 'hello' and 'goodbye.' "

"That might prove problematic, living in Italy."

He smiled faintly at her with a sort of weary but fond exasperation.

"Always my practical Jane. What would I do without you?"

You seem to be getting along just fine with Izzy. But the deepened lines on his face told her she wouldn't be saying that.

Already, she could feel herself softening toward him in his desperation, and wondering what it was about the seemingly harmless man from California that had caused it.

"Would you come with me?"

"What?"

"If I ran away to Italy. I might get lonely not being able to talk to anyone. You could come with me. You'd love Italy."

"I don't have a passport. Mr. Rosen, what's wrong? Is there anything I can help you with? Should I tell that man to go away, that you're ill today?"

"No, no." He pushed away from the door with a sigh. "It'll be okay, Jane. I've just had a nasty jolt. Come and sit down. I ordered you your roast beef; eat some of it."

Mollifying though it was to hear the food order had been deliberately for her, it couldn't distract from the strange behavior of the past ten minutes.

"Mr. Rosen . . ."

"All right, all right, yes, you can help. Here's what I need you to do." He paused to seemingly gather his thoughts. "I'm going to take Steven out for lunch; we'll be gone for an hour. I need you to go to the accounting department, go to the director of finance, Harjeet Singh, give him this note I'm about to write. Then go to Jason Mantford—you know who he is, he's chair of the firm's partnership board—show him the same note. Do not read the note, do not show it to anyone else, do not speak to anyone else. Destroy it as soon as they've both seen it. Then go down to reception and ask them to give you the east boardroom, the farthest one down the hall. Put it in my name, and reserve it for the whole afternoon. No one is to go in or out of that boardroom without my authority. I'll bring

Steven there, and Singh and Mantford will join us. If anyone asks about my whereabouts or pushes you for information, you cite an ethical wall, okay? Do you have all that?"

He was writing on a legal pad hurriedly. As he finished talking, he tore it out, folded it over thrice, and handed it to Jane. "Do you have all that?" he asked again.

"Yes, Mr. Rosen, I do."

The corner of his mouth kicked up in a small smile. "First time I've had an accomplice on this." Jane raised her eyebrows. "Figuratively speaking, of course; you know I'd never involve you in anything that wasn't aboveboard."

"If it wasn't aboveboard, I don't think anyone will incriminate me for booking a boardroom and delivering notes to firm members, when I have complete deniability as to the note's contents."

He grinned. "I would have preferred an answer somewhere along the lines of 'Yes, Mr. Rosen, because I trust you completely.'"

"Oh, would you? Well, beggars can't be choosers. Do you want me to do your evil bidding or not?"

"Yes, you fiend. Go." Jane mentally patted herself on the back that their banter seemed to have restored some of his composure and helped him bury his badly concealed panic a little deeper. She took the note and left his office. Accounting was not somewhere she had had to go since her first tour, so it took some consulting of the floor plans to ascertain where to find Jason Mantford before she took off.

Disturbing two of the most powerful people in the firm, with no explanation as to why she was barging in urgently, was a little daunting, but being the emissary of Mr. Rosen had its advantages in that he, too, was one of the most powerful people in the firm, plus everyone was used to his assistant having to carry out orders on his often inexplicable stunts and uncertain temper.

The note seemed to do its trick; though neither man changed color or evinced the panic Mr. Rosen had upon seeing Steppenwolfe, they both became intensely alert, told her they would need to gather a few things and clear their schedule and then would be down to the boardroom promptly, the boardroom that Jane then proceeded to book with the tortoiseshell glasses.

"I don't understand why there isn't a client file number to record for this meeting in our booking system." Tortoiseshell wasn't having Jane's explanation of complete privacy.

"I told you, it's an ethical wall."

"That's to shield from other lawyers in the firm, not from reception. And I'm supposed to record the names of guests. Who from inside or outside the firm is joining him?"

"This is highly confidential. There will be absolutely no further information on this meeting, and I am following Mr. Rosen's orders. Would you like to take it up with him? He'll be here shortly."

Tortoiseshell sniffed and muttered to herself, but the threat did the trick.

Jane debated waiting around to see Mr. Rosen and Mr. Steppenwolfe return from lunch and safely into the boardroom, but Tortoiseshell was eyeing her, and Mr. Rosen's manic need for secrecy on this convinced her the fewer people around to draw attention, the better. She returned to Mr. Rosen's empty office where, under the reconciling glow of their mutual endeavor and because she was truly hungry as it was now past two o'clock and the adrenaline of the episode had burned through her, she devoured two roast beef sandwiches, cold.

Five o'clock came and went. Then six. Jane stayed at her cubicle in case her services should be needed again, but everything was quiet. No intrigued firm partners came round demanding answers; no one queried the presence of the Californian man, or even seemed to know he was in the firm apart from those three men ensconced in the boardroom with him.

At six thirty, the phone rang through on Mr. Rosen's line, a California number very similar to the one Mr. Steppenwolfe had called on back in November, save for two different digits. Same firm then, but different extension.

Jane answered with her customary greeting, and a low, sultry woman's voice replied.

"He's not in? What a shame I missed him, but I think my brother is there, Steven Steppenwolfe? Measly sort of man?"

Brother? Jane held the phone away from her in shock and stared at the receiver.

"Hello? Hello?"

"Yes, sorry, I'm here. Must have been a glitch with the long-distance connection." With the connectivity of modern phones, that wasn't even a good lie. "I'm afraid I don't know the status of your brother. I really couldn't say if he's in the firm or not, but if you'd leave your name and number, I'll be sure to have Mr. Rosen call you back as soon as he can."

The voice on the line gave a little laugh, and Jane got the distinct impression she was the one being laughed at.

"Oh, that's all right. You can tell him Julie called looking for her little brother and her erstwhile summer romance. He'll know what it means."

"Um, okay. Did you want to leave a last name as well, or is it also Steppenwolfe?"

"Oh, he'll know who Julie is. Ta, sweetheart." She hung up.

What the actual fuck.

Chapter 14

Jane got no explanation for either Steppenwolfe or Julie that night. She waited until eight before finally emailing Mr. Rosen to see if he needed her and got a curt It's all fine, go home in response. She relayed the message from Julie and waited a full twenty minutes before she received Okay.

The next morning passed in a blur of make-work projects Mr. Rosen had dumped on her desk bright and early, presumably to keep her out of the way and too busy to ask questions. He disappeared in the afternoon to "see Steven off at the airport." He showed no elation or relief at having this potential threat out of the country, but was conspicuously matter-of-fact about it. He told Jane the round trip to Pearson Airport would probably take the afternoon, so she could head home early at three.

Back and forth to Pearson did not take that many hours, Jane decided, even with traffic, not unless he was planning to spend a few hours with Steppenwolfe at the airport, discussing . . . who knows what. Was this to buy time away from Mantford and Singh? But that didn't make sense. Mr. Rosen had invited them into their confab.

Jane huffed, although not entirely due to frustration. She had decided to follow through on her plan to practice marching up and down the stairs using the fire escape in her apartment building. Being home early, and frustrated at the mystery, letting off steam seemed like a good idea, so she'd laced up some sneakers and threw on an old pair of high school gym shorts and went at it. Three stories didn't seem like much compared to the sixty-five she would soon have to do, but after finishing only two rounds of the three flights she was already winded.

She paused for a breather, and then pressed on again.

The more she thought about it, the more it didn't make sense. Why would Steppenwolfe even use Pearson Airport? During her time at the firm, Jane had learned that the wealthy elite and the corporate jet-setters always used the Billy Bishop airport on the Toronto Islands for the very reason that it was downtown and handy. Customs between the U.S. and Canada was much quicker there too. Why all the secrecy in the first place? She had googled Steven Steppenwolfe; he was exactly as he seemed: a California lawyer from a slick, successful firm. Yet he wasn't a managing partner, nor particularly renowned. He had authored a few pieces on certain changes to legislation after the '08 crisis, he had spoken at the odd conference, and his list of public clients on the website was standard.

"The hell is all that clanging noise?"

"Practicing. I have to walk down sixty-five sets of stairs for a fire drill at work. Problem with that?"

Her downstairs neighbor quickly retracted his head back through the window.

And who was the mysterious Julie? She'd googled Julie

Steppenwolfe and gotten nowhere besides an old obit for a ninety-year-old woman who'd died in Texas. The California firm was large—there were two Julies with different last names to be found on the website after scrolling through lawyer bios. One was a Nordic-looking blonde along the lines of Isabelle who was titled a "consultant"; the other was a redheaded partner. Both were beautiful, but neither turned up anything extraordinary or unusual in their particulars.

Maybe this really was just a run-of-the-mill albeit hypersensitive and confidential client issue. But then why had Mr. Rosen gone so ghastly white when Mr. Steppenwolfe unexpectedly appeared? Did Julie know about Isabelle . . . ?

"Eugh. Gross." A blister had been slowly bubbling up while she walked and thought and now had popped. She felt the slight damp of fluid inside her sock.

She sighed. A shower, then. She was getting nowhere with this mystery tonight.

Jane spent the weekend walking the stairs, both her heels protectively covered with Band-Aids, until her legs ached. It belatedly occurred to her that crippling herself with practice stair-climbing would leave her in worse, not better, shape for the upcoming drill.

On Monday, she went to lunch with Adele where, feeling pent-up and for the first time in a long time feeling the lack of someone to confide in, she poured out her fears about Isabelle in as detached and clinical a way as possible, wishing that she was also free to talk about Julie and Steven Steppenwolfe.

"I just think if they're going to keep dedicating all these firm resources for this client project, they should tell us how long it's going to run. It's a lot of running up and down to the sixty-fifth floor for everyone, and Anita and Alison are supposed to be floaters to support lawyers when their assistants are away. How can they do that if they're perpetually helping out Isabelle and co.?"

Jane huffed and sat back, covering her lapse in restraint by poking at her wilted salad. The Irish Embassy Pub and Grill had been her idea for their lunchtime visit. She had passed its white stone, pillared facade on Yonge Street often, just a block or so away from the famous intersection of the streets of Bay and King. Its old-world elegance, wedged between modern buildings, reminded her of the National Club, and, feeling adventurous, she suggested they try it. The inside did not disappoint; it was glowing and noisy, with a lively lunch crowd filling up the space between its yellow walls, wood furniture, and wall sconce lighting. Only, in a moment of indecision while ordering, she'd gone with a plain Caesar salad instead of one of their hearty sandwiches or traditional Irish pies. Now she felt grumpy eyeing everyone else's lunch.

"What are you really complaining about? Your workload is no more no less than normal, n'est-ce pas?"

Jane hesitated. "I think Isabelle and Mr. Rosen might end up together. Y'know, *together* together." *Sound more like a high schooler if you can. Great job.*

"Ah, I also suspect it is so. But they are being discreet with their courtship, no? They are not making you uncomfortable."

"No, they're being . . . okay about it, I guess. I mean, I'm not even sure what's going on. I think she definitely wants him, but sometimes I'm not sure she even likes him. Why go after a guy you don't like?" Despite believing Clémence's assertions, Jane couldn't shake the feeling that she was missing something about their romance. Was it wishful thinking, or did it just seem *off* somehow?

"He is the foremost partner in the firm. Liking *him* may have nothing to do with it."

"What do you mean?"

"They don't call it 'arranged marriage,' but among the elite, old families sometimes it is nearly the same thing. There's free choice, bien sûr, but only if their adult children choose from among the approved people. When I first started at the firm, there was a new, young female partner. The week she started, the girl's mother called her friends—the ladies who lunch—and the next thing you know, all those ladies' sons who worked in the firm were stopping by to take the girl out. She picked one she liked well enough, and voilà. It is often the case."

The idea of having that much social currency and expectation was so foreign to Jane.

Adele shrugged. "Sometimes there is love, sometimes love grows, and sometimes it is more a partnership. A power couple is a powerful thing. And Mr. Rosen, he is very powerful, from a very old family, and so is very . . . appropriate for an Isabelle. Mr. Rosen has always ignored these things before, but perhaps he is getting older and changing his thinking. How does he respond to her?"

Jane stopped to think. She had been so quick to look away, to mentally block up her ears when they were near her that it took some work to draw up the images and conversations to examine them.

In her determination to be always out of the room and not bear witness to the sight, Jane really didn't have much to draw on besides those flashes of Isabelle's flirtations that burned in her memory and made her grind her teeth, but Mr. Rosen?

Jane admitted to herself that nearly no experience with adult romantic relationships made her spectacularly unqualified to make these judgments However, even though she wasn't an expert on romance, months of close contact had made her something of an expert on Mr. Rosen. She knew how his face softened and changed when Professor Graham's name flashed across the phone, knew how he relaxed when she herself approached him.

But did he like Isabelle?

Jane couldn't recall a single instance of his smile touching his eyes, of his laugh sounding warm and genuine. She had seen him catalog Isabelle's every flirtatious glance at him or other men, had watched him systematically step back to stay clear of her habitual hair flick. For all that he paid attention to Isabelle, he seemed curiously . . . untouched by the lure of her presence. But, while his usual vim and vigor was still in his speech, and his lightning-quick temper was still at play, it was mellowed with Isabelle, she decided, and his usual client-charming best version of himself was put out on display for her.

Ah, just like a client he needs to get onside.

So Adele was right. This was some sort of rich people mating ritual, like a corporate merger. Jane had just been too ignorant of their elite culture to understand.

"I don't know if he's into *her* exactly, but he's so attentive and courteous to her. If he wasn't interested, why wouldn't he shut down her flirting? He's never had a problem being direct before. So yeah, I guess he's going for it," she said to Adele at last and felt a sinking in her stomach at the knowledge. She thought of his face when he'd seen Lamp, newly restored. His caring love for Graham. He was soft inside, she was almost sure of it, something that must have been denied when he was young. Jane knew what it was to nurture a secretly warm heart and receive nothing from the world outside to revive it. For the first time, she acknowledged to herself that distantly, covertly, in a place kept hidden even from herself, she had been picturing how she and Mr. Rosen could have been happy together. She could have loved him well.

Oh god. She was so much further gone than she'd thought, back in January.

She pushed away her salad, feeling a little sick.

"Qu'est-ce qu'il y a? The salad is not good?"

"No, not good."

*B*ack in her cubicle, Jane put her head down on her desk, grateful for the cool and the quiet.

"Jane! I need you to scan and copy these . . ." Mr. Rosen rounded the corner, a sheaf of documents in his hand, and came up short. "Jane, are you all right?"

She was in love with him, no denying it to herself. *What an awful, stupid thing to do. Stupid. Stupid. Stupid.* She wanted to cry.

"I'm okay, just a bit of a headache." She pulled herself into an upright position and put on her best polite, professional smile, the one she wore every day when she was a waitress.

"Are you sure? You look a bit wobbly." He moved forward and gently laid a hand on her shoulder. "If you need to go home . . ."

"No. I've taken an aspirin. I'll be fine." She craved his touch but refused to be moved by it. "I'll take those documents and get them right back to you."

He handed them over, but his dark eyes stayed on her, serious with worry.

"I'm fine, Mr. Rosen."

Just do the job you were hired to do.

A miserable evening preceded a sleepless night. Jane tossed and turned in her bedroom with its yellow walls that seemed to mock her now. Loving a man who couldn't or wouldn't love you back was just stupid. Working for a man day after day and uselessly pining for him and watching while he made a loveless match with someone else was pure masochism. Any way she looked at it, she was going to be left heartbroken and alone.

Throwing away her first real job because she couldn't keep her emotions in check was equally stupid, but her instincts screamed to get away from the firm, away from Mr. Rosen, to stay intact, insulated, to survive, and keep going.

So she was going to be brokenhearted, lonely, and looking for her next job. Fantastic.

Less than a year into my shiny new career and it's already fucked-up. If she loved him less, she might be able to hate him more for derailing her plans so thoroughly.

Longing for anything other than what was, was counterproductive, she told herself sternly, and feeling sorry for yourself was worse. Keep putting one foot in front of the other. Some people have it better than you and some people have it worse, and that was just life. Life was unfair. Better to focus on the little things, like a clean apartment, the grocery list, going to the movies, small routines—these things were solid and dependable, unlike people, who could leave you heartbroken and alone.

It was a bleak thought, but she'd done bleak before—hell, she'd done bleak in spades, and she could do it again she told herself.

The next morning dawned gray and frosty, a brutal March denoting a still long-off spring, something Canadians were habitually used to but still grumbled about every year.

In her preoccupation with her own miserable future, Jane forgot her scarf and gloves and was left shivering and huddling inside her coat waiting for the train. She was halfway to Toronto before she realized today was the fire drill and she'd left her flats at home. It was going to be a choice of wearing her sturdy boots and clumping down every single step, or wearing her heels and hoping for the best, or going barefoot and walking over countless dirty surfaces and having the feet of her pantyhose completely ruined.

The man in the seat next to her chose this moment to completely descend into sleep, and slumped sideways into her. She growled and pushed him back. Maybe Adele would have a pair of gym shoes she wouldn't mind loaning her.

By the time she stepped out of Union Station onto Front Street, a freezing drizzle was starting to come down, misting her hair, face, and coat. She should have taken the underground PATH, but she didn't think nature was going to take the symbolic reflection of her heartbroken mood this far.

Typical.

She hurried over the cobblestone pedestrian walkway and across the street where she dodged the line of taxis pulling up in front of the Royal York Hotel. She'd discovered last week while wandering on lunch break that by walking up the hotel's circular driveway into an alcove where the valets lounged, there was access to a small footpath filled with bike racks that short-cut onto Adelaide Street, and from there, King Street, saving her from the press of foot traffic. She took that course now, favoring the sides of the building where the awnings provided some protection. By the time she made it into the office, the toes of her pantyhose were damp, and tendrils of her hair were starting to stick out and frizz. She was shaking from the cold.

"What happened to you?" Mr. Rosen demanded in lieu of a morning greeting.

"It's freezing rain."

"And you didn't bring an umbrella?"

"Amazingly, weather divination is not part of my skill set. You can take that up with HR for hiring me so carelessly."

Mr. Rosen's eyebrows rose at the uncharacteristically acid tone of her snark, but a smile still pulled at his mouth. He sauntered away, hands in his pockets, and returned a few minutes later, just as Jane was getting settled in at her desk, with a hot cup of tea.

This small act of kindness—though not really small, not to her—made her feel both further irritated and emotional. She wanted to tell him to stop being nice to her, but of course she couldn't do that. How could he understand that what others would consider to be small, humane acts had a disproportionate effect on her when they came from him?

"Thank you, Mr. Rosen."

He said nothing, only handed her the tea and retreated to his office, giving her space alone with her bad mood.

At ten, Isabelle came round and disappeared into his office, and Jane gritted her teeth as she listened to the sound of trilling laughter through the door. Finally, she went over to Adele and inquired about the shoes, in desperate need of a respite.

"Quoi? The fire drill? Oh no, we don't actually do that." Off Jane's blank look, she elaborated, "Of course we *should* do that, and some of the young people do it for the exercise, and I think the marketing department is all made to do it because their boss says so, and new employees *used* to do it at least once just so they know the way . . ."

"Okay, so when you say we don't do it . . ." Jane said, slightly irritated, having less than her usual patience for Adele's meandering.

"I mean most people in the firm just stay at their desks or go out for coffee ten minutes before the drill and come back when it's all over."

"Isn't that illegal or something?"

"HR used to monitor us, reprimand the truants, but that job was given to Diane, and so . . ." Adele shrugged. "Mr. Rosen is a bear about it, though, so most of floor sixty-five disappears for coffee."

"Great. So I've been prepping to walk down sixty-five flights of stairs for nothing."

Adele patted her arm. "I'm sorry, I did not think to tell you. But I will pick you up and we'll go down for coffee together. Look on the bright side: I'm sure your glutes must now be very toned. You should start wearing more pencil skirts!"

Jane stomped back to her desk, startling Isabelle who passed her in the hallway, and unsuccessfully attempted to stuff down the guilt she felt for snapping at Adele.

Not for years had Jane allowed this level of emotion to bleed past her exterior. Pulling it in was how she'd always survived, and on some level she knew, in the not-too-distant future, she would be alarmed at this loss of control, but right now she was finding it difficult to care.

She drank the remains of her now-cold tea and answered Mr. Rosen's emails, losing track of time. At eleven o'clock, an earsplitting wailing sounded throughout the office that made Jane jump and momentarily forget there was no need to panic.

Heart pounding despite herself, she covered her ears with both hands and tried to carry on reading, grumpy that Adele hadn't collected her for that coffee run.

"JANE!" Mr. Rosen was suddenly in her field of vision, roaring to be heard. "WHAT ARE YOU DOING?"

"WHAT? IT'S JUST A DRILL."

"WE HAVE DRILLS FOR A REASON, JANE, OR HAVE YOU FORGOTTEN 9/11?"

Jane's stomach dropped.

"GET TO THE FIRE ESCAPE RIGHT NOW OR I WILL THROW YOU OVER MY SHOULDER AND CARRY YOU THERE."

Jane jumped out of her seat. Mr. Rosen never made threats he didn't follow through on.

He strode down the hallway and around the corner, Jane scurrying in his wake. True to Adele's prediction, the office was already suspiciously empty, and those left behind were seated at their desks, headphones or hands over their ears as they carried on with their work.

At Mr. Rosen's furious bark, they jumped up like they'd been scalded and rushed ahead to the fire exit stairwell.

The office fire escape was not like the metal latticed stairs that wound around the outside of Jane's apartment building. It was a wide interior chute of concrete, almost like a large, empty elevator shaft. The stairwell was cold and quiet, insulated from the rest of the building, with endless flights of stone steps twisting downward in a zigzag pattern that rendered its users dizzy. Each level was marked by clear floor numbers: 65, 64, 63 . . . In a pinch, when the elevators were slow and the main staircase was busy, or people were trying to avoid their bosses, staff were known to use these stairs. Jane had always avoided them, disliking their tomb-like industrial feel that gave them a Hitchcockian horror vibe.

But there was no gainsaying Mr. Rosen's stony face as he held the door open for her. The other unfortunate staff members had sped ahead and were already clanging down several floors below, clearly keen to put some distance between themselves and the famously cantankerous senior partner.

As Mr. Rosen followed her in, the door slid shut with a hollow boom, and they started down the stairs. The stair flights were quite narrow, and the space that she and Mr. Rosen occupied felt alarmingly intimate. She could hear the rasp of his palm skimming the metal handrail, and the sound of his breathing as it started to pick up ever so slightly from the exertion.

They passed floors sixty-five to sixty without incident, but she could see he was unimpressed with how few people were participating. As they passed fifty-nine to fifty-two where other companies leased, he growled.

"Fire drills used to mean something. These stairwells used to be packed on a day like today; you had to go to the assigned meeting place on King Street, get your name checked off on a list by HR or there'd be hell to pay. Now everyone feels safe and they've forgotten. Fools."

On the fifty-first-floor landing, Jane paused to take off her heels, and Mr. Rosen took them from her and stuffed them in his suit jacket pockets without a word. The slight break meant that they were now completely alone in the stairwell.

To distract him from his dark thoughts, and to fill the air that felt too close, Jane cobbled together a question about the history of the building, knowing it would set him off on a tangent. He was a sucker for historical detail.

By the time he finished telling her how the BMO tower had once been the sixth tallest tower in the world, and they were reaching floor thirty-five, he seemed more sanguine. "Pride of Toronto, this old beast of a tower." He patted the concrete wall affectionately.

"You'll miss it if you move to Montreal, then."

"Montreal?"

Shit.

Focused on her aching calves, the rumbling sound of his voice, and the hypnotic and slightly dizzying effect of stair after stair after stair, Jane had let the thought slip out.

"I just thought, perhaps maybe, you might be spending more time there, in the future. Sir." She tacked on the "sir" in halting awkwardness. She hadn't called him that since their relationship's rocky beginning. God, why this, why now, why open a can of worms when there was literally no escape? *I'm a freaking masochist.*

He looked at Jane, genuinely baffled. "Why would I be going back to Montreal?"

"I thought, uh," Jane stammered. "It's Isabelle's home, isn't it? Or is she transferring permanently to Toronto?"

His eyes flicked across her face like he was trying to decipher a puzzle, and Jane fought down a miserable blush. And then realized they were both a little red-faced from the stairs anyway so what did it matter.

"Oh, I see." He looked down and away for a moment, thinking. They were on floor thirty before he spoke again. "So you think I want the lovely Isabelle, then. She is lovely, isn't she?"

Jane had expected the worst. She had braced herself for the worst. She had taught herself to unflinchingly monitor every possible sign that signaled the worst was imminent. And yet she somehow still felt caught unawares, and her stomach sunk. Her sleepless night, this whole miserable day, her whole lonely life felt like it was all coming to a head as sweat trickled down her back and endless stairs unspooled at their feet.

"Is that what you think, Jane? Should I make it official with her? Cry uncle and let her do what she wants with me, civilize me, make me a domesticated man?"

Jane said nothing.

"I think domestication might suit me. Of course, I'll have to get used to certain things, like wearing a proper tie every day. Izzy doesn't seem the type to let me go around without one; she's always so impeccably turned out, she'll have expectations. Yes, I can see it now." He clapped his hands together jovially, as if picturing it, as they rounded the twenty-eighth floor, but his voice held an anger Jane didn't understand. "She'll want fancy dinners, cloth napkins, proper silverware, a home that looks like a high-class hotel. A professionally run Instagram account. Yoga. The right set of people for our friends. Less mess, better manners, I'll be an altogether more refined man. I suppose that will make me more likable, don't you think, Jane?"

"Likable?" she croaked.

"Well . . . for some people. You always like me at my sloppy, cranky worst, don't you?"

She gave a tremulous laugh.

He grinned. "What, none of your usual sass? Or even a meek little 'yes, sir'? It's been a while since I've had one of those. You used to say it all the time. I can't decide if I miss it or not." He paused before continuing. "When you're reassigned to someone else—I assume you'll want to be reassigned, of course, if I'm constantly jetting back and forth to Montreal—I know I'll miss more than that."

So Clémence was right. Isabelle was talking him into moving to Montreal.

Resolutely, Jane stayed silent, but a traitorous lip trembled. It was unclear what emotion she was even trying to keep in check. Rage, grief, hurt, longing were all jockeying for attention.

Mr. Rosen continued. "I'll miss a lot of things"—his voice grew gentler—"like how you greet me every morning, and that exasperated look you get when I miss a meeting. I'll miss your compulsive need to color-code everything, and how you rescue dear old Lamp when I've knocked him over. I'll miss our lunches together, our chats."

Hot tears were starting to well in her eyes, and her insides felt molten and bubbling, rising up with the truth, but still, she clamped it down. Still, she remained silent. The balls of her feet ached, her legs ached, everything hurt.

Out of the corner of her eye she saw Mr. Rosen wet his lips and hesitate—his one and only nervous tell—and then plow on. "I'll miss other things too. Things a boss isn't supposed to miss. That hair, watching you think, and I've never met anyone who could be so benignly stubborn. I can't stand my ground without exploding and you can't stand yours without being completely calm. How is that possible?" A corner of his mouth curled up in a rueful grin.

"I'll miss the sound of your voice on the phone when I call from an out-of-office meeting. Knowing you'll be there waiting for me when I get back and I'm tired and grumpy and just the sight of you makes it better." His chest was rising and falling rapidly now, voice cracking on the last syllable. Jane fought the urge to look up, her mind spinning with confusion. *Why is he saying these things?* "It's strange how that works. No matter what's happening in my day, just you, standing there and breathing, existing, suddenly makes it better. Maybe you only have that power for me." With a slight shake, Mr. Rosen threw off his intensity and at once resumed a jarringly jocular tone. "Of course, I doubt you'll miss me at all! Once you have your new boss you'll forget all about . . . Jane? Jane, are you crying?"

"You ass!" she burst out.

Silence was no longer an option. The churning waters had bubbled over and were spilling out. To her horror, the verbal diarrhea began to flow. "You absolute asshole! Stop talking!

Just stop talking! Don't tell me these things. I don't want to know. It hurts! You think I won't miss you? You think you'll be happy trussed up in a proper suit and served at fancy dinners like a turkey? Telling me how you'll miss . . . how you'll miss . . . you goddamned fool, idiot, lumbering wall of a man!"

Sputtering and crying, feeling righteously indignant and utterly mortified, gesticulating wildly as she ran out of words to berate him with, she tried to turn away to face the wall so that she could salvage what was left of her dignity, when she was spun back around to face the wall of his chest.

"Jane . . ." He caught at her hand. "Jane . . ." She flung him off, but he gently grasped both her forearms and kept her upright as she nearly overbalanced on the stairs. "*Jane . . .*"

"Idiot!" she repeated. "You're better than this! You're better than Isabelle and you know it, and if you're going to just . . . what, because she has the right last name and the right family and she looks like a magazine cover? Idiot! *I'm* better than this. I don't care if everyone in this firm thinks I'm dirt on the bottom of their shoe, or that I'm only here to fetch coffee, or that I'm sleeping with you, or whatever it is they think . . ."

"What?"

". . . I'm mad about you. *You*, not your social standing or status. You're grumpy and rumpled and adorable and brilliant and secretly kind and weirdly wonderful, and if you're too stupid to look for a woman, *any* woman, who actually cares about you and would love you, rather than someone who wants to use you, then go ahead and walk blindly into your fate. I hope she makes you wear a damned tie every day and pose for a thousand Instagram posts and you hate every second of it. Idiot!"

"You're mad about me? Not mad at me, but *about* me?" he asked.

"That's your only takeaway?!" Jane bawled, still crying, still angry, still heartsore, but now also exasperated, because when was she not exasperated by this man?

"You're mad about me?" he repeated, persistent and urgent.

"Yes!"

"You're sure?"

"Yes!"

"Can I kiss you?"

"Yes!"

And suddenly, he was grasping, pulling her into him and bending down to frantically kiss her, his lips sliding in the wetness of her tears but undeterred, pressing his mouth to hers over and over again even as she sputtered in shock.

Then she shocked herself. She kissed him back.

She kissed him back with a wild sense of abandon, with a hedonistic pleasure she hadn't known she was capable of, clutching at his lapels to anchor herself to him and feeling like she might fly apart at the seams, like every nerve ending was suddenly brilliantly alight. His kiss was messy and warm and enthusiastic and wonderful and so much like him she just cried all the harder.

"Jane, Jane, stop crying," he said hoarsely, pulling back. "I've never kissed a wailing woman before and it's killing my confidence." With a visible effort he calmed himself and tenderly cupped her face. "Jane Raine, I goddamn adore you."

"What?"

"I'm in love with you . . . Have been for ages. Couldn't be helped. I'm sorry."

"What?" She was sniffling now, trying to make sense of him.

He kissed her again, this time gently, carefully, and Jane sunk into it with a sigh, one hand reaching up to stroke his stubbled cheek, fast becoming addicted to this new way of communicating with each other.

"I'm in love with you," he said when they finally pulled apart after several long moments in which Jane nearly forgot the thread of the conversation. "I don't want you transferred, I don't want you gone, and I certainly don't want to be the lapdog of Ms. Isabelle Ingram."

"*What?*"

"Are you going to say anything other than 'what'?"

"Then . . . why now . . . ?"

"Ah, yes, well." He looked embarrassed and ducked his head. "I couldn't really just come out and say I was; I had romantic feelings for you. There are workplace harassment laws, and they're meant to protect you from, say, a boss hitting on his assistant. And even if there weren't—I mean I'm a decade older than you, I own the firm, and you need this job. If I got it wrong and you didn't reciprocate how I—this is an unequal power dynamic—you're too inexperienced in the corporate world to know just how much—and I would never want to take advantage of you because, well, because I love you. And when you love someone, you kind of want them to love you back without all that other stuff getting in the way. I wasn't kidding at the holiday party. I want you to know there will never be repercussions for saying no to me."

"You . . . love me?" She felt faint and incredulous. Staggering under the dual intoxication of his kisses and his words,

Jane felt like she was grasping for a sobriety she didn't really want, but needed.

"Then *why* . . ."

"Why what?" He carefully tucked an errant strand of hair behind her ear.

"Why have you been flirting with Isabelle?"

He gave his great barking laugh, and Jane nearly reared back to smack his arm again, but he pulled her closer and kissed her before she could.

"I have *not* been flirting with Isabelle. I have been *enduring* Isabelle. Clémence is the one I needed for the deal. She's brilliant."

"You certainly didn't treat her like that! Dancing off for lunches with the client and leaving her behind to work."

Mr. Rosen wrinkled his nose. "Is that what you think? Is that what she thinks? God, I'll have to have a talk with her later. Jane," he said, forcing her to focus, though adrenaline, hope, and anger were all still surging through her, "Clémence is a brilliant lawyer, but she was an even more brilliant journalist before she became a lawyer, and she made a name for herself doing big exposés on companies and their financial dealings. Some people kicked up a fuss when I hired her—I told them to go to hell, obviously—but this particular client has a long-standing relationship with Isabelle's family, and Clémence's history makes them nervous. I needed to keep Isabelle sweet to keep them sweet, so they didn't fuss about Clémence working on the deal, and it seemed prudent to keep Clémence out of their sight, *and* to keep Isabelle in my sight so she didn't swan off with all the credit for Clémence's hard work like I heard she's been doing lately. It's a shitty game, I know, but this deal will be huge for the firm and huge for Clémence's career if I can manage it right."

Jane's head was reeling. "Why did Clémence give up being a brilliant journalist?"

"Journalism is crappy pay. She's divorced and a single mother. I told you I love you, and are we really still talking about Clémence and Isabelle?"

"I thought you and Isabelle . . ." she began again only to be cut off emphatically by Mr. Rosen.

"Jane, believe me when I say I never gave a flying fuck about that woman. It wasn't until a moment ago when you were busy packing me off to Montreal and tortured domestic bliss that I even realized what must have been pinging around that mysterious brain of yours. I thought . . . well, I hoped you'd finally understood me at Christmas, and that maybe you weren't totally averse to me. The Montreal trip was rotten timing, I know, and then having the two of them always around, and you were already hurt by the office gossip, so I just . . ."

"Rambling," Jane said, amazed. He never rambled.

"Right. Well, I wanted you to want me, and I wanted you to say it first so I could be sure my feelings were welcomed. You started talking about Isabelle, and I suddenly realized jealousy might do the trick. Clever, right?"

Jane reeled back, stunned. The last few days played in her mind, moments sliding apart and fitting back together in new patterns. She rewound their conversation about him moving to Montreal in her head.

Her anger flared. "You sneaky rat bastard manipulative . . . *lawyer!*"

He smiled adoringly down at her. "I love you too."

He can't possibly mean that. "I don't believe you." She made to pull out of his grasp again, and the smile dropped off his face.

"No. I've waited months to have you in my arms. Would you fucking stay put, please?"

"You can't just randomly say you love me! And expect me to believe it! During a fire drill!" She choked, incredulous.

"Why the hell not?"

She leaned back—as far as his total envelopment of her frame would allow—and studied his face.

"Because normal people don't do that!"

"Jane, our meet-cute was me attacking a coffee machine. Our big declaration of love is sweating in a stairwell during a fire drill. We don't do normal."

"Well how 'bout you try believable?"

"How is this not believable?"

"I'm all soggy!" Jane wailed, feeling there was no dignity left to salvage at this point.

"Ah, that I can fix. I think I have a tissue here somewhere." He kept one arm wrapped around her as the other dug in his pocket and produced a slightly rumpled tissue that Jane took and tried to mop up her face.

"Professor Graham always carries a proper handkerchief," Jane said petulantly.

"Yeah, well, Gerry's a much better man than me." He kissed her temple just as she was blowing her nose, and it was that grossly romantic act more than anything that made Jane begin to believe him. But with that belief came the fear. She never got to have nice things. And this was too nice to have and then lose.

"It won't work," Jane said, mind already fast-forwarding to practicalities and logistics, even as a part of her was still reeling at this news.

"What, us? Why not, Miss Pragmatic?"

They'd been stopped in their position for some minutes now, and clanging overhead told them some other diligent employees from another company were climbing down and catching up.

"C'mon, let's get going. We still have to finish this drill." He took the demolished tissue back and shoved it in his pants pocket and, with a casualness that flummoxed Jane, like he did it all the time, tucked her small hand in his and started down the stairs again. "We have twenty more floors to go. You have until we reach the ground to explain why you think this isn't a fantastic idea."

Chapter 15

Well?"

They were on floor eighteen, Jane having taken the last two floors in silence as she tried to calm herself from the emotional high, and reconcile both the fear and the joy slowly spreading through her.

"I'm your assistant. I work for you."

"Yes, and as much as I'd love to keep you as such, obviously HR would never allow it, and I'm not wild about being in this morally gray area either. If you're happy at the firm, they can reassign you to another partner, one I don't normally deal with. Adele would probably have some good recommendations of who would treat you right. Or you can have a glowing reference and walk into any other firm on the street. I'd happily take myself to another firm to make things easier for you, but, well . . ."

"You own the firm," Jane supplied.

"Sort of own it," he corrected softly. "Jane, I know it's not fair that your working life has to be upheaved, but I want us to have a relationship, not a fling. I want to make that very clear."

"People in the firm will still talk." Maybe if this wild idea of his actually worked and they had a proper relationship people would realize . . . She immediately threw up a mental wall, as impenetrable as any ethical wall the firm created. That was too much to hope for; that was thinking too far ahead. Jane gave herself a minute to pack that thought away and focus on other immediate concerns.

"They already do. Let 'em."

Hard to argue with that logic.

"I'm not from your type of people, the Upper Canada College and country-club set. I can't golf or play tennis, I'm not educated, not really, I don't come from anything. How are you going to introduce me at a dinner party?"

"I'll say this is my lovely girlfriend, Jane, who is far too good for me. And if you absolutely feel you need some sort of credentials, I'll say she's famous Professor Raine's daughter, and we met at work. Anything else is their problem. And believe it or not, I don't go to many dinner parties. Jane, I'm exactly what I appear to be, a grumpy workaholic, because believe it or not, I am definitely getting the better end of this bargain. My own set tolerate me, and I go among them only when I need to. I'd rather spend my time with you and Gerry and people I like. If anyone turns up their nose at you, I say fuck 'em."

Jane mulled that over.

"Five floors left. Any other objections?" They were both quite sweaty by now, but he didn't relinquish her hand.

"No more lying, no more tricks, Mr. Rosen."

He looked away. "Deal, on the condition that you call me Edward."

Edward.

The thought gave her a little thrill. It was something real, something intimate, even after his confession and kisses. She'd known for a while that the E. W. Rosen stamped on everything stood for Edward William Rosen, but not many people used his first name. Per some old boys' club pseudo sports team tic, most of the partners called one another by their last names. He was usually just "Rosen" in the firm if not "Mr. Rosen."

"At least call me Edward when we're outside the office."

"We're not outside the office."

"No? Well we're about to be."

They took the last step off the stairs and onto level floor once more, Jane's legs rubbery, and followed a short corridor tilting slightly uphill to a metal door, almost like they were leaving an underground bunker, to emerge blinking into the still slightly drizzling rain and faint streaks of sunlight. Their journey had brought them to a grassy patch at the back of the BMO tower, facing Adelaide Street.

A group of people were standing there leisurely, still a little sweaty like Jane and Edward, but starting to shiver now. A fire truck was parked nearby on the street, lights and sirens silent. A firefighter stood nearby, enviously eyeing one of the employees' lit cigarette before he shook his head and addressed the crowd.

"All right, folks, looks like we've got nearly the last of the people participating out. Then we just need confirmation of the relay signal from the tower security team and we'll be good to go. You can return to your offices momentarily, and I promise you can take the elevator up!"

The weak joke was met with a few polite chuckles.

Jane had dropped Edward's hand as soon as they were outside. He'd frowned but allowed it, and wordlessly handed over her shoes before extending an arm to balance against as she hopped from one foot to the next to slip them back on.

The wailing of the building alarm could still be heard faintly from the outside. It gave one final pitch of noise and then blessedly died off. There was a collective sigh of relief.

"Okay, folks, thanks for taking the time. You all have a nice day now, eh."

People turned back toward the glass atrium entrance on the north side of the building, chatting lightly as they went, glad to be leaving the cold and rain.

Edward was unusually silent beside her as they followed the group in and queued for the elevator. He was quiet for the ear-popping ride up to floor sixty-five, and for the long walk down to their end of the office corridor. When they reached where they would normally part ways to go to their respective desks, he instead gently circled a hand around her wrist and drew her into his office, where he shut the door and promptly kissed her, and like each time before, her mind short-circuited in favor of blindly reveling in the warmth and nearness of him.

"So that's a yes?" he asked, when they both came up for air.

"Yes."

"Say, 'Yes, *Edward*.' You have to use my name."

Jane laughed. "Yes, Edward. And that's the only time I'll use your name in the office."

He scowled. "No one actually expects assistants to use formal titles anymore unless they're crotchety and old. You were the one who started saying Mr. Rosen."

"Because that's what most of the firm calls you. Ground rules, right now—in the office, you're Mr. Rosen, and no kissing."

"I don't like your rules. I think your rules stink."

Jane gave him a stern look and he relented. "Fine. I fully submit to being ruled by you, so I might as well start as I mean to go on. Anything else, Mademoiselle Raine?" He nuzzled her.

She experienced a surge of such overwhelming happiness and relief it felt almost like panic.

"Can we ask for my transfer in a few months? I agree we can't keep working together, ethically we shouldn't, but can we slow down the big changes so it's just one at a time? We keep this quiet and out of the office for now, see how it goes, and then at the start of May we take it to HR."

"You want me to prove that I can behave and that I mean what I say, don't you? All right, little skeptic, done. Anything else?"

"I may or may not have reminded Clémence how the time-keeper apps works, and she may or may not be planning to use it to expose Isabelle's lack of team effort . . . so you might need to get in line on that."

Edward roared with laughter. "Of course you did. In one subtle move you accomplish what all my blustering and planning hasn't yet. Classic efficient Jane, fixer of coffee machines, printers, and now office politics. Well, I'll still put in my two cents on Clémence's behalf. Now, anything else?"

Jane shook her head and he grinned. "Excellent, if we can just resume . . ."

"No, you don't! You said you'd behave and we'd keep this out of the office." She backed away toward the door, smiling.

"Just this once. It's a special occasion." He prowled toward her.

"What, the fire drill?" Jane teased.

"That's right. I'm very passionate about . . ." He caught her and pinned her to the door, leaning down for another kiss. ". . . fire drills."

The day passed in a whirlwind. Edward wanted dinner together that night, but Jane begged off and was appreciative when he seemed to pick up on her need for space, to process things. He well knew her methodical mind, and Jane was grateful that he understood that big changes were hard for her to take.

She rode the train home in a happy glow and breezed into her apartment with a sigh, kicking off her shoes and peeling off her pantyhose, hopelessly ruined by climbing down sixty-five flights of steps, partially shoeless.

Sitting at her kitchen table with a cup of tea, she tried to take it in. Nearly eight months ago she was at this same table, seeing her diploma, listening to the voice mail from the agency, and expecting nothing more than a lot of hard work in the hopes of moderately improving her life, dreams so small and concrete. She had depended on no one but herself since she was thirteen. Having someone like Mr. Rosen—*Edward*—offer himself and his love and his care was . . . it thrilled her and made her ecstatically happy, but it made a small, embarrassed part of her want to cry with relief, to have someone else to lean on, to have a partner and one that she could trust.

Having trust issues was the hallmark of a foster kid. She knew it, and she hated it. She hated falling so neatly into that category along with all those other kids, hated being a stereotype, hated how it dogged her every move. And she didn't need any help understanding it: as a child, everyone entrusted to look after you had failed you, homes and guardians evaporating, so as an adult, placing trust in anything or anyone external to yourself felt doomed to end in betrayal and failure.

But it also doomed you to a life alone, she knew, and what could sometimes feel like backbreaking self-reliance. Family and a home became the things you secretly wanted most in the world, and wanting it made it all the more difficult to trust when it was offered—how could you know if an oasis was real, or just a mirage you'd conjured up to hide the yawning desert? Better to walk on by than endure the heartbreak of finding out what you thought was sparkling water was just a handful of sand.

But she'd spent seven months seeing this man all day, almost every day. She'd cataloged all his worst faults, and then reluctantly, later, all his best attributes. He'd never lied—in fact, his brutal honesty was often more than polite society tolerated. He was right: he was what he seemed. She trusted him; she just had to trust that this, this idea of them together, was real and practical and not a romantic fantasy.

She looked around her apartment, proud of how she had brightened it with paint and little touches, but also recognizing it was shabby and sad next to the fancy, sleek places he frequented. How would she ever bring him in here?

She was just on the verge of doubting everything again when her phone buzzed with a slew of incoming texts. Edward had been adamant that afternoon, in between his deep kisses, that he was going to take full advantage of having access to her all the time, including blowing up her phone.

"I'm very needy and insecure," he'd teased, relinquishing

her lips in favor of nuzzling at her throat. "I need lots of contact and affirmation."

"I'm surprised you held back before," Jane had said rather breathlessly from her position sandwiched between him and the door. "Restraint is not exactly your forte." She'd gestured vaguely to their current position intending to make a joke of it but was distracted by his mouth, hot on her pulse point.

She'd heard of touch starvation before, but she'd never wondered if she suffered from it in her largely isolated life. This greedy feeling that he engendered, though, this heart-pounding thrill that made her feel like close was never close enough—was that normal? Was that just how it felt, when the person you were mad about was actually within reach? Did every sensation become hyper-focused like this until you were dizzy with it?

Edward had chuckled at her reply without raising his head, and the deep vibrations passing through her made her whimper in a way she'd be deeply embarrassed about later.

"HR policy. Personal contact information is locked down." He kissed delicately behind her ear. "Not available to a boss after hours unless personnel has a company-issued phone and compensation for the extended availability, etc. Otherwise"—he paused to nip at her earlobe and Jane shuddered—"it'd be considered *inappropriate*."

"HR policy is very, oh, thorough." Jane gasped, tilting her head to give him better access as he returned his interest to her neck, pressing closed-mouth kisses down its length.

"*Mm*. Labor law is an interesting field." He nudged at the neckline of her dress, his stubble scraping the thin skin over her collarbone.

"Did you study it at, uh, law school?" Her fingers clutched at his shoulders to pull him closer, with no idea why she was trying to hold on to a conversation.

He pulled back to look at her, his eyes dark. "Do you really want to talk about labor law right now?"

"No."

"Good," he'd grunted, and then returned to the all-important task of kissing her again.

Well, she had given him personal access to her now, and her phone buzzed with eight texts in quick succession.

> Just saw on news, renaming Air Canada Centre to Scotiabank Arena.
>
> Wtf, you can't just rename Toronto landmarks!
>
> Well, guess u can. SkyDome = Rogers Centre
>
> But does anyone actually call it Rogers?
>
> They have to redo all maps and street signs and tourist crap now? Didn't think it through :S
>
> Fucking banks. Too much power.
>
> Not that an airline owning the home of the Raptors was any better.
>
> Ever been to a Raptors game? I'll take you. Do you like basketball?

Jane grinned, remembering the delights of that afternoon, and told herself again to trust this. Then she set about replying.

Chapter 16

$\mathcal{E}$dward was as good as his word for the rest of the week. Though his manner was more flirtatious and affectionate than usual, he kept his professionalism mostly intact. He didn't try to touch her or kiss her again, although he called or texted every night. On Friday afternoon, he insisted he be allowed to take her on a Saturday date, and so Jane agreed to a simple dinner and a movie. He offered to come out to Port Credit, but still mindful of the humble nature of her personal space, she convinced him she'd rather spend time in the city than the suburbs.

Saturday morning, Jane put on a simple blue cable-knit sweater and denim skirt with knee-high boots, having pre-emptively agonized over her outfit the night before, threw her coat over it, and ran to catch the train.

They met outside Union Station, on the same cobblestone pedestrian walkway she had hurried across so miserably the morning of the fire drill. The day had dawned clear and gray, several degrees warmer so that it felt like spring was actually on its way.

Edward was standing there waiting, and Jane almost did a

double take. She had never seen him out of a suit before, or straying too far from the professional backdrop of Bay Street. He was wearing worn and soft-looking jeans, a dark green cotton T-shirt, and a faded black peacoat that hung open in a very Canadian male disregard for the cold. The simple, casual apparel took several years off his age, and his dark features and broad shoulders were all so handsomely pronounced by his attire that Jane wasn't surprised to see several women give him looks.

More than that, he looked comfortable and relaxed, and when he caught sight of Jane, his face lit up and he appeared . . .

Happy. I make him happy.

"Hello, sweetheart." He bent to kiss her, keeping it a chaste greeting.

"Edward," she replied softly, and he suddenly grinned wolfishly and bent to kiss her again, his former restraint gone. Jane had a fleeting moment of concern about PDA before her mind went blissfully blank. His large, warm hands sought out the slight dips of her waist through her lumpy coat and used them to grip her and pull her tight against him. Jane, off-balance and stretching up on her toes, fell easily into his solid warmth, letting him take her weight and keep them both grounded with his strength. He immediately took advantage of the new proximity to angle and deepen the kiss, and Jane responded eagerly, threading her fingers through his messy dark hair, as she'd been dying to do for so long.

A nearby wolf whistle finally brought things to a halt. Edward broke off and blindly flipped his middle finger in the direction of their interloper, his other hand still keeping her close.

"Using my actual name," he rasped in her ear, his voice deep and gravelly, "I'd say we're off to a good start."

And they were. He pecked her cheek innocently, like he hadn't just made her seriously contemplate jumping him in public, took her hand, and they set off toward the Scotiabank movie theater on Richmond Street. As they walked, he picked up his rant where he'd left it several nights before about the renaming of the massive sports arena that stood behind Union Station, as if it were any other day between them, while Jane sought to get her heart rate under control. Apparently, he'd done further research on the phenomenon of renaming Toronto city landmarks for their new sponsors and was riled up.

"Y'know what's going to happen next? Someone's going to up and buy Lake Ontario. It'll be Lake Uber."

"I'm not sure that wouldn't be an improvement. You have to admit, naming the lake after the province wasn't exactly a stroke of creative genius," Jane said.

"You're taking the other side just to goad me. No popcorn for you."

"Lake Pepsi. Lake Abercrombie and Fitch."

"How about Lake Rosen, Haythe and Thornfield?"

"Even your firm doesn't have that kind of money. You need American levels of big money for that."

Edward looked funny for a moment and then turned the conversation another way. Had she offended him?

No, I said I'd trust this.

Adele had been significantly less sanguine.

Although they'd agreed to keep the news hidden at work,

the one exception had been Adele, who not only had an uncanny ability to pick up on different kinds of tensions, but whom Jane felt unequal to deceiving and insufficiently equipped to dodge her motherly instincts.

She and Adele had gone for a quiet lunch during the week, farther away from the office than usual. When Jane finished recounting the tale, Adele was strangely silent.

The waiter refreshed their drinks, and Jane waited for her to gather her thoughts. It was obviously a big U-turn from their last conversation about Mr. Rosen and Isabelle, but surely it was good news.

"Then you are together. And you believe him that this is what he wants?"

"Believe him? Yes, of course I believe him."

No you didn't, not at first, her brain whispered back, but in the face of someone voicing her own doubts and thoughts, she felt her hope dig in its heels.

"Forgive me, it is just very strange."

"What, strange that he might want me with beautiful Isabelle standing nearby?"

"Chérie . . ." Adele sighed, clearly unsure how to go on. "It is not a case of you versus her. You are a very nice girl. I have seen that he is very fond of you. Protective. The firm talks of how well you get along, when he frightens so many others."

Jane looked away, all too well acquainted with how the firm talked about them. But certainly being talked about for being in a relationship would have to be better than being talked about for supposedly just screwing the boss. Adele read her look.

"Yes, some of the talk is crude. But I never worried about

you that way because you were so . . . eh, sensible. You are not romantique. Not foolish. Not setting your cap."

"You thought I wasn't one of those women, the ones you said don't get hired for this reason because they make problems by flirting with the men."

"You are not one of those women. But those women don't get hired because it *doesn't work*. Yes, once in a while you will get some, *pft*, some senior citizen partner who falls for a young thing, leaves his wife for her, makes a mess. They will talk about that until the day he dies. But that is the exception, not the rule."

"And I'm the rule," Jane countered, trying to contain her hurt.

"Jane." Adele leaned across the table and took her hand. "I do not doubt Mr. Rosen is a good man, and that you are a lovely girl. But I don't want to see you hurt. Men in his position do not marry their legal assistants."

The lunch had ended with a certain froideur between them, after Adele gave up her small attempts at reconciliation by telling funny stories about Diane as the plates were cleared. They skipped dessert and returned to the office quickly, like two people for whom a first date had gone badly. It took all of Edward's teasing that afternoon to banish the dark cloud the lunchtime conversation left and renew Jane's dedication to having faith in them.

She shook off the remembrance now. She was on a date, a proper date, and it was going well. It would be reasonable to expect some awkwardness between them in this new dynamic, but aside from a little skittish nervousness, there was none. They talked and bantered, Jane blushed and he grinned, always with an arm around her waist, a warm hand on her hip, or tenderly tucking a strand of hair behind her ear. Any use of his first name got her thoroughly kissed, and Edward ended up repeating his rude hand gesture several times as they got told off for holding up the ticket line and the concession line, and for blocking a doorway with their antics.

Jane couldn't have said what movie they saw or what meal they ate afterward, or how long she stood kissing him, the open panels of his coat wrapped around her in a warm cocoon, waiting on the platform for the train that was to take her home, only that she was beyond happy.

This blissful state quickly became something of a permanence. March bled into a gently balmy April, and days, evenings, and weekends were filled with Edward Rosen.

He took her to the promised Raptors game. He took her to an art gallery, and for an evening in the Distillery District where copious fairy lights strewn between refurbished industrial buildings twinkled down, and portable outside heating stands warmed the wine drinkers that lingered on cobblestone patios. He took her to the symphony and asked her to wear the green dress from the holiday party he so admired. He took her to the theater, where they saw a production of *Much Ado About Nothing*, and Jane avidly watched the stage while Edward delightedly watched her.

"I've never seen you so excited," he teased her afterward. "If I'd known Shakespeare was the way to get your attention, I would have tried it months ago."

"It's not the Shakespeare specifically. It's . . ." She paused, trying to tease out her feelings. "You know my father was a professor. Our home was always filled with students and literature and bits of poetry. I always took it for granted, or maybe I was just too young to appreciate it. I'm only just coming to realize that I miss it. I wish I remembered more of it."

Edward chuckled. "You're remembering more than you might realize. I'm not sure you're aware how often you're quoting this and that."

Jane thought it more likely that she was quoting this and that because she finally had someone to talk freely to.

"Not many people bring up Caesar's burial speech at a holiday party, or know about Caesar's burial speech," he added.

"*You* knew what I was talking about."

"Yes, which was lucky for me because I wanted to impress you. But I only knew it because we studied the speech as a rhetoric example in law school. That's the limit of my Shakespeare. You leave me in the dust."

"I wish . . ." Jane started, after a few moments of contemplative silence, and then stopped herself.

"Wish what?"

"I don't know. That I could have more of that again."

"You can. It's called school. It's called university and being a nerdy, adorable English major."

Jane raised her eyebrows dubiously. "It's called crippling tuition."

Edward just smiled at the bite in her tone. "You'd find a way. And in the meantime, how about you pick any and all plays you want to see. Hell, I'd even do Shakespeare in the Park with you, and if that isn't proof of my devotion, I don't know what is."

They stayed in as well. Jane continually refused to allow him into her place, though he insisted on driving her home most of the time.

("Is that a toilet on the front lawn?"

"And that's why you're not allowed to come in. You've no taste for plebeian decor."

"Seriously, how long has that been there? Please don't tell me people on the street use it."

"They renovated the bathroom in the unit below mine, and the garbage men just haven't picked it up yet."

"Yet? How many days has it been there? Is it still 'too soon' to talk about you moving in with me?")

His condo was in the luxe neighborhood of Yorkville, where shops like Chanel, Cartier, and Burberry lined a glossy section of Bloor Street known as the Mink Mile, and exclusive hotels like the Four Seasons and the Windsor Arms—favorite Hollywood celebrity haunts during their annual pilgrimage to the Toronto International Film Festival—bookended the area. Edward lived in an ornate brick and glass building, in a spacious unit with two separate patios, impersonally decorated in dark colors, but he was as careless of his wealthy surroundings as he was in his office. The first time he invited Jane in for dinner, they ate scrambled eggs and toast on the couch; Edward insisting on cooking despite having next to no skills.

"It's a little bit burnt," he said, scraping the singed eggs from the frying pan onto Jane's plate. "The smoke detector probably tipped you off on that, but I think I salvaged the edible parts."

"It looks delicious," Jane said dryly.

"Liar," he laughed, and kissed her before sitting down and

tucking into his own plate, which was mostly a massive stack of toast.

"Is learning to cook something you're actively working at, or should I stock up on antacids?"

"Pipe down and crunch on your eggs." He grinned.

"Just to be clear, I'm really fine with ordering in."

"But how else will I impress you with my domestic skills? Show you I have long-term potential?" He batted his eyes at her.

Jane speared the blackened eggs on her fork and held it up in front of him with her most deadpan expression. "Edward, these eggs are the ones with the long-term potential. They're like industrial glue. They will outlast the both of us."

"Smart-ass." He leaned in to kiss her again, and Jane tasted toast. "Right, I will read a cookbook for next time, and this time"—he pulled out his phone—"there's a sushi place downstairs. They can deliver super quick."

"Thank god," Jane said. "And if you really want scrambled eggs, next time *I'll* show you how to cook them."

Edward placed their order, then cleared their plates away, and Jane heard him whistling as he scraped the blackened egg mess into the garbage can and replaced the batteries in the smoke alarm he'd dismantled during his cooking trial the third time it went off. A rap at his front door a few minutes later announced the arrival of sushi, and Edward came back to the couch with a bag of small containers and two glasses of red wine.

"Dinner."

. . .

Things still frosty with Adele?" Edward asked curiously later, as they ate and drank. Jane had mentioned their disagreement in very broad brushstrokes.

"A bit better," Jane answered. "We're agreeing to disagree on certain things right now."

"She'll come round," he said confidently, but Jane wasn't so hopeful; Adele continued to look at her with poorly veiled concern and Edward with suspicion, whenever she saw them together.

But Jane's thoughts were preoccupied; things between them had been progressing, and her mind was nervously flitting over the evening's potential.

She did have some very minor experience with sex—there had been a fellow waiter at the restaurant when she was nineteen, but she'd viewed it back then as more of a clinical experience. Something to try once or twice to satiate her curiosity and so that she'd feel like less of a child thrust into this adult life. The partner in question was safely out of the restaurant and out of her life by the end of his university semester, and Jane never bothered herself then or now in wondering what he thought of her. It hadn't completely succeeded in erasing her feeling of perpetual virginity.

I never thought I'd think this, but maybe I should have actually listened to Marianne's sexcapade ramblings once in a while. Ugh.

The evening was getting late, the night sky dim. A few table lamps gave a soft glow to the living room, and Edward looked handsome and relaxed on the couch in his soft buttondown. Despite her nerves, Jane still wanted to climb onto his lap to be closer, to tousle his already messy hair and stroke his cheek.

They finished dinner and were enjoying a second glass of wine, picking at dessert, while Edward questioned and teased her about her own cooking skills, and Jane knew she was giving increasingly distracted answers.

He switched topics.

"Hey, I don't think I've shown you my amazing view." He stood from the couch and held out a hand. She followed him through the darkened condo out onto a patio facing north. Light pollution from the downtown core to the south obscured the stars and made the night sky hazy, but a breathtaking view of Toronto stretched out far in front of them, a shimmering mirage of a thousand city lights dancing just past the patio's stone wall, and Jane leaned against the cold brick and sighed in appreciation.

"Not bad, eh?" Edward's low voice rumbled from behind her.

Jane smiled, though he couldn't see it. "Not bad at all," she agreed.

She felt the heat of his approach, and then his arms wrapped around her waist, drawing her back against his chest, and though he'd embraced her just like this a dozen or more times in the past weeks, her pulse quickened. She clutched at his strong forearms where they lay against her, feeling the contrast of his rough hair and warm skin and the smooth cotton cuff of his rolled-up shirtsleeves. His size always made her feel completely enveloped by him, jittery but safe.

He laid a kiss just where her neck met her shoulder, slow

and deliberate, and Jane exhaled hard as her eyes fluttered shut. She forced herself to speak.

"So, is this your seduction routine?" The aim was to sound playful, but it came out breathless and wavery. She reached back to curl her fingertips around the nape of his neck, steadying herself under his caresses as he pressed another kiss into her skin. "Invite a woman to your condo, burn some eggs, and show her the view?"

He chuckled, dark and low, and dragged his lips up the length of her neck. "No, Ms. Raine, my burned eggs are only for you." Jane laughed weakly, and then his lips found that magic spot behind her ear he'd first discovered after the fire drill, and her laughter died instantly as her knees buckled slightly.

"I did actually intend to make you a decent dinner, but I fucked it up. Not quite the suave service you were expecting."

Something in his voice tugged at her gut and caused her to turn in his arms. His eyes were dark, his pupils large, but there was a hint of nervousness there too.

Oh. We're both nervous.

It calmed her a little, settled something. And with that settling, her want for him spiked. She slid her palms up his chest and gathered her courage.

"Fuck 'suave.' I like burned eggs better."

He gave a sharp bark of laughter, and then his hand was on the back of her neck, reeling her in for a kiss that started slow and soon turned frenzied.

Jane pressed against him mindlessly, curling into the wall of him, wanting more.

Somehow, they landed in one of his patio chairs, Jane

straddling his lap as he groaned. Clumsily, she began undoing the first few buttons of his shirt, kissing the newly exposed skin as his hands roamed her figure greedily. She had a moment's insecurity, remembering her slight curves, the disparaging remarks of the women at work, Isabelle's contrasting shapeliness, her own inexperience. Lost in her head, it took her a moment to realize he was talking.

"... wanted you so fucking much, all those months. So gorgeous. You were so fucking calm and *kind* all the time even when I pissed you off. How do you even . . . Jesus, Jane . . . and then you fixed Lamp, and you're so clever and stubborn and adorable, drove me up the fucking wall that I couldn't . . . love you so much . . . and I just . . . I wanted you to want me too."

She cut him off with a deep kiss, the last of her nerves evaporating.

"Bedroom," she gasped against his mouth.

"Yes," he growled.

He bundled her securely in his arms and shot to his feet. Jane clung tightly to him, fingers crumpling the soft cotton of his shirt and finding purchase in the hard expanse of his shoulders beneath it. The immovable, careless strength of him would always be her undoing.

He walked them back into the apartment; in his enthusiasm for kissing her, he paid scant attention to where he was going and mistakenly carried her into a closet, a bathroom, and a wall, before successfully navigating the doorway of his bedroom.

"I thought we were in a hurry," she teased, feeling breathless and brilliantly alive and carefree. "Was this the scenic route?"

Edward laughed, sounding equally breathless, as he lay her down on the bed. She missed his heat and weight immediately as he pulled back, but it was only to divest her of her shoes before his calloused fingers gently circled an ankle and he began a slow exploration of her legs, bare under her simple dress.

"What are you doing?" she asked, shifting impatiently under his hands.

"Taking the scenic route." He laughed, and the low, warm rumble of his voice became the bass note to the tenor of her own jumping heartbeat, loud in her ears.

It was different, it was so very different with him, with love and chemistry and trust and every glorious inch of skin lit up with sensation. She knew Edward, she knew his deep focus and intensity, the furrow of his brow when he was absorbed by something, but she hadn't known, could hardly comprehend, what it was like to be intimately at the center of that attention. She didn't know he could also be endlessly patient and savoring, and that the combination of all these things together could be so devastating, so wonderfully shattering, until her mind whited out with pure sensation, vision blurring at the edges, and there was nothing but the solid feel of him under her hands to ground her.

The next morning dawned bright and warm, the muted sounds of traffic and city noise drifting up through an open window, as Jane stretched luxuriously in wonderfully soft sheets, spring sunshine warm on her face, the haze of sleep receding slowly.

A languid yawn sounded behind her, and a heavy arm tightened around her.

"G'morning," Edward rasped, pressing a lazy kiss to her shoulder blade. He made a sleepy snuffling noise that Jane found endearing, and then settled deep into the mattress again, fully prepared to drift back to sleep. Jane already knew from countless early meetings that he was most definitely not a morning person.

That was fine. Every inch of her was sated and warm and happy, and she felt an uncharacteristic urge to giggle, thinking how far a gulf there existed between what she knew of sex before and what she knew now. She twisted under his arm to face him, stroking the backs of her fingers along the shadow on his jaw, darker before his morning shave than it was at the end of a long day at the office, and across the broad planes of his chest and its dark trail of hair. A small smile twitched up the corner of his mouth at her touches, as he kept his eyes closed and his face half buried in the pillow. Yeah, they were definitely spending the whole day in bed.

Behaving at work became exponentially more difficult, and though Jane kept them to her imposed rules of professionalism, she knew they were both counting down the clock each day until they could race back to Edward's condo and their exclusive bubble of two. Edward, she knew, was also counting down how long until they went to HR. Though he had agreed to her initial request for a few months of privacy, his discomfort with the secrecy was palpable at times, especially since they were now sleeping together.

Staying in with Edward meant plenty of *very* enjoyable time in bed, but it also meant semi-disastrous cooking adventures and TV marathons and almost constant touching. Really, he was nearly as starved for touch as she was, and Jane was left to calculate just how little affection he might have had in his past.

There was one other person they allowed into their bubble, the night they had dinner with Professor Graham. Gerry, as Jane was now to call him.

"Well, he finally made a move, did he? Or you finally figured it out?" Gerry started the evening off with, after kissing Jane on her cheek. "All I've been hearing is Jane this, and Jane that, some woman he was 'mad about' at the office. Neglects to tell me the poor thing is his beleaguered assistant, that she's got no clue about his crush on her. First time I was in the office and heard him call you Jane and put two and two together I didn't know whether to throttle him or laugh my ass off. How the hell did you manage to get through law school?" This last part was addressed to Edward with a friendly cuff to the shoulder. Edward beamed.

"My charm is unique. It takes a little while to unfold."

"Uh-huh, like a cheap lawn chair. Exactly how many months did this take to unfold? When we had lunch at the National Club I thought for sure you'd have made your move by then. Poor Jane still had no idea. My dear, you're far too good for him."

Jane did not expect, once they would eventually go public, to receive such a warm welcome everywhere. But it was certainly nice to be embraced so thoroughly by a man they both looked up to.

"He's like a father to you," Jane posited later that night when they lay wrapped up together. The weather was growing warmer still, so tonight they were sharing a Muskoka chair on his balcony, enjoying the night lights of the cityscape.

"More of a father to me than my actual father was."

Jane thought back to Adele's and Gerry's previous remarks and the tremor that ran through her the night Lamp broke when he spoke of hospital runs. Were they there yet, that she could ask such a personal question? He knew her sorry background, but not the details, not the intimate pain.

Edward sighed and wrapped his arms around her tighter, pressing a kiss to her hair. "I can hear you thinking and worrying. I guess you've heard some of the old gossip about my father."

Jane said nothing, only waited patiently.

"He was a miserable bastard, exactly what you'd expect from someone so cold and ambitious. Everything was about the firm, the legacy of the firm. He was only ever affectionate or proud of me when I got good grades, when I agreed to go to law school. Mum was lovely, though. Gerry helped me with her funeral when she died."

"Did your father ever . . ." She couldn't ask it, but somehow he knew what she was trying to say.

"I'd say he was emotionally abusive, to us both, but otherwise . . . just once. I spilled something on his paperwork in the home office. I don't even remember what I spilled. I must have been nine. He grabbed my arm, I was a skinny runt back then, so just that grab was enough." Jane burrowed closer into him, wordlessly trying to comfort, and blinked back tears. Edward soothingly rubbed her back, as if it was her awful memory and not his. "Honestly, I think he was more surprised at himself than anyone. Mum took me to the hospital, had it reset."

"She stayed with him?" Jane was incredulous. She was no stranger to violent tempers in the foster system, though she'd luckily navigated around them, but those were a motley collection of adults paid to look after her. Mild mannered and feckless as her father had been, he had deeply loved her; she couldn't imagine him standing by while someone hurt her.

Edward's mouth quirked sardonically. "It was over twenty years ago, and my mother was from an older time period still. I was a late-life child for her. Women in that era, from that set, didn't usually do divorce if they could help it, not with all the assets in his name. When we came home that night from the hospital, though, she moved both of our things into a separate wing of the house. They never shared a bedroom again. We were already living pretty separate lives, but we were really just roommates after that, not a family. Albeit roommates in a six-thousand-square-foot mini mansion. Anyway"—he shuffled and resettled into Jane and the chair in a way that let her know this particular conversation was nearly over—"Gerry's about as great a dad as I could get, so in a way, I'm lucky. I wish I'd listened to him more often early in my career, instead of my father." He pulled back to look at her seriously. "And now you know *my* Dickensian childhood tale." He kissed her twice and then sighed, tipping his head back to look at the night sky.

Jane reached up to stroke her fingers through his hair in the way that she knew he loved and thought about his story. She felt particularly tender toward him. She knew from the armchair psychotherapy of social counselors speaking to the victimized foster companions of her youth that children of abuse often found it difficult to separate manipulation from love. It made her rethink Edward's brief trick in the stairwell, using her jealousy to prod her into declaring her love for him, in a new and softer light.

She thought about what it must be like, to be raised with such incredible wealth and privilege, and to fear your father. She thought about Edward's explosive ways, how he bellowed and slammed doors and was short-tempered, despite his secret good nature, so that everyone in the firm was slightly afraid of him, the biggest, loudest growling bear in the woods. When she first started, he'd been more than growly, actually; he'd been borderline cruel, and Jane wondered if that response was born of trust issues that were as deeply embedded as her own. Whereas his mother's response was a study in contrast, a discreet method of separation, to quietly remove herself and her child to another part of the house, maintaining her silence to ensure a form of security for them both. Jane thought of her own instinctive response of maintained wariness and silence in all her years of solitude and fear. A silence she had only recently begun to throw off, thanks to Edward.

She supposed the only conclusion to be drawn was that women had a habit of expecting and enduring their victimhood, when men railed against it. She wondered what it said about her, that she rather envied Edward's ability to rail against it.

When she said as much to him, he turned his face away with something akin to shame. "I didn't rail hard enough, or soon enough. I wish to god I'd started kicking and screaming against his authority earlier."

211

She took her time when they went to bed that night, murmuring endearments into his skin in between pressing kisses to his shoulders, his neck, his chest. She told him that he was wonderful and strong and smart. That he made her feel safe. That she loved him very much.

Chapter 17

A certain coolness had sprung up between Edward and the beautiful Isabelle, who no longer took to sashaying around the sixty-fifth floor but kept to a new temporary office on the sixty-fourth floor, often using junior associates as a go-between. Jane knew Edward must have put a stop to her flirting, and it made Jane feel pleased and guilty at the same time.

"I don't like her, but now I do feel a bit bad she has to work with you and feel rejected," Jane said out of the blue one night.

They were at the driving range. Edward generally disliked golf, Jane had found out, but was particularly fond of the driving range. (Jane figured this was mainly to do with the opportunity to knock the crap out of something with a large metal stick, and Edward more or less agreed. "It's like a batting cage, but the ball stays still when you swing at it. It's brilliant, Jane!") She wasn't similarly enamored of it but did enjoy swinging the club a few times before giving it up in favor of watching the ripple of powerful muscles in his shoulders and back as he swung, sipping an iced tea from the vending machine and enjoying the quiet of the late evening. Marianne had been right about the joys of visible back muscles, Jane decided, trying not to let on that she was ogling. The way he preened and posed, she figured she was failing.

Edward stepped back from his practice swing now. "Feel bad for who?"

"Isabelle! I'm glad Clémence will be able to hold her own against her work-wise, but Isabelle was flirting with you and now she obviously knows it's a no, and it must be so embarrassing and awkward for her."

He snorted. "Oh, please, she won't waste time on feeling rejected. Do you really think I'm that heartless?"

"I think you have a sneaky lawyer brain that schemes to get what you want and doesn't always consider collateral damage or consequences."

He laughed and nudged a few more balls on his green into place. "Sounds about right. But no, in this particular instance, Mademoiselle Isabelle is neither hardworking nor is she genuine. If her daddy wasn't the CFO of a multimillion-dollar oil magnate's company, I doubt we would have hired her when she graduated law school. I told you we needed her on this deal for her client relationship, and that I had a longtime suspicion she'd been piggybacking off of Clémence's deals. I wanted to see how that would all play out if I got involved: she thought if she flirted with me enough, I wouldn't notice that she does no work. She doesn't actually give a damn about me." He shook his head. "It's an ugly thing, Jane, ambition without substance to back it up."

"Still . . ." Jane protested.

"All right, well, I also hinted to her that I wasn't fully comfortable with partners in the workplace dating and that I think best practices are for one person to join another firm, so that neither can use each other for material advantage. And I told her what a spectacular job I thought Clémence was doing and how the Montreal regional managing partner should know about it, and didn't she agree? She definitely didn't like that. She was gone from my office with a dust cloud in her wake." He laughed heartily over this last bit, and Jane joined in with a semi-reluctant smile. "A very modern woman, love just isn't enough."

"All right, then, so long as no one's getting hurt."

"No one's getting hurt. And in Montreal, Clémence just played her ace card with the timekeeper app and got promoted. You can expect a gift basket."

Work continued on as planned, but Jane now felt her self-imposed deadline of taking things to HR and requesting the transfer drawing nearer like a doomsday. The hesitation she felt wasn't about giving up her daily interaction with Edward . . . okay, it wasn't *just* about that. It was mostly that, as many times as she told herself to trust, still that cold-blooded whisper of reason in her head insisted *wait and see. Wait and see before exposing yourself, before risking it all. You can't afford to lose.*

Adele's ominous words about things not working out had somehow nettled and stuck. If they went public, there would be talk, but it would eventually be understood as a relationship and respectable. *But*, if they went public and broke up, she'd be known as that woman who had been sleeping with her boss and fooling herself into thinking it meant something. Diane and her cronies would have their proof now and it would spread like wildfire, and he'd be known as another creep who took advantage of an employee.

No one would know the truth of what they had been to each other. Whoever she was working for then would start looking at her differently. Anyone who might hire her later would look at her differently. The Bay Street world was small; it would follow her around. She'd be miserable. The safest route was to keep their relationship quiet, and if it all went wrong, she could slip away to another job with good recommendations. No one would think twice about another assistant who had quit working for the untenable Mr. Rosen.

She hated that she was thinking in terms of escape routes but she couldn't help it.

And Edward, she knew, was chafing at the delay. He was doing his best to be patient and go with her timelines, but as he said, it was a morally gray area. The fact that they were both consenting did not eradicate the fact that she still worked for him. He seemed to have no fear of things not working out between them or any repercussions, but he wanted everything aboveboard as soon as possible. When Edward gently pressed her on the topic, she told him she dreaded changing her workday. It wasn't a complete lie. She had a terrible presentiment that she was going to be *bored* working for another partner. Edward had been a brutal taskmaster since day one, but in the winter months when he'd been gone and Jane had helped out Adele and worked in the floater pool, there was an opportunity to compare, and the result wasn't favorable. The learning curve in her new profession had been decidedly shorter than she anticipated, and the monotony that chased her from waitressing was nipping at her heels again.

She expressed this to Edward one night over scrambled eggs in his condo, successfully cooked this time.

"Of course you're bored. Jane, you're too smart by half."

"There are lots of smart assistants in that firm."

He pulled back from massacring some button mushrooms at her irked tone. "Don't misunderstand me. I know there are lots of smart assistants, and there are lots of dumb lawyers. Adele could run rings around most of our upper management, but I'm talking about you, not them. You should go to university. I'm the last person to insist anyone follow in their father's footsteps, but you . . . You can run from that legacy of your father's all you want, Jane, but you belong at a university, if not to study English then at least to figure out what you'd actually like to be doing, instead of just doing what you need to survive."

Jane pondered that as he finally dished up his creation: scrambled eggs with mushrooms and ham. She'd insisted there be at least one vegetable with the meal.

"You really think that?"

"When we walked past that protest rally the other day you started reciting Yeats. Something about hurling the little streets upon the great. That's not a normal thing to do," he reminded her, with a raised eyebrow. "Grab the ketchup?"

"Ketchup with scrambled eggs is for heathens."

He kissed her in reply.

At her desk on a Friday, Jane looked at the calendar again. She was almost ashamed to be feeling unfulfilled when Edward was filling up her life, but maybe he was right. Either that or face some fundamental flaw in herself that meant she'd be secretly restless all her life.

Thinking back to those happy years on the campus with her father wasn't as exquisitely painful these days, and she could examine with some interest the feeling of longing that came with them.

The phone rang and jolted her reverie.

"Mr. Rosen's office."

"Jane?" It was Tortoiseshell from the front desk. "I have a 'Julie' here to see Mr. Rosen, but she doesn't have a boardroom booked. Was he expecting a client?"

Jane spun lazy circles in her chair. "Oh, hi there, no, I don't think so. I've got nothing in his calendar . . . oh!" She came to an abrupt halt and sat up straight. *Julie? Julie from California?* "Hold on a sec, let me check with Mr. Rosen. Did she give you any other details?"

There was a pause and a muffled murmuring. "No, she just said her name is Julie, that she's distant family? And that he'll know who she is."

"M'kay, hold on." Jane knocked on Edward's door and pushed through. He looked up with a smile.

"There's a Julie here to see you, says she's distant family . . ."

"FUCK." He shot out his seat in such a violent way that Jane actually took a step back.

"Fuck, fuck, that fucking . . ." He leaned down over his desk, his clenched fists supporting him against the wood as if he wanted to punch through it, and breathed deeply, trying to bring himself under control.

"What's wrong? Should I tell them to call security?"

"No! No, sweetheart. I'm sorry, I'm . . . I'm fine. Listen, I need you to do something for me."

"Do something for you like when Mr. Steppenwolfe came?"

"No, not like that. I need you to leave the office."

"What?"

"Yes. I need you to leave the office, no questions asked." He came around the desk and drew her with him out the door. "Go home early. It's Friday anyway. Go home to your place and stay there. Don't check my email or dial in to retrieve the phone messages, just go home and put your feet up, watch a movie. I'll call you later tonight or early tomorrow."

Jane dug in her feet and temporarily halted their progress. He was handing over her coat and bag. "Is the firm in trouble?"

"No . . ."

"Then what's going on? Are you in trouble? Are we in danger? You're acting panicked."

"I know, I know." He sighed and slowed, drew her into a hug, ignoring their office rules, and pressed his forehead to hers. "I know I owe you explanations. I know you're too clever to just accept this at face value and move on, but I can't. I can't explain right now. I'm just asking you to understand that I can't explain right now, but I will, I will in the future, soon, I promise, but right now I just want you safely clear of this whole mess. Because that's all it is: it's a fucking mess come to town and I need to put it back on a plane again."

He tucked a tendril of loose hair behind her ear and kissed her lightly. He sighed again. "I promise I'll explain, just not now."

It was clearly not nothing—it was clearly very much *something*—but Jane couldn't for the life of her fathom what it could be. What exactly caused this response of terror and rage? Because she could see it; she could see something had him frightened, or if not frightened, at the very least spooked. His eyes were darting over her face, asking for acceptance, but he was vibrating with nervous energy and clearly desperate to get away, to get down to the lobby and deal with the ominous Julie. Jane was itching with curiosity to see her, to see if she was one of the women from the California firm website and whether it was the icy blonde or the sizzling redhead, to see with exactitude what the precise degree of relationship was between them, and what matter she and her brother kept bringing to the firm door that would pull in not only Edward, but the firm's partnership chair and the director of finance.

She could circle back. She could lie and say she'd go home and then come back to her desk to try to eavesdrop or check his email. She could alert Adele and ask her to try to glean some details; she was certainly much better at sussing things out than Jane, but . . . she sighed. No.

"Okay. Okay, I'll go home. But you really can't pull stunts like this anymore. I couldn't ask when I was just your assistant, but now I'm something else and so you can't just keep me out of the loop all the time."

"Thank you, thank you, sweetheart. Okay, I love you and I'll see you later." His relief at her departure was tangible. Jane thought about that fact all the way home.

It was midmorning the next day when he finally called. Jane was in the shower and found the missed call with an accompanying text after she stepped out.

All okay. Thanks for being understanding. Love you.

Jane didn't answer, feeling put out. *Let him stew.*

She made herself a cup of tea and ran a load of laundry before she took herself to task for passive-aggressive behavior. She'd never really understood the games people play in relationships. The other girls working at the restaurant were always bursting full with a flood of drama and relationship angst, just waiting for the casual inquiry to pinprick it, about how he sent that text, and she replied with this DM, and his friends said, and her sister said, and then how he didn't call for three days and they never *said* they were exclusive but shouldn't it be obvious that . . . it was dizzying. Marianne called them "drama-llamas."

If it was clear you both wanted each other, why try to negotiate? Why the subterfuge? Surely, you could just be together and work everything else out.

How soon her own theory was falling apart in its practice. She thought their relationship was beyond things like this.

She texted him back a simple message, then ended up taking the whole day at home, trying to relax enough to luxuriate in an unexpected long weekend, though in truth she missed him. It had been a while since she'd spent so much time at her own place, and alone.

Sunday he drove to Port Credit, and Jane met him at the Starbucks at the base of the lighthouse. She felt better on her home turf, but wasn't ready to have him in her apartment, now for different reasons than its humbleness.

He looked more himself than he had on Friday, but there was still something ill at ease in his expression, and tired lines lay heavy under his eyes.

He smiled weakly at her across the table, and Jane frowned

back, trying not to soften right away, trying to quiet her heart and let her head take the reins on this one.

"Edward, I don't think I'm being unreasonable in asking for an explanation," she said carefully, "when you react like that."

"I know. I know," he cut her off. "I know how erratic it must look on the outside, and I'm asking a lot for you to go on blind faith, but there is an explanation and there are reasons for keeping things—well, it has ramifications for the firm, and it's not that I don't trust you, I do, you're the most trustworthy person I know, it's just, I'm not ready to tell you *yet*."

Yet, she thought to herself. He was planning on telling her eventually; that was mollifying. And it affected the firm; that more than anything else made her pause and remember that his first impulse when Steppenwolfe arrived was to call Mantford and Singh. Personal or professional? She was demanding an explanation as his girlfriend, but if this was a firm matter, did she have the same right to demand answers as an employee? Confidentiality in the firm was stringent. Was this simply her inexperience making her so uneasy?

Or were these swirling thoughts just a way to gloss over anything that disrupted her seemingly perfect relationship? Lying to herself was not a luxury she'd ever indulged in before.

"Jane, I will tell you. I promise. I just need time."

She sighed.

"Six months," he offered, looking increasingly alarmed at her reticence. "When we've been together for six months, I swear I'll tell you everything."

He was only asking for time, she told herself, a finite

amount of time. They'd been together now nearly two months. "Six months," she agreed, and he visibly relaxed.

"I'm all in with you, Jane, for the long haul. I promise."

He held her hand across the table, and she remembered every good thing about him. She forgave him completely. Almost.

Chapter 18

A week of relative calm passed. Their dates, their banter, their daily work resumed. Although Jane's head insisted something wasn't right, her heart couldn't be brought to heed the advice. Both head and heart agreed he was a good man, both believed he truly loved her, but head would diverge and insist that a secret, a secret that had to do with her, not just work, was fermenting. Twice more he had renewed his promise that he would tell her everything, but "not yet" was still the watchword. Her mind picked at it like a scab.

She couldn't imagine what a brother and sister from California, a Toronto lawyer, a mysterious file number, and herself could amount to that would be in any way intertwined or able to put that look of pain in his eyes. If it was a personal matter, she couldn't fathom if the secret was kept to spare her pain, or because he feared her judgment, or because it was somehow too intimate to yet introduce in their fledgling relationship (although almost from the first date, and also because he voiced the sentiment so often, it felt like there was nothing "fledgling" about it).

But he told me about his father, and even Gerry doesn't fully know about that.

Jane didn't like to be kept in the dark. She couldn't make him understand she'd rather be informed than coddled. How could she protect herself and plan for the future if she was to be blindsided? Protection was in having the information, not being guarded from it, however bad it might be.

She took to checking her bank account every day once more, a habit she'd suppressed since Mr. Rosen became Edward, having then reduced the tic to only twice a week. She dug out the business card from the woman at the placement agency, and updated the feeble CV the college had helped her put together, slightly less feeble now.

She caught herself doing these things with a fair degree of shame, although ostensibly the agency and the CV would be useful if, once they came out with their relationship, she did indeed decide to change firms rather than transfer to another partner. There were merits to the idea; it was sensible to have the resources prepared.

Instead, she was suspicious of herself, that these were the steps of someone getting ready to run.

In the second to last week of April, Jane's work was cut out for her. Taxes were due April 30. Her own had been neatly filed last week, a simple thing given the straightforward nature of her finances. In typical fashion, Edward was procrastinating. She spent the morning laying out receipts and copies of personal and firm expenses that might have overlapped on a credit card and trying to decipher the notes and organizational systems of the many assistants who had kept his records in the past years.

The phone rang and a California number flashed across the screen.

Jane paused a moment—Edward was away from his desk—then answered.

"Mr. Rosen's office."

"Hello there." It was Julie. "Is Edward available?"

"Mr. Rosen isn't in right now. May I take a message?"

"Yes, please do. It's just a simple question. I forgot to ask him last time I was there and we were discussing things." Her tone of voice made it sound like discussing things was an intimate act that Jane might become a voyeur to if she were imprudent enough to inquire after details.

"If you could just ask him if we're filing our taxes as husband and wife this year, or no."

For one wild, desperate moment, Jane thought "our taxes" was referring to *herself* and Edward, that somehow this woman knew about their relationship and was presuming them to soon be husband and wife.

Then the crater opened up beneath her.

The woman, his *wife*, was still talking. It was hard to hear over the ringing in her ears. ". . . so if you could just tell him that, and ask him to phone Julie back. Ta." She hung up.

Jane sat staring at the phone in her hand.

Married.

She felt light-headed. She dropped the phone and pushed her chair out from the desk. Then she dropped down to sit on the ground and tried to breathe.

He has a wife.

A wife who sounded posh and breezy and free. She was either the blonde or the redheaded lawyer, most likely the blonde. A beautiful California blonde with a law degree. Of course.

The pain was unbearable.

She sat and she fought to shore up and contain it, she fought for so long she lost track of time, far surpassing her self-imposed mental timer of three minutes.

It was pain and humiliation and shame and heartbreak and *stupid, stupid,* **stupid** *girl* . . .

The miasma swirled around her, overwhelming, disorienting. She didn't cry—it was too great for that—only fought it back and fought it back, trying to surface. Finally, she was aware of her surroundings once more, and she got up and sat unsteadily at her desk. Edward would be back from his meeting soon. She didn't want a scene. At all costs, she must avoid a scene. Every move was critical now. She could leave, before anyone knew. Just pack up her desk and go.

If this was the running she'd been prepping to do, you'd think it would come as less of a shock.

No. She wouldn't run; he might misinterpret that as his cue to chase her.

Her hands were shaking and she knew her face must be very white. All the blood in her body had left her extremities and was now pounding in her heavily thumping heart. Her fingertips tingled and felt numb.

She heard his footsteps in the hallway.

"Jane! That pissant from the securities commission is coming in tomorrow. Brian what's-his-name. I'm planning to

tell him to go to hell. Can you find out if there's a fine for verbally abusing government representatives? I mean, it's not like
we're in court—hello, Lamp, what's up . . ."

He breezed past her, focused on a file in his hand. She
heard him grunt as he threw himself into his desk chair and
knocked over one of the many stacks of floor-bound papers.

Her heart must be leaping out of her chest now. She felt
her blouse quiver with its thumping. His voice must be from a
decade ago, something normal from way back when.

She quietly stood up and walked to his doorway. She could
walk no farther.

"Mr. Rosen."

"You've got it? Fine, no fine?"

"Mr. Rosen. Your wife called."

It was as if all the air had been instantly sucked out of the
room. Jane trembled and felt light-headed again but stood her
ground.

"Jane . . ." he rasped.

"The message was very simple."

"Jane, please . . ."

"She wants to know if you'll be filing your taxes together
this year. If you could please call her back. I'm assuming you
have her number. I'm sorry, but I didn't take it down."

Edward looked haggard, like he'd aged ten years. His
harsh breathing sounded loudly in the room. He wouldn't look
at her.

It was her father's funeral all over again, when no one
would look at her. Funny how this, too, felt like a kind of death.
She waited for him to make the next move, but he just sat
there.

Coward.

"Coward."

His head shot up. Now he was looking at her. He wet his lips, his nervous tell. "Yes," he agreed, his voice hoarse. "Yes, I was a coward. I should have . . . I should have said . . ."

"We're not doing this here. We're at work." The last word cracked like a whip, and Edward flinched under its lash. His eyes darted across her face, as they always did when he was trying to gauge her. Jane shuttered her expression. The waitress mask. His eyes grew wide.

"No, don't do that, don't hide. Jane, I can explain."

"I said we're not doing this here, Mr. Rosen."

"And I say we are. If I let you out of my sight now you'll shut me out and I'll never get in again. Jane." His old impetuosity was rising, tinged with panic. He got out of his seat and moved toward her, and Jane instantly took a step back. Hurt cracked across his face, but he stopped and held up both his hands in surrender, a pantomime of their scene at Christmas, when all she had to worry about was Diane from HR gossiping that they were sleeping together.

Edward unfroze, rerouted to the spare chair by the window, pushing all the papers off and drawing his own chair over, a little ways away, and sat down, clearly indicating that she should join him.

Jane lingered in the doorway. They would have to have this conversation out. Could she handle it now? Disinfect while the wound was still open? She closed the door behind her and took the proffered chair. She clasped her hands in her lap to stop their trembling.

"Do you know how law firm partnerships work?"

"What?" That was not how she expected him to begin.

"Law firm partnerships. People all say I own this firm, but I don't fully own it, only partially."

He explained. A "partnership" was really a business model for sharing profits. Partners of the firm were invited to buy in, put up a certain amount of cash for a certain percentage of ownership and profits. That cash was part of the necessary capital to keep the firm running; it served as a guarantee with the bank, with their professional insurance, and more. Mr. Rosen's grandfather, and two other men, Haythe and Black, had pooled their money to start the firm. Black had left for New York, and another man named Thornfield had stepped in. The firm grew and more partners joined, adding to the capital and retaining a share of the profits, but the three founders maintained the biggest shares and so had controlling stakes. Mr. Rosen had passed his controlling stake down to his son, who had passed it to Edward. The other two men's progeny weren't interested, or died out, and so the Rosen family bought out their stakes. The partnership board, of which Mantford was the elected chair, was to allow the other smaller percentage owning partners to also have a vote in certain decisions.

Eight months working in the firm, and this was the first time Jane was hearing this. It would have been so much more useful than spending three hours learning how Outlook works with that IT guy.

"But what does this have to do . . ."

"I'm getting there. You need this background to understand. Our portion of the capital that gives us a controlling stake, it's not just like cash in the bank. It's part of a larger portfolio with real estate and stock market bonds. It's the value of the portfolio that makes up the Rosen stake."

"Okay," Jane said, following along but still not understanding the relevance.

"When the 2008 collapse happened, things were bad. Businesses and law firms started going under. Big ones, ones you never thought you'd see in trouble. The Rosen portfolio was bleeding money. It was next to worthless, almost overnight. Partners lost their shirts, started pulling their money out. We were losing capital; the firm was going to be bankrupt. There wasn't even enough to cover payroll, severance packages for laid off employees, the big bonus for long-term service a lot of people here count on for retirement. It was going to ruin lives. Did you know when unemployment goes up, so do suicide rates?"

Jane shook her head.

"My parents were both still alive back then, and my father found a solution. Not every business was going bust. In fact, out in California . . ."

Jane felt a drop in her stomach as she suddenly saw where this was going.

"Out in California, in the tech sector, some companies were having a nice, quiet little boom. Silicon Valley was rising up. Steppenwolfe's law firm had invested smartly in a few new companies, and it was paying dividends, money right in the bank."

"Your father asked them to invest in the firm?" Jane asked, drawn into the story despite herself.

Edward gave a weak smile. "And lose the controlling stake? No, it was the Rosen firm and it was going to stay a

Rosen firm. He wanted their money, but he wanted it in our family, so *we* could use their money. I was just finishing law school, and single. Old Mr. Steppenwolfe had a lovely daughter, six or seven years older than me and already established as a lawyer at their firm. My father saw his chance."

Jane remembered back when Edward first declared his love during the fire drill and spoke about age gaps and power imbalances being his reason for trying to provoke her affections, rather than demand them. She didn't need to hear another word about his marriage to know where that lookout had come from. It made her soften toward him, just marginally, that he had sought to spare her that, but then in the next moment she reminded herself that she had been actively deceived, and if that wasn't an abuse of privilege and power then it was at the very least an abuse of her love and trust.

"And so you agreed to marry her for the money?"

He drew back, stung. "Of course not. I had no idea that was the scheme. I was told it was a graduation trip. Go to California, lie on the beach, enjoy yourself, and oh, while you're there you'll stay with my old friend Steppenwolfe, he has kids around your age, they'll show you around. His daughter's a real beauty." He spat the last part out bitterly. "I didn't know my father's ambitions and the firm's solvency were riding on it."

"But did Julie know? Why did she agree to this?" Jane asked.

"She knew, and she had her own motivations; would you believe it was as simple as the fact that a bunch of her friends were having weddings and she was pissed off to be left out? Her narcissism and cruel temper had lost her a previous engagement already, and she was getting a reputation as a liability as a lawyer, so the dating pool in her elite circle was drying up. And here I was served up on a platter. I would look good on her arm, I was of the right type of people, and she liked the idea of adding to her family's empire. Maybe she actually thought we could grow into having a real relationship, but I think the other items were more of a priority."

Jane thought back to her conversation with Adele, about the pseudo-arranged marriages of the elite.

"Everyone was in on it but me," he continued. "It was all daiquiris on the beach and Julie in an endless parade of bikinis, and people talking of what we could build together, a career, children. Her brother acted like my best friend; her father treated me like a son—well, you know how hungry I was to be someone else's son. And once I was in a relationship with her, my father all but put the ring in my hands and shoved me down the aisle. You would have thought it was a shotgun wedding, he moved so fast. Six weeks and I was married. If we'd dated a little longer, I might have found out what a foul character she is. Her family was eager too; they thought a stake in Toronto was a good idea. Our firm was bigger than theirs and had more assets. Sure, the firm was in trouble at the moment, but they were hedging their bets that the Canadian economy would bounce back faster than the U.S., and they were right. Our recession wasn't quite as severe, and there was more business on this side of the border, at least for the next few years. They also got to diversify their own portfolio because they were edgy over whether their currently profitable Silicon Valley investments were going to boom or bust. The nineties' tech bubble and dot-com crash were still fresh on everyone's mind back then. I won't bore you with the financial details of how it was done, but assets were put in our marital name to make this all happen."

He paused and looked up, visibly pulling himself from the dark memory. A touch of wonder lit his face as he took in Jane's expression.

"You look like you pity me. Jane, don't you understand what a sniveling idiot I was? I barely knew her, just a hot, ambitious blonde in a bikini, and I was married by September. A worse version of Isabelle, equally talentless as a lawyer—oh, I found that out later; she was constantly being disciplined by the ethics board, that's why she's a 'consultant' on their site instead of a partner, and she's using her mother's maiden name professionally now to shake off some of the bad rep. Grossly ambitious with no means to achieve it except through Daddy and his arrangements. When I see how obvious Isabelle is now, I can't believe I fell for Julie back then."

"You were lonely, and they offered you a family. I understand why you grabbed for it. Family is what you offered me, and look at the red flags I was willing to ignore to have it."

He flinched. "Jane, I never meant . . ."

"Finish your story, Mr. Rosen." She wanted information, not apologies. Only knowing "why" might take this pressure off her chest.

"We were married, and the firm was saved. And I realized just whom I had married and lived stewing in my own regret, but by then it was too late. My father died not long after the marriage took place, and my mother shortly after. Julie convinced me I should come back to California after the funerals, where I'd be happier. We could work on our failing marriage;

I could grieve my parents. Just six months, she said, an extended holiday. Do you know what a fifty-fifty divorce state is, Jane?"

Jane shook her head.

"It means it's a 'community property' state, and that all marital property will be divided in a fifty-fifty fashion according to the court unless otherwise agreed. It means everything is considered 'up for grabs,' including the firm capital if we divorce under California law. My father, in structuring the deal, never presumed we might divorce. Why would he? Look at his own marriage. We were married in California, we lived in California, I came into my rights as a firm partner while in California, a lot of our financial agreements were drawn up in California, and it's a hell of a lot easier and faster for her to start divorce proceedings and keep the case in her state than for me to get it to Ontario. By the time my fantasy of our marriage was over, the firm was profitable again, and I would have happily let her walk away with any amount of money. But she wanted the firm. She wanted to asset-strip it and dissolve it, or stay married and keep me and the potential of lifelong alimony on a leash. It's a divorce on her terms, or not at all."

"But why keep it a secret?" Jane asked. "A permanent separation . . ."

"If I fought her in court, at best it would be a long, ugly public battle, but even without that, if word of our mucky financial arrangements got out—that there was someone just over the border who could pull strings anytime—it could have the same effect. Reputation is everything on Bay Street. Partners would start pulling their money out fast rather than wait for the outcome and see if the business still stood. Clients would take off too. It could start something tantamount to a bank run. Any way I look at it, Rosen, Haythe and Thornfield LLP would be over."

Jane felt a chill at that. The dissolution of the law firm of Heenan Blaikie was four years ago, and the devastation it left behind for all those who looked to it for employment was still a cautionary tale on Bay Street. It was one of the first things she'd learned from Adele.

And this firm, which she had worried was the equivalent of working for the devil when she started, had come to mean something fundamentally different since then. It was its own ecosystem, a place that housed new Canadians like Adele and students like Alec with steady, self-respecting jobs with benefits and security, that gave millions in charity and opportunities for marginalized lawyers. The class hierarchy was still there, the country-club set, and it still represented some truly reprehensible clients, but under Edward's captaincy and the slow absorption of the young, forward-thinking junior lawyers, it was displaying potential for so much more. A positive use for its economic power and privilege.

Beyond that, she knew the personal history, that the firm was founded by Edward's German grandfather who had fled to Canada before the second world war only to discover that, even after anglicizing the family name *Rosenthal* to *Rosen*, his religion would have him turned away from the traditional law firms of that time, and so he founded his own. That despite Edward's history with his father, the history of the firm was something he wanted to maintain. That his protective, possessive instincts ran deep of everything and everyone that came under his purview. That she herself, when only just his assistant in that first week, felt the wall of Edward standing between her and any real threats, like that man in the boardroom, and was glad of it.

So no, he couldn't give up the firm. He couldn't lose more to other people's greed than he'd already lost.

But if he wouldn't give up the firm, and Julie wouldn't give up the claim, then . . .

"So you stayed married," Jane concluded for him. "You're staying married."

He sighed. "Her brother's a reasonable sort, more to be pitied. He's pretty spineless, does the drudge work of the firm and tries to keep her ambition and temper on the rails. He comes up here once in a while to check on the business, goes back and convinces her it's fine as is, no point in trying to battle me for it. But she won't let me go. Not without handing over the firm. She would drag it out. Even now she's costing me a personal fortune in payments just to keep quiet."

"Does anyone else know you're married? Does Gerry?"

He looked away. "Mantford, the partnership chair, knows. Singh in finance only knows there's an involved third party, file BW 5232-8. Gerry doesn't know. He would never have let you near me without a warning if he did. I told you he's a better man than me. The wedding was quick, and I spent most of our actual married life over there. By the time I came back to Toronto, we were on the outs with each other, permanently. Then there was still the fallout from '08 and the rebuilding; everyone was distracted. Trust me, more people were recalling how Lehman Brothers went down than remembering I had gotten married. If they did remember, I think they just assumed the marriage had ended and were too polite to ask for the gory details. I let it be buried. It kept my and my family's professional reputation intact, and it let me convince myself I was free to meet someone new."

"You might have told me."

"That would have gone over well on the first date."

Jane shot him a look and he cowed. "I didn't think you'd give me a chance or believe me that I've had nothing to do with that women for nearly ten years. You needed persuading that we could work just as we are. I *was* going to tell you, though, once we were more established as, well, us."

They sat in silence, the wreckage of his life, their relationship scattered around them. Jane wondered if he could see it as clearly as she could, but his next words proved he was looking not at the wreckage but at hope.

"I'm sorry I lied, god, I'm so sorry. But nothing has changed. I love you, Jane. I want to be with you. This is unconventional, I know, but it's not a real marriage. We could still have a life together and down the road some kids. We can still have all that. This isn't a fucking Jane Austen novel where the village will turn up their nose at the morality. People do common-law living all the time."

It still wouldn't be classified as common-law for us. Not with a wife in existence. He would never be mine.

"Jane." His tone was pleading. He reached for her hand, and she allowed it. She felt exhausted, drained. A strong desire to sleep for a week was on her; maybe then she could process everything. The outside world, their surroundings pressed in on her again, and she breathed deeply as if coming up for air.

"You have a meeting. It's nearly two o'clock." He looked at her incredulously. "We're still at the office, Mr. Rosen. Life doesn't stop for a broken heart."

"I'll make it stop."

She creaked out a laugh at his usual bombastic way. "I'm tired. This has been a lot. You have that meeting at two and you'll be in it for the rest of the day. I'm going to finish my workday. We can talk more tonight." She could see him latching on to that promise, that if the conversation wasn't done then maybe neither were they. In that moment, she felt like she was wielding an invisible headsman's axe.

Edward smiled at her practical way and agreed, but his smile was thin and bitter. He didn't try to kiss her or touch her again, but he let her stay in the relative privacy of his office and took himself out to the corridor where she heard him pacing until he obediently went to his meeting at two o'clock.

She sat in the chair and looked out his window at the cityscape and Lake Ontario beyond. Lake Rosen, Haythe & Thornfield, he had joked. The firm that had cost him his freedom.

When she was sure he was gone, she carefully put the chairs back in their usual place, and then closed the door behind her. At her desk, she copied down the contact information for HR, for Shirley, head of secretarial services, and for Adele. Then she packed her bag. She touched her fingertips lightly to the desk.

Pens and papers she let lie exactly as they were. If things were disturbed, he'd clock it when he came back from his meeting and get worked up before this evening.

One elevator ride down, and then out on the sidewalk, then around the corner to the Mövenpick Café. Jane sat on the low couch facing the large street-level windows and watched the people go by with the same interest as her first day on

239

Bay Street, enjoying a numb, detached calm that she knew wouldn't last. She sent Edward a text at six, saying she would meet him at his condo, and then walked north to Yorkville, knowing he'd beat her there.

The doorman recognized her and buzzed her up, and then it was just her and Edward alone in the living room. He was in his worn jeans and a blue sweater—her favorite on him, soft and inviting.

On the way there, she tried to pretend there was another option open for her, another way. But she'd known almost from the moment of his explanation how this would play out, what her own self-discipline and self-respect would demand.

She took a deep breath as he fairly vibrated with nervous energy.

"I'm leaving the firm. Please let me do this quietly. No fuss. I'll email HR this evening with my resignation. I'll state personal reasons. I won't be serving notice. I'll ask Shirley to give me a reference."

He nodded. "I wouldn't ask you to stay at the firm, knowing what's involved, but we already talked about separating our working life from our personal."

This was the hard part.

"Mr. Rosen . . ."

"*Edward*. We're outside work."

"Edward, I'm leaving." She could not bring herself to finish, to say "leaving you" and bring the headsman's axe down, but she saw he understood her anyway. The silence was deafening.

She saw his throat work convulsively as he tried not to look away.

"We can leave Toronto. I can work anywhere the firm has an office. We can go to Vancouver. No one will know about her. We can have a whole new start . . ."

"Edward, you're married."

"I'm *not*."

"You're married in the eyes of the law. We can never be married; our children would have no protection legally. I would have no protection legally, not even the protection of common-law partners. If you were in the hospital, if you needed medical decisions made for you, she would be allowed to make them while I could only stand by and watch. She'd always come first. I'd always come second. If something happened to you, everything would be left to her mercy."

"I didn't think marriage and security meant that much to you. I should have laid out my finances on the first date." She could see he didn't really mean that, but she addressed it head-on anyway.

"They don't, not in that way. I love you . . ."

"It's fine. I understand."

"No, I don't think you do." Her calm was dissipating, emotions splintering through. "I don't think you know what it's like to have nothing. I mean *really nothing.* Can you even wrap your head around that? No home, no family, no money, no future, nothing. When I was a waitress I used to think, 'If I break my arm, I'll be on welfare or starve until the cast comes off and I can serve tables again.' Welfare wouldn't have even covered rent on my shitty apartment—believe me, I looked it up. So, eviction. And then you come along, and you offer me everything. But it wasn't real, was it? And I can't depend on it . . ."

"Yes, you can depend on it! On me," he cut in roughly.

"No, because you lied! You lied to me, and I can't trust you anymore. You live in a different world, and I won't be your project. Now you love me; maybe tomorrow you'll change your mind. If we move in together, can I pick a fight with you and still have a roof over my head? I don't know. If I want to leave, where will I go? Will I be worse off than I was before? My whole world depended on my father, and when he died, the earth cracked open under my feet. I can't afford to rely on one man like that again . . ."

"That's different, you were a child . . ."

"All I've got in the *world* is me, and my own two feet, and the ground I stand on."

She uttered the words with such vehemence they resounded around the room, and both of them were momentarily taken aback. Edward recovered first. "You could love me, be with me, and still have that. I wouldn't . . . I'd never . . ." He was pleading with her now, voice breaking.

"No. How could I keep up without your wealth, without your help? Without even having the legal status of being your wife or at least your common-law partner? Go to dinner parties and be labeled the mistress, the other woman, living off your wealth—you've kept the secret this long, but if California keeps popping into the office then it's just a matter of time before the truth comes out. And you'll still have to stay married to her. This will always be broken, and I'll break with it. The risk and the stakes are too high for me."

"You love me." It was an accusation, a desperate bid for reassurance.

"Yes." Her lip trembled. "I love you with all my heart. But

I'm a modern woman"—he grimaced at his own words played back to him—"and I know love isn't always enough. It doesn't guarantee a happy ending."

"Jane." He reached for her, skimming the bare skin of her arm with his hand.

She'd gone so many years without that human touch, in that moment it was the worst thing he could do to break her. "Jane." He was holding back tears, voice trembling.

Was it wrong? Her decision was founded in logic. That harsher part of herself, which always saw things in the cold light of the worst day, wouldn't let her run from the truth that this was the necessary thing to do. But was it wrong? When it was clearly breaking them both so badly?

She tried to picture a life with Julie dropping in like she had at the office the day Edward had sent her home, Julie calling with her snide little questions about taxes. People whispering, laughing at her, the poor little nobody living on Edward's dime, a woman desperate enough to make nice about a man who already has a wife. She tried to picture children—and Edward had always talked assuredly of their future children, but until this moment she hadn't realized how desperately she also wanted them—children whose stepmother would be Julie, at least on paper. Children who, if she ever brought them into the office, to pick Dad up after work, as she'd seen other families in the firm do, would be looked at as . . . No.

Her relationship with Edward at the start seemed like a fairy tale, a happy ending too good to possibly be true. Now it seemed entirely ephemeral, gossamer thin and dissolving into the air.

"I love you, Edward, I do. And in another life we could

have been happy. But in this life . . . I don't blame you for doing what it takes to keep the firm alive. There are so many souls depending on you. I understand, and I honestly wish you well."

"You wish me well?" he snarled. "Just like that? Practical to the last. You go your way, and I go mine?"

"I think . . . I think that's how this was always going to end," she said softly, feeling her way around the thought. "We're two very damaged people, Edward. We don't know how to trust. I've spent my life trying to be invisible to keep people at bay. You've spent yours kicking and clawing at anyone that came near you—you clawed at me when I first met you—and even when we got past all of that . . . well, we didn't, did we? You didn't trust me with the truth. You put *your* needs first, you put wanting me first; you didn't put *me* first. I don't trust you to stay, and I couldn't stand to watch you leave, so I have to end this now. I've got just enough skills to survive on my own, but I don't have the skills to be falling in and out of a fantasy life with you. If you fall too many times, you don't get up again. Maybe people who have families, who have other loved ones and people to pick them back up, can do it. But people like me can't."

In loving him, she'd exposed her soft underbelly and had been betrayed. She couldn't stay and wait for the next time the knife slid back in.

He could see the decision was final on her face—he could always read her so well—and he turned away, the picture of abject misery and grief.

"You'll find someone else, someone not as fastidious as me about . . . well, someone with the resources to feel secure in this alternate arrangement. You'll find someone else."

"That's insulting and you know it. I want *you*."

"I'm leaving. Please don't try to find me or contact me. Please respect my wishes on this. A clean break is all that I can manage."

He sat on the sofa, head in his hands. Jane walked over and planted a gentle kiss in his unruly dark hair. It was the only mercy she'd allow herself, the only balm she had to give him, and as she did it, she heard her heart break in two.

Chapter 19

Alone once more, back in her shitty apartment with its mockingly cheerful walls, Jane gazed around blearily. Up until now, she had kept the thundering tide of her feelings—just barely—at bay, only letting herself skim the surface after that first blow of discovery. She had had to react, think, plan, decide, but now she let herself *feel*, and the rising swell of her grief came down on her like a dam bursting free.

She lay on her lonely bed and sobbed, great wracking sobs such as she hadn't experienced since her father died.

He loved her, used to love her, might love her still, unless . . . but no, he would move on, was that possible? He had truly loved her, but that was all over now. He would find someone new, someone without her baggage and fears and stupid, *stupid* principles. Someone who could be with him as an equal and not feel herself a mistress. He could start again. But there was no new beginning for her. Just back to the life from before.

Security for fear. Love for loneliness. Comfort for scraps and bare edges. Recognition and familiarity for invisibility and strangers. A bright future swapped for . . . nothing. Existing.

There might be other men, but never again like him. She felt sure no one would ever quite . . . love her the way he did.

Her sobs were choking her now. She heard a broken keening noise and realized it was coming from her; the raw sound of an animal in pain.

Night turned into day, and back to night again, and back to day again. Jane lay curled in on herself, getting up only to use the washroom or sip some water in between her bouts of crying and listless sleep. She hadn't emailed her resignation in to work, hadn't let them know she wouldn't be showing up. It was grounds for dismissal and no reference, but she couldn't find it in herself to care. She felt as if everything was very far away, everything that was once critical—even paying rent— existed somewhere else, and she couldn't quite understand why it had once mattered.

Eventually, grief wore itself out. She felt drained, weak. Her mouth tasted like sandpaper. She needed food. Shuffling to the kitchen, there was nothing but some moldy bread in the cupboard; she'd spent so many days eating at Edward's place. Tearing away the fuzzy bits, she swallowed the remainder in ravenous bites. She needed groceries, had to go out—a shower, yes, a shower was in order. The old pipes creaked, and a shock of cold water hit her before warming up, but it had the desired effect of rousing her a little. Washed, dressed, she sat at her small kitchen table and with heroic effort focused her mind on a grocery list. Life had to resume.

Self-pity is not a luxury I can afford.

She had given herself the deadline of two hours to outright grieve, and instead she had taken two days.

It was this terrifying lapse in self-discipline that woke her up more than anything. If she couldn't rely on herself, then she really had nothing.

A grim acceptance of what needed to be done. It was time to be rational again, sane. No more big dreams. Get back into the mindset of when she first realized the inevitable need to leave the restaurant—small, achievable goals, a concrete plan for what comes next, careful footing. Self-preservation.

It was like exchanging the loveliest plush, warm bed for the hard park bench you once knew, but Jane curled her mind around these thoughts and derived a kind of cold comfort from them, like a person blinded who, with a fumbling touch, seeks only the familiar.

She wasn't going to marry . . . him. And she couldn't stay at the firm; that fact remained certain. And she couldn't stay in this apartment, or this city . . . or anywhere else that would be a reminder of him, or where he might find her. It wasn't certain that he would heed her request to give them both a clean break.

Legal secretary was a good job, but already, and even with the excitement of him, there was the creeping discontent and boredom. He was right: she needed more, and she wondered how she had lived with that feeling as a waitress for so long. (Even now, when every moment was a struggle to cleave him from her thoughts, his knowledge of her, nearly as good as her own, was shining through.) Well, she now had office experience, Jane was confident she could do any number of administrative positions; no need to be restricted to law firms (where *he* had a network, and might walk in the door as opposing counsel).

Office work it was. And she should get more education—

many of the higher-paid secretaries at Rosen, Haythe & Thornfield talked about their degrees. Jane felt she should have one too. From a more recognizable institution this time, somewhere respected. She could take classes part-time while working, maybe even literature classes—the tuition wouldn't be such a wrench this time with savings in the bank. Now that she'd experienced her own earning potential, maybe a student loan wouldn't be quite so scary.

It felt a bit bold, a sort of leftover bravery from the time with him, but Jane knew she was more capable than she let herself believe before, when life's memories were only foster care and waitressing.

So, another job and a respected school, both somewhere away from the city.

The dean's office was exactly as Jane remembered it. Over ten years ago she stood here as a child, listening as Dean Richards spoke of preserving her father's legacy.

Strange that no one thought of me *as his legacy.* But then she heard her father's voice echoing in her memory . . .

"Plato, Socrates, Chaucer. These men are long dead and gone, but their sounds remain." And here he lovingly caressed a book. "Books outlive men, Jane. Ideas and beliefs and writing outlive all those who cherish them. They are passed on like a torch to light the way, always for someone new."

Dad's books outlived him, and they'll outlive me.

Being in this place was unsettling. It was a long time since memories of her father had risen up without any accompanying urge to tamp them down. Now Jane let herself linger on the thought and tentatively explored with a probing, delicate touch the sad-sweet ache the memory brought, still faintly traced with anger from that long-ago abandonment.

Dean Richards's secretary had showed her into the office and told her to wait, that he was held up in a committee meeting. The secretary was not the one Jane recognized from her youth, and the old appointment ledger that Mrs. Bramble diligently kept had been replaced by a shiny Mac laptop along with the newer model of secretary, but here in the dean's inner sanctum everything remained the same.

The door creaked open behind her.

"As I live and breathe, Jane Raine."

He was bulkier, balder, older, but still somehow the same. He spread his arms out wide, but whether he expected a hug or if it was to punctuate his statement, Jane couldn't tell. She settled for a slightly warmer-than-polite smile in return, holding herself as she would before one of Edward's clients, shoulders back, firm, calm, confident.

"It's good to see you again, sir. It's been a long time."

"Ages! You were still a little girl. Now you're all grown up! You look . . ." His gaze swept over her black sheath dress, plain but impeccably made and fitted thanks to Adele, and soft blue cardigan. Her hair was down, simply parted to the side, and she wore her usual minimal makeup. Her face was still young-looking, despite the days of crying, but her expression was opaque with a quiet watchfulness of his reaction to her. "You look . . ." He didn't know what to make of her. *Good. Let him be off-balance.* "You look like yourself. Only grown-up. And maybe a bit like your father. Much prettier than him, of course!" He chuckled and Jane smiled in return, lowering her lashes just for a moment in a show of inadvertent modesty. It was a trick she often saw Isabelle do, when she wanted to set men at ease by letting them feel their comments landed the mark, before persuading them to do something for her. It had worked every time, except on Edward.

"Sit, my dear, sit." He gestured to the wingback chair opposite his desk, facing a fine view of the greens outside his window. The greens where she had played as a child.

"I can't tell you how pleased I am to see you. Does my old heart good to see your father's only child. Oh, while you're here, you must let me show you—I know we said it would just be a bench, but we actually erected a whole new wing of the library in his name. The Joseph Raine Memorial Hall. It's just grand! Do you have time to tour it? How long are you here for?"

This was arriving at the point more quickly than Jane anticipated. She had hoped to strengthen the bridge with a few fond reminisces before asking the favor, but oh well.

"Well, that rather depends on you, sir."

"Oh?"

"Yes, on whether you can help me . . ."

Adele's advice rang in her head: *Don't ask men for a favor; it sounds like a chore and implies repayment. Ask them for "help." If we need help it is because we are helpless, and if we are helpless then a man can save us. He gets to be a hero; you get your favor, chérie. This is something all women know.*

But Dean Richards didn't look superior; he looked nervous as his eyes darted around the room.

"What do you need, my dear? And how can I possibly help you?"

"It's about a job," Jane plowed on, and his expression instantly cleared. She wondered what it was he feared she might have asked him for.

"A job?"

"Yes. After I left foster care"—his flinch was nearly imperceptible—"I worked as a waitress. I went to night school and trained to be a legal secretary." Jane felt humbled, telling her story before a man with two PhDs, but she remembered Adele's advice about men wanting to play the savior and continued. "I got a job at a large firm in the city and did very well there. But now I would like to get a real education, at a highly respected institution like this one"—*flatter him*—"my father's school"—*pluck the heartstrings*—"and yours."

"You want to attend Lowood University?"

"I could only attend part-time; I need to continue working to support myself. I have some money saved to cover tuition, and I know there are some bursaries for students with low income. I don't expect to be waved in based on my father's name. I would apply and everything . . ."

"But you said you need help with a job?"

"It's a big campus; there must be many secretarial positions. It would be helpful to have a job nearby if I'm attending school. I was hoping you could put in a word for me. There are a few postings on the campus website. I have a good reference from the firm where I worked; I'm really just hoping for an interview . . ."

"Oh, but of course! Jane, just say the word. The Classics Department has a shared secretary for the professors there— all three of them." He chuckled. "She's going on maternity leave before the summer term starts. I'm sure that would work out splendidly. Let me just . . ." He pulled a substantial legal pad of yellow paper across his ink blotter-topped desk and jotted down some information with his heavy ballpoint pen before tearing it off and handing it to her.

"That's head of admin. I'll shoot her a quick email so she'll be expecting your call. Let's try that for starters. Now, about your schooling . . ."

Jane's head was whirling. Would it have always been this easy, if she'd asked for help at eighteen? In the long, lonely years of her adolescence and the gaping silence from the population of her old life, she'd thought the message had been pretty clear.

When she left the dean's office that afternoon, she had a potential new job and a choice of classes to attend next Monday. The summer semester was luckily light on attendance, so she was to be registered as a "mature non-graduating student," a designation for people trying to return to school but without the necessary transcript, and so permitted to complete a few classes in the hopes of proving their academic competence and thus being accepted to pursue a full degree. It felt rather strange to be designated "mature" when she'd been viewed as so inexperienced at the firm, but as she saw a group of nineteen-year-olds leave the campus canteen, she had to concede that the designation was relatively appropriate.

At home, she packed up her meager belongings, feeling like part of her permanence was being erased. She'd arranged a sublet on the apartment and accepted her own sublet lease of an apartment near campus from a student who was gone for the summer. She continually reminded herself as she packed that this was necessary, campus being too far to commute, and a good thing, progress in her life, a new chapter, though the strangeness of sleeping in someone else's bed while a random stranger slept in hers brought back bad memories of the impermanence of her foster years. When she found a borrowed sweater of Edward's she'd worn home one night, she gave herself leave to cry in the tub.

Two minutes maximum.

She emailed Adele, feeling she owed her a goodbye of sorts and, mindful that this was being sent to a firm account, explaining in the broadest possible brushstrokes what had happened:

> Adele, I've left the firm and him. Both exits are completely my decision. I know you're too kind to say it, so I'll say it for you: you were right. Please don't worry about me. I'm completely fine, and I'm even enrolling in school. Thank you so much for all your kindness and for showing me the ropes.

It was definitely stretching the truth, and Jane cringed over the cryptic wording that she knew would invite Adele's most dramatic interpretations, but she hit send before she could second-guess it.

She got on the train at her usual stop, the Port Credit station, but instead of heading east to the city, she went west again, this time for good, past Kitchener and Waterloo, into the rolling green hills, and to Lowood University.

Chapter 20

The three classics professors that the dean found so amusing in their sparsity were exceptionally kind. Professor Karian was a woman of about forty whose PhD thesis was on Cassandra the prophetess and the frustration of all-seeing women and the subsequent legacy of witch hunts. Her wife taught graduate-level mathematics. Professor Martin and Professor O'beyga were both older gentlemen whose primary need for a secretary was to repeatedly explain email and the online portal for student records and grades. The office was really one large room, with Professors Martin and Karian sharing a double desk pushed under a window, while Professor O'beyga, by virtue of being the most senior, enjoyed a private alcove in the room, the size of a walk-in closet. Jane's desk was a clapboard Ikea number, shoved near the door.

The work was far from taxing, and the professors, in their pleasant, studious ways, were perpetually ghosting shades of her father. She might have been bored except for her classes.

The summer timetable was limiting, but with the dean's encouragement she had signed up for Introduction to Poetry, Shakespeare's History Plays, and Narrative Theory.

"You'll enjoy the poetry class. It's being taught by Daniel Holland, a very promising new PhD graduate over from Oxford."

She tried not to feel guilty she hadn't signed up for Introduction to Classics when the trio asked.

The first few days were as nerve-racking as her first time on Bay Street. She should have fit in immediately due to her early upbringing, but so many of her classmates were bright, hopeful, happy young things, that they felt entirely foreign, and more foreign still from the working single moms and basement-dwellers that had populated her evening classes training to be a legal secretary.

But Edward, damn him, had been right—*this* is where she was meant to be. The stories and teachings of her father, she now realized, were a patchwork of inconsistencies thanks to his wandering attention and her childish interpretation. Having things explained to her, the whole long skein of books and history and stories lain smooth, was intoxicating and, she must admit, a form of escapism. There was no self-consciousness when she was knee-deep in deciphering scansion. She was running to keep up and it was glorious.

"Did you know that someone once wrote a whole essay on the difference between the lines 'a blue sky' and 'a sky of blue'? A whole essay on how that choice affected the poem!"

Professor Karian smiled. "Is that from your poetry class, or your narrative theory class?"

She was taking a break from marking papers to chat with Jane, who had come into the office after her lunchtime class overflowing with notes.

"My poetry class. Oh, but yesterday in my narrative theory

class, we learned about this medieval stained glass window and how it affects narrative structure . . ." and Jane was off, uncharacteristically running at the mouth in her excitement.

Professor Karian laughed and shook her head. "I'm glad you're enjoying the class so much. A lot of people find narrative theory tricky. It makes you think, doesn't it? How to reframe a narrative, what agency characters have, how we determine what's a happy ending and what's a tragedy. I have a colleague in the English department that will swear up and down that the first separation of the lovers in Austen's *Persuasion* is actually a good thing, since when they're finally reunited, they're on more equal ground. Changes the book if you look at the narrative like that."

"That's a bit far-fetched," Jane said, but later that night, she thought about it some more. If you could reinterpret a story in different ways, then you could reinterpret your life as well. Instead of stringing together all your tragedies and clinging to your will to keep walking, why not look at it as something that kept making you stronger? Resilience. Maybe she wasn't just plodding along and pounding in crooked nails over and over again. Maybe she was getting stronger. It was a thought to cling to on those rare nights when she allowed herself to cry herself to sleep, when the work of the day wasn't enough to keep at bay thoughts of Edward and all she'd lost.

My heart can be broken, but my spine can still be steel. That's something.

The moniker of "Professor Raine's daughter" was not something Jane had really contended with before, besides Edward's short-lived and disastrous celebration of it. But here at the university, among the professors and some of the grad students that came to visit the classics trio, it carried its own small brand of celebrity.

Her father's books, an ongoing treatise on the study of technology being imbued with mythical powers like the creation of Frankenstein, and several highly theoretical science fiction novels that were considered high art literature, were still studied on campus and a standard part of many professors' critical reading lists. So being Jane Raine was something. That the something meant nothing did not dawn on people. There had been a very small sum of money in the bank from his last book when he died, and a few banked paychecks, the latter of which had gone to his funeral costs, but nothing else. Whether that was because her father had been careless with money or because the returns on academic publishing were so meager (he was hardly a *New York Times* bestseller) Jane couldn't say, but she always suspected it was a combination of the two. Edward had asked her once why there wasn't some kind of trust left to her, but she had shrugged it off. There was a lingering hurt and embarrassment over her father's shortcomings as a parent that made her shy away from such inquiries, and it seemed a fruitless line of questioning.

People asked her lots of questions about her father—what he was like, what he thought of things, the inspiration behind his books, and worst of the lot, had he been working on anything when he died?

That a thirteen-year-old girl would be shortchanged on the kind of academic knowledge they sought about him didn't seem to cross their minds. She knew her father from the things he taught her, bits of poetry and logic studies, speeches and some philosophy. She knew a little of his books, had thumbed through them once as a curious ten-year-old, and had gleaned some of their meaning. She knew what his study had looked like, where he disappeared to write them. She knew he liked oatmeal for breakfast and always dressed her in sturdy overalls when she was little, because he thought covering little girls in showy dresses and lace was counterproductive to a child's curiosity of the world and going out to get muddy and play.

Their questions made Jane feel distant from her father—their curiosity was for an adult's life that she never really knew—and worse, they made her feel embarrassed. That the majority of her own adult life was spent as a waitress, that she was on trial as a "mature nongraduate" when her father was so feted. That she had never again touched his books, finding the memory association painful, despite still having a few of his personal copies with his notes in the margins buried in a box in her apartment.

Professor Karian caught on to Jane's discomfort early and spoke to the graduate students who came by for her office hours. They stopped asking questions and greeted her with an oversolicitous politeness instead. Which was not great, but certainly not worse.

The professors of two of her classes still persisted in the odd remark, and Jane was grateful Daniel Holland's class was a reprieve.

Daniel was possibly the most pretty-handsome man Jane had met in real life. Pretty-handsome was the only way she could think to describe it. His features were by no means feminine, but they were so precisely, so classically cut and symmetrical that handsome didn't seem to cover it. Handsome was more Edward's rough-hewn jaw and stubble, and Jane realized how quickly he'd become her measuring tape for other men's aesthetic and physique.

Try as she might, she still thought of him.

But Daniel was so different; he was quite tall, broad shouldered but incredibly lean like a swimmer. His jawline was a clean-cut, but the gaze was drawn more toward his proud nose, his bright blue eyes set deep in sculpted sockets that gave him a look of perpetual intensity, and a high forehead topped with smooth, dark blond hair. The entire effect was attractive yet aristocratic, with a kind of leonine, coiled power. His voice was deep, melodic, and lightly accented, with tones of Oxford posh.

Jane felt, as she often did around well-built people, child-like standing next to him. She had to crane her neck back to speak and take two steps to match every one of his. He was very serious, listened carefully, and always paused to think before he spoke.

The Oxford thing seemed to intimidate everybody. "Left-over effect of Canada being a former colony," Jane joked once with a classmate, and then realized that despite them both being Canadian, she'd offended them. *Whoops.*

Someone had clearly pointed out to him that she was the progeny of the famous Professor Raine and therefore someone of note, and Jane was relieved that though he took pains to speak with her and be especially acquainted with her, he did so away from the gaze of her classmates, and showed no marked preferential treatment in class.

She figured he'd realize the special designation bestowed

upon her was a misnomer, none of the late great professor's brilliance to be found, but in repeated chats lingering on the steps of the lecture hall after class, Jane found that they did in fact have much to talk about.

She was clearly the student to his mastery of subjects, but without the rest of the class there, he moved more quickly between topics, dived deeper on details. Jane listened, rapt, as he taught her about how dawning studies in phrenology and physiognomy had informed eighteenth-century literature, the origins of scatological humor that featured in books like *Tom Jones*, whether Shakespeare's sonnet 116 or 121 was the truest indication of love.

And here, with her broken heart, Jane could do more than just learn and follow the content.

" 'Looks on tempests and is never shaken,' immovability isn't his most complex idea when it comes to love, and ending the volta with love's longevity is an obvious bookend. But in sonnet 121 . . ."

"In sonnet 121," Daniel countered, "he promises to love her warts and all; that's hardly more sophisticated. But in 116 the language . . ."

"I think sonnet 116 isn't as focused on the object of the love as . . ."

He sighed, patiently, and Jane felt silently reprimanded, as she often did with him, for her impatience that she had cut him off. She ducked her head in apology.

"I think when we're further along in the course, you will come to see things as I do on this topic."

Jane found that a bit condescending, but she held her tongue.

"For now, though, I see you're passionate about it, and while that's good for enjoying poetry, it makes it a little trickier for academic study. Can I recommend some background reading for you? Not as part of the course; just something that I think will guide you."

Jane nodded, pleased to be given this extra consideration and forgetting her earlier offense. Daniel reached into his leather messenger bag and withdrew a small Moleskine notebook, in which he jotted down some titles and then tore off the page and handed it to her.

"Thanks," Jane said, and tucked it carefully away.

"No problem," he replied, and Jane tried to not feel self-conscious next to his pristine, professorial look.

Chapter 21

If there's one thing Adele taught her—okay, scratch that, there were many things Adele had taught her—but one of the earliest lessons was about looking the part. She'd be forever grateful for the results of their first shopping trip, when she'd been forcefully transitioned away from the baggy blouse and shapeless skirt combo that had made up her entire office wardrobe. Looking the part had gone a long way to easing her path on Bay Street, though she hadn't wanted to admit it at the time. And while some of her blouses and shift dresses would be okay for her work as secretary to the classics trio, it made her stand out as a student, especially when she already felt marked for being mature.

So it's once more unto the breach.

The breach this time was a small strip mall a short bus ride from campus, and now Jane had a brief list of items, having studied some of the girls' wardrobes in class, to efficiently accomplish her plan.

A denim jacket to throw over her blouses on working days. A pair of dark, smart jeans. A light summer cotton dress with a tiny floral print. White sneakers for walking some of the wooded paths and fields around the campus, and a pair of tan wedges to replace her Bay Street black pumps. If she was still a student in the fall, maybe she'd come back for a few colorful sweaters.

It was a source of pride that this shopping trip had gone so well. She wanted to boast to someone of the accomplishment and with a pang realized she missed Adele, and felt a renewed appreciation for her friendship. Jane hadn't expected a reply to her hasty email, but Adele's generosity of spirit had surprised her yet again; a reply had been almost immediate, and it was a testament to Adele's restraint that she had responded only with warm reassurances and no questions. She had included a phone number and instructions to call when Jane felt ready.

Jane dialed the number now, standing at the bus stop to take her back to campus.

Adele answered on the second ring.

"Jane! Chérie, so good to hear from you. Are you all right? Are you in the city? I wanted to give you space, but mon dieu, so much to talk about. Come by and we'll have dinner."

Jane chuckled and felt a little watery. "Hi, Adele. I'm sorry it took so long for me to call you. I know that email was bull . . ."

"Non," she was cut off, "you are entitled to your space, my friend. Especially after what happened."

Jane breathed. "You know?"

"That there was a wife? Quel surprise, now the whole firm knows! The California girl came to the office, some weeks after you had gone—and Jane, Mr. Rosen—ah merde, I promised I wouldn't speak his name but . . ."

"You can say his name, Adele. I'm not that fragile."

Yes I am.

"How is he?" and Jane congratulated herself that her voice only quavered a little.

Adele paused. "Not good. He was not good, after you left. Very not good. Doesn't say anything. No one knew where you'd gone. He only asked me if you'd been in touch, and if you were okay. Then that . . . Californian showed up." Adele said "Californian" with the same disdain she reserved for polyester. "We had all seen her before over the years, but no one knew who she was; some thought maybe a long-distance girlfriend. Then, in front of the whole lobby, he shouts at her and then it all comes out. We were all in shock! What did you used to say, 'drama-llama'? More so a whole drama menagerie!" She paused to draw breath, clearly reliving her surprise.

"And of course no one else could know, but I immediately thought of my pauvre Jane, and what must have happened."

Jane nodded to the bus stop wall. "Well, you tried to tell me it wouldn't work. You think I'm stupid and old-fashioned to walk away, just because he's married?"

"Is that a dig at my French sensibilities?" She scoffed. "Every woman takes love on her own terms, Jane. I only tried to caution you because you were so inexperienced, and he knew so much more, but I would not worry about you now. You stood by your terms. Eh, I don't think I am saying this right—I need French to explain—but I hope you know what I mean. And now, tell me what you have been up to."

Jane told her about meeting the dean, and about school and her new job, and tried not to revel too much in Adele's praises.

In turn, Adele told her about her new lipstick, an art installation at Union Station that irritated everyone by blocking the doors, and how Diane had thought she was exclusively dating Alec from IT only to find out he was also seeing a girl from marketing and another girl from the Genius Bar at the Apple Store.

"Adele," Jane interrupted, laughing from her last story, "listen, I've got to go—my bus is pulling up—but I'll try to call more often and keep in touch, if that's okay." Suddenly, she worried she'd overstepped, now that they were no longer colleagues, but Adele's response came back warm and enthusiastic as always.

"Of course, you must call! I look forward to it."

"And . . . if you see him, Mr. Rosen, in the hallway, and he asks again, you can mention I'm okay."

"Oh, of course, you do not know. He has gone to the Vancouver office. He was already packed for leaving before this wife showed up. And now he has gone, and he is there to stay."

Vancouver. A five-hour flight and a three-hour time difference. As far away from Toronto as one can possibly get while still being in Canada.

Adele was saying her goodbyes, and Jane hung up, distracted by this fresh wave of misery. It was stupid and irrational. Jane sat on the bus and fingered the bright brass buttons on her new denim jacket.

They were equally separated, whether it was two hours to Toronto or five hours to Vancouver, but his erasure from the city felt like another helping of pain.

. . .

Daniel had this habit of encouraging Jane away from what she considered to be compelling female poets. Emily Dickinson, Sylvia Plath, or Mary Curer Elliott. Daniel said of course they were incredibly important poets and he would encourage anyone to study them, but she, Jane, felt too much when she read them, emoted too much in her essays. He said reading poetry for pleasure and to feel connected and found was one thing, but academic scholarship of a poem was another, and for that she needed to detach.

Jane thought that was bullshit.

"The class is Intro to Poetry: you need work on deciphering scansion, meter, use of . . ."

"I can do that and feel Elliott's pain."

He sat back, eyeing her coolly. On any other man, his look would have been skeptical. "Feeling her pain is for drama class, Jane."

One year ago, a remark like that would have cowed me. You wanna go toe-to-toe on female pain? Bring it.

"Empathy, then. I can find empathy and scansion. It's like a silent scream, like Edvard Munch but in text. Look at the spaces she leaves in each line, the conscious abstinence from using adjectives. You know why? You know what this poem's about?"

"The predominant theory is the political unrest at the time . . ."

"No. It's about being attacked. It's not about the political unrest in the streets; it's about being roughed up in the streets, trying to physically get through them. It corresponds with an entry in her diary . . ."

He raised one eyebrow and Jane paused. "What?"

"You read her diary?" Jane thought he might be impressed but couldn't be sure.

"You said to cover all primary sources." They were sitting in the student café after class, having a cup of coffee. Jane wasn't sure how it had come to pass, only that they were here now. Up close, Daniel's features were even more perfect, in a chilling kind of way.

He nodded for her to proceed.

"Anyway, I understand, I do. It's about . . ." She gathered her thoughts. "It's an absolute rage, which comes with being buffeted on all sides. It's more than physical; it's having your autonomy taken from you. The ability to say I will exist here, and I will do this, or I won't do that. It's so basic in its right. That loss of self, that loss of control. And it's followed by rage. An impotent rage, which is the most frustrating part of all. Because without socioeconomic power, without physical size or strength, there's no way to make your rage felt. You want to pummel with your fists, but there's no impact; you're just windmilling in the air, so you keep it inside you. It's a silent scream. And that's the part you can't move past. That's the worst part; that's why you can never let it go. Because this thing's been done to you, and there is no way to express how it felt."

Jane sat back, flushed and a little embarrassed. Not since chatting with Edward had she unleashed her personal feelings like that.

Daniel was eyeing her contemplatively. "Have you ever thought about writing?"

"What?"

"Writing. Like your father. If I can't dissuade you from being passionate about the subject, then you might as well put that ebullition to good use."

This seemed odd and off topic. "I don't have that much to say. And even if I did, who would read my ramblings?"

"I think publishers would sit up and take notice if Professor Raine's daughter had something to say. An old legacy, a new voice."

Jane sat very still, refusing to squirm in her discomfort. This wasn't the first time he'd brought up her father's publishing or spoke with a degree of calculation about her identity that made her want to shy away. She didn't know why; Daniel was just being nice in his own way. And more than once she'd called Edward out for having a calculating lawyer brain. But his manner had been different, Jane thought; he only calculated on the probability of what was likely to be, or how to get his own way. *I never felt like a bargaining chip with him.* But that was silly. What would Daniel be using her to bargain for?

"There can be a decent amount of money in publishing, you know. Nothing grand, but then again we're neither of us in a position to turn up our noses."

"I think if there'd been any money from my father's publishing it would have come to me when he died, as I'm his only living relative."

Daniel, despite his crisp accent and refined ways, was, as Jane had discovered, from modest origins. He'd attended Oxford on a scholarship. Completing his PhD still incurred some debt, and he'd taken this teaching job in Canada as the first offer, and the most lucrative one, that came through. Jane in turn made an offhand remark about her own strain with

269

money (though the lower rent of the sleepy university town and the income from her sublet of her Port Credit apartment was helping to cover the reduction in wage from working at a Bay Street firm to answering the phone for the classics trio).

Daniel had been a mine of information about bursaries, scholarship applications, and the reasonable rates of education-related government loans in Canada. Jane still wavered at the thought of going into debt, but the other options sounded feasible if she continued her part-time student status in September. Dean Richards had even promised to write her a reference for some of the applications. The dean had been rather keen on keeping tabs on her, checking in on her progress, how she liked the job. It made Jane feel bad for the all the years she'd thought meanly of him.

"Exactly. As his only living relative, your identity has value. If you don't want to write, you could give talks on him, or write his biography and sell it. That sort of thing. Just something to think about." Daniel smiled and sipped his coffee.

Another date with Handsome Dan?" Professor Karian smirked when Jane let herself back into the office that afternoon.

"They're not dates. We're just chatting," Jane said.

"Hmm, I suppose that has nothing to do with the new outfit?"

Jane was wearing her new summer dress, the one that she thought made her look more like a student, and she jolted internally at the idea that her intention might be so misconstrued.

She shook her head at Karian and took her seat at her rickety desk. "It's the start of your office hours in twenty minutes and you have two appointments, one with Crying Girl—you gave her a D on her last paper, so prepare for real waterworks—and one with Mr. SparkNotes. Might want to pace yourself on the witticisms."

Karian groaned.

Chapter 22

The non-dates kept happening, almost organically. It was never more than simple coffee or an offer to walk together after class. Daniel never flirted with her, so far as she could tell, and certainly never touched her, so she deemed it a safe friendship. She liked talking to him, liked learning from him, though more and more she had to bite her tongue.

He liked her to be calm, rational, dispassionate about topics, all the things Jane thought she had in spades, in order to be academic. But time with Edward had infected her with some of his playful ways, and it took Jane a while to realize that Daniel found these bouts of nonsense puzzling, rather than entertaining, and so she endeavored to weed them out.

("Hey, you're teaching on the third floor at the same moment I'm secretary-ing on the third floor across the courtyard. Next time I'll wave at you."

"The courtyard is too long. You couldn't possibly see me. Why would you wave at me?"

"It was a joke. Never mind.")

He might have liked me better back when I was a stone-faced waitress was an uncomfortable thought that kept reoccurring.

Still, he was the only friend she'd made thus far, and she was grateful for the company. And if he was a bit overly serious, then really she ought to forgive him because he, too, had been disappointed in love.

The topic came up when they were out on the quad one day and an incoming alert on Daniel's phone had made his jaw clench and his face tighten.

"What's wrong?"

Wordlessly, he handed his phone over. It was an Instagram picture of a smiling brunette flashing a massive diamond engagement ring, her apparent fiancé beaming at the camera from over her shoulder. The woman was exceptionally pretty and delicate-looking.

"Ex-girlfriend?"

He nodded.

"Want her back?"

He smiled sardonically and shook his head. "*I* broke up with *her*."

"What went wrong?"

"Nothing. We just weren't a good match."

"Like mismatched socks?" She knocked her shoulder against his, but he didn't smile.

"I'm an indebted academic. I couldn't run with her upper-class set."

It was strange to hear her own objection echoing back at her.

"And you couldn't compromise?"

Now he did laugh. "I just kept picturing taking her to a faculty dinner and her trying to snap selfies and talk *Real Housewives* with the dean. Her last post was about which celebrities have houses in Malibu and if they were close to the wild-fires. She'd be a blow to my career."

"If you think so little of her then why were you with her?" His dismissive tone was at odds with the pained expression on his face when he'd seen the picture.

"Because I loved her; it's not a rational thing." He struggled for a moment then relented. "She may be vacuous but she's sweet and kind and charming. She thinks the world's a wonderful place, and when you're with her you get to also live in that wealth and beauty bubble. She's very attractive. That 'gram doesn't do her justice. But I've always known my career needs to come first. By the way, did I use that term correctly? ''Gram'?"

Jane shrugged. She was thinking of Edward, who had defied her fear of being his embarrassment at a dinner party, and said he'd knock out anyone who looked down on her. She still believed he would have done so.

"But the picture still hurts," Jane said.

"Yes, the picture still hurts. But I'll get over it. I distract myself with thoughts of tenure," he said half-mocking.

"Very romantic," Jane agreed.

"You should read Dickens for examples of 'in love' but ultimately mismatched and ill-fated marriages. In *David Copperfield* there's a famous line—I won't have the exact wording but it's something like: 'the first mistaken impulse of an undisciplined heart.'"

Jane repeated the line, and then added, "So you think your beautiful ex was a mistaken impulse?"

"Don't get me wrong: the sex was great, no mistakes about that impulse." That made Jane grin. "But we had nothing in common, nothing to talk about. You discipline your heart; you choose who to love based on mutual goals and shared interests."

"Well, that sounds very . . . practical. But pardon me if I don't take my romantic advice from a Victorian novelist who was himself divorced with ten kids, had a secret mistress, and died over a century ago."

He smiled a thin, flaying smile and shook his head. "What about you? I'm assuming from the amount of time you spend with me or alone there's no boyfriend?"

"Also unlucky in love. Not because it wasn't practical, just, y'know, outside circumstances." She was impressed with herself that she could say as much without wavering. Daniel, with a show of tact and discretion that Jane deeply appreciated, did not inquire further and instead moved the conversation along.

"Are you free this evening? There's a concert at Jamison Hall; some of the graduating music students . . ."

She was free, unsurprisingly, and so Jane found herself that evening in the antiquated concert hall—roughly the size of two classrooms put together and likely built when chamber music was still a thing—seated beside Daniel, listening to students perform Beethoven's Symphony no. 7 in A Major, and doing a fairly decent job of it.

She liked the menacing sound of the music and let the growing swells fill her as she looked around the wood-paneled room and the people in it. She'd already spotted Professor Karian and her wife seated two aisles over, and she waved and mouthed that she'd catch up with them after the show. She saw a fellow undergrad miming the flutist's role in her seated lap, saw the music professor sitting to the side, glued to his phone and ignoring everything in favor of what was clearly a soccer match playing on it, saw a trumpeter take advantage of a brief pause in his part to empty his spit valve on his neighbor's shoe. Jane turned to Daniel to nudge him over this comedy of errors he must be seeing too, but Daniel was diligently reading the program with his usual concentration and intensity for all things informative, and Jane knew he would not like to be disturbed. She sat back in her seat.

They finished the evening with a rousing rendition of the national anthem, which would have made more sense to start the evening with, but apparently there was a mix-up with someone forgetting their sheet music for the anthem and so things had to be switched around to stall until their roommate could bring it to them. This was according to Professor Karian's wife, who was friends with the music professor.

Jane laughed and even Daniel chuckled as the four of them stood on the steps of the concert hall, enjoying their red plastic cups filled with cheap wine that were provided as part of the reception.

Jane liked Professor Karian's wife, Camila; she was beautiful and statuesque but entirely self-deprecating and so friendly and informal that Jane forgot to feel self-conscious standing next to her. She was from South America, with only a light accent, and a broad, mischievous grin that irresistibly reminded Jane of Edward. She, too, had caught the despicable saliva-related act of the trumpeter, and as the four of them walked across the campus lawn after disposing of their cups, she linked arms with Jane while her wife and Daniel walked behind them, and she laughed merrily to hear that Jane had also seen it.

"My wife gushes about you. Says you come in from class

every day excited about the lecture and full of new ideas; it's refreshing for those of us who have been teaching for so long to have someone for whom it's all new and exciting."

"Oh." Jane smiled. "That's nice to hear. I worry I bend her ear too much when she has work to do."

Camila laughed. "Not at all. We're professors—we love to talk; it's part of the profession. And she's glad you're chatting. She said you were so quiet and reserved when you started with them."

Jane shrugged and played it down, saying that she was merely used to working in a more formal environment and needed time to adjust. She changed the topic and inquired about what areas of mathematics Camila taught.

"Analytical geometry." Off Jane's blank look, she laughed and explained, "I'm an engineer by trade, or was, so now I teach things like calculus and analytical geometry, which are essential courses for any engineer."

"Why did you move into teaching?"

"Oh, lots of reasons." She flapped her hand around airily. "I met my wife, and I liked her academic lifestyle—you'll notice a lot of professors are married to each other. I genuinely liked teaching. And life as a female engineer is tough, even more so when you're Colombian. Sometimes you get a little tired of fighting and working twice as hard."

Jane frowned in sympathy.

"I imagine you're tired of being labeled as Professor Raine's daughter."

Jane nodded.

"No escaping the identities others put on us. Stereotypes. Archetypes are something my wife likes to talk about. Makes you think, if you had to answer, 'What do I foremost consider myself to be?'"

Foster kid immediately popped into Jane's mind, and she grimaced at her answer. Except no, she wasn't anymore. That label had dogged her long enough; that period of her life was over. She'd made it to school, not once, but twice, first to be a secretary and now to get a degree. That had to count for so much more.

That's a shitty thing to have happened to you, Edward had said when she'd told him about foster care. Something that happened to her, that she had overcome, nothing more. If she were studying that line like a poem, she'd mark the separation of herself, the noun, from the verb. She tried to adopt his point of view. So what was she now?

Student, she tried supplying instead, and that made her smile. Yes, *student*. She thought of Edward's admiring glance, *my practical Jane*. *Competent* might come next. And *resilient*. Unfortunately, *heartbroken* was also somewhere on that list.

"Anyway," Camila was still talking, "it's more types like your boyfriend back there that have to worry now. His traditionalist ways are outmoded." She indicated with a gesture of her head to Daniel, who was deep in conversation with Karian, still walking behind them.

"He's not my boyfriend," Jane said automatically.

"Hmm," said Camila, but thankfully, she changed the subject. "Have you seen the news lately about those California wildfires? Terrifying stuff . . ."

.   .   .

The heat of August was oppressive. Jane had spent so many years now living by the lake with its cool breezes that she'd forgotten how hot it could be so many miles inland.

"That's Ontario for you," Daniel said when she complained. "All my money on my heating bill in the winter, and the rest of it spent on air-conditioning in the summer."

The apartment she was subletting didn't have central air, or even a box window air-conditioner, and Jane spent many nights sleeping in the cooling porcelain of the bathtub, with every fan she could buy pointed at her.

The next apartment I get will have air-conditioning, she decided. Returning to her sunny yellow walls in Port Credit was seeming less and less likely.

She wasn't fully at home here, on this campus, not quite, and once or twice she thought of what it might be like at another university where her father hadn't been a professor, and maybe enjoying a degree or two more of anonymity; but she'd thrown herself on the kindness of Dean Richards to get started, and it felt churlish to leave for potentially greener fields now. She liked her job with the professors, which was hers if she wanted it for another six months, she liked the little campus town, she liked her new friend Daniel and her new friend Camila (who had apparently enjoyed their chat and mentioned inviting her out for coffee or for dinner at her and Professor Karian's house sometime), she liked walking alone under leafy trees, so radically different from Toronto's concrete bustle, and she completely loved her classes.

Already she was filling out the application to be a student

in September and calculating her finances. She would have to restrict herself to two courses per semester in order to work enough hours to cover all her costs. With her job, plus the sliver of income from her sublease in Port Credit (and how long would she be allowed to keep that arrangement?), plus her savings from the law firm and the generous severance package that came out of nowhere, despite the fact that she had quit, plus the low-income funding she was eligible for, and if she could get that essay scholarship, well, then, she might just miraculously pull this off.

Life felt full, hopeful, and yet . . .

She'd never felt lonely before, or rather, she amended her train of thought, she hadn't fully realized she might be lonely until she met Edward. Between Daniel and Karian and Camila, really her life was as populous as it had been at the law firm, and more so—at the firm her only real friend had been Adele. And yet, it couldn't quite touch the sides of the affection, the care, the level of understanding, of balance between their personalities that she had with Edward.

She sighed deeply. It seemed too much to ask the universe that she be allowed to have university, maybe a different university, *and* Edward. She wondered when she got so greedy.

In an effort to escape her hot apartment, Jane took to spending more free time at the student café, sipping on ice water once she finished her first iced tea (and wasn't it nice to be among other students who worried over every dime like her. No one looked askance at you for taking up a table for hours on the price of one iced tea at the student café), working on her essays, completing class-required reading, or poring over the fall semester's course catalog. The latter occupation was how Daniel found her one Thursday afternoon.

"You're staying on," he said with a smile that suggested she had only confirmed what he had already anticipated.

"I must be mad. I was only just starting to build some real security, and now I'm going to go and live on the knife's edge again, financially speaking, although you were right—the university provides a lot of aid, more than I realized there could be, otherwise I might have found my way to this school sooner.

"Sometimes it's not just the money; it takes some courage."

"That's true," Jane conceded. She paused to speak, turning something over in her mind that she wasn't sure she wanted to air. "You've never asked me why I took so long to get to university, where I've been in the interim years between my dad dying and here."

Daniel looked at her with his trademark serious expression and said, "I assumed if it was something pleasant, you would have shared it. Since you haven't, I conjectured . . . Well, you're not secretive or melodramatic. If you give or keep your information, I trust you have your reasons. You're a pragmatic kind of woman. I was surprised when you said there was no money from your father's work left for you, but then you wouldn't believe how in England death duty swallows bank accounts whole. I've no idea how it works in Canada."

"Nor do I." Jane laughed, though something niggled at her brain . . .

"Show me what courses you're thinking of taking," Daniel said, gesturing toward her course catalog.

Jane grinned, eager to share on this subject. "Well, I'm

looking for things scheduled in the evening or early morning, so I don't have to break up my workday. I mean, the trio are great about me nipping out for class now, but it's just the summer session. I bet everything picks up speed in the fall and I should be at my desk."

"I don't know what kind of traffic you're envisioning in the Classics Department, but I take your point," Daniel said.

"So that restricts my options to these five here, or these three here." She indicated two columns on one page and then turning the page and pointing, "and this one" before flipping the book toward him. He made a strange face like he was thinking about laughing.

"What?" Jane demanded.

"I think you're the only person I know who still uses the course catalog instead of the information available online. I didn't even know they still printed these. Are you sure this is fall of this year and not 1980?"

"Very funny," she deadpanned. "I'm choosing between: Intro to Shakespeare and the Works of Jane Austen, *or* Narratology Part II and the Works of the Brontës. What do you think?"

He made a small moue with his face and then asked, "My honest opinion?"

"Uh, yes? It's course selection. I didn't ask you if I look fat in this dress."

"You look lovely in your dress. I would take the course on Intro to Greek Literature and the Narratology Part II."

"Really?" Jane was dubious. "That sounds like a heavy load. I remember some of my father's lessons on *The Odyssey* and *The Oresteia*. That's slow reading, and so is the Narratology Part II. I'm still just starting out and I have to balance it against my day job."

"You don't consider yourself capable? Because I think you're more than capable. Or is this really about how you'd rather read Austen or Brontë?"

Jane ignored the compliment, piqued by something she found dismissive in his tone. "What's wrong with wanting to read Charlotte Brontë?"

I've been effing living it.

"Nothing at all. She's a classic English author—I'm English, I have all the respect in the world for her. But if you want to be taken seriously as a scholar, if you think ahead to your applications to graduate school . . ."

"Whoa," Jane interrupted. "Who said anything about graduate school? I'm just working part-time on getting through my first year of undergraduate. At this rate it'll take me five years to graduate, if I keep taking summer courses, and it'll be six years if I need to scale down to pick up a second job if I can't get the scholarship."

Saying it out loud made her own head reel. There was a reason she kept her plans limited to one foot in front of the other, to keep plodding on and not overwhelm herself with the scope of the project.

"You *will* get the scholarship, and the bursary," Daniel reassured her. "I don't know why you're questioning this. It's obvious you have the ability, and the background for this. I think you'd be very useful as an academic."

"Useful?" Jane queried, thrown by the word.

"Useful in your contributions to scholarship. Useful to the university. Useful to yourself." He hesitated as if he was going to say something further, and for one strange, fleeting flash Jane could have sworn he was about to say "useful to me." Her pulse picked up but . . . "useful to me" was far from a romantic declaration. And would she even want it to be? If Edward was married and gone forever, then . . .

"I just think you're a practical person and you should look at this practically. Long-term."

"And the Brontës aren't practical long-term?"

Daniel sighed, and not for the first time, Jane picked up a flash of irritation from him, as if this path for her life was something they'd already agreed on and she was suddenly and without reason swerving. But that made no sense. They talked about classes and books and touched lightly on their own lives, but she'd never discussed her future with him.

"I'm merely advising you as to the breadth and depth any academic committee would look for, if you continue with your studies. If you're choosing courses merely for pleasure"—and here his lip curled—"then so be it. Or you could save yourself the money and just join a wine-drinking book club."

"Wow," Jane said, rearing back. "Just wow."

She grabbed her bag and began to stuff books into it with angry movements.

"Jane . . ." he remonstrated.

"No, it's fine. I just think that's all the honesty I can take from you today. I'll see you around."

"Jane, I apologize." She turned back. He didn't sound particularly remorseful, but he did sound sincere. "I have exacting standards for people, and I've been in the academic game longer than you. I see how things are evaluated, the games you have to play. My advice may be harsh, but that doesn't make it incorrect. But I am sorry for upsetting you. I see your potential and I want to help you. That's all."

Jane sighed. Sometimes conversations like this just became a case of missed targets.

"I appreciate that you would like to help me, and I hear what you're saying, I do. But I've worked really hard to get here, so don't ever speak of my studies dismissively."

He didn't nod or acquiesce, but he had an air of studying her words, so Jane left it at that. Shouldering her bag, she headed for the exit of the café, passing a group of young men who were sniggering and not so discreetly nudging one another and gesturing at Jane. A collection of books and papers and beaten-up laptops was spread across the table in front of them, and wedged open against a ketchup bottle with multicolored sticky notes splaying out of it like peacock feathers was one of her father's books.

She paused a moment, arrested by the sight and not sure why. Buried among the plates and papers she saw that each boy had their own copy of the book. A study group, then. Two of the boys had the same edition, off-white paperback covers with a generic landscape image on the front, old and well thumbed. They had the green stamp from the campus bookstore of re-sold books; books that were sold back to the store at the end of each semester, and purchased for a lower cost by the next incoming student to take the same course. It was common for perennial required reading. Most of the books in Jane's own bag had that same green stamp. The boy with the book propped up against the ketchup, the one that first caught her eye, clearly had the newest edition. It was a handsome hardcover in dark blue, the lettering of the title stamped into the front, rather than printed, and it was twice as thick as the others, no doubt containing appendices and study guides in the back that often accompanied expensive versions of scholarly texts.

A curious sensation, intuition sparking swept through Jane again, stronger than before, pushing her quarrel with Daniel to one side. She stood stock-still in front of the messy table, ignoring the boys glancing nervously at one another, feeling caught out for their earlier gawking, but Jane simply stared hard at the book and thought.

What was it that was tugging at her mind, ever since she stepped foot on this campus and realized she was a minor celebrity and she had repeatedly denied that to people . . . And in a flash, the light bulb went off.

And immediately, she wished it hadn't.

A sense of calm, cold rage washed over her. If she was right . . . then she'd just stepped over a cliff, and a tenet of her life was about to come crashing down.

"Jane?" Daniel, seeing her paused, had left their table and come up behind her. He lightly took her elbow, pulling her out of her trance.

Jane stared up into his face, coming back to herself. "I have to go," she said and shook him off.

The campus bookstore wasn't far, just around the corner, actually, from the building that housed the office of the classics trio, and Jane made a beeline for it.

The top two floors were devoted to paperbacks, grouped haphazardly by author or by subject, according to the whims and effort levels of the undergrad part-timers who worked there for the summer. Come fall it would be the headache of a new third-year supervisor.

Navigating it was a nightmare, and Jane stalked up and down three different aisles before she found what she was seeking.

There. Three full shelves of her father's books. Above them was taped a handwritten sign, torn from loose-leaf, listing all the courses for which these books were required or recommended reading. The books looked shiny and new.

Jane carefully picked one up and flipped it over: the price read $20.99. A thumbnail of her father's face was printed above it. She fanned the first few pages until she found the publisher information: *Latest edition, 2018, now with an illuminating forward by Professor . . .* which apparently was the reason for the reprint.

She picked up another older-looking copy of a collection of Professor Raine's essays: $22.99, collected and printed in 2017. Another for $14.50, third edition in 2018. Another one, a hard copy mistakenly jammed in the paperback shelves, for $25.99, printed in 2016.

She stood still as a statue in front of the shelves, thinking, then with a sweep of her arm collected half a dozen of the books and marched to the checkout. She didn't even flinch at the total on the register. Purchases made, she immediately headed for the dean's office.

She brushed past the secretary, who barely looked up from her shiny Mac, past the creaky double doors, and straight into the inner sanctum.

The dean looked up from his book, surprise on his face.

"Jane, my dear. This is an unexpected visit, not that it isn't welcome."

"Sorry to barge in on you," she said, not sounding very sorry at all. The dean turned abruptly at her sharp tone, a tinge of nervousness creeping onto his face.

"Not at all. You're always welcome here. How's the job? How are classes going? I hear from your professors that you're doing exemplary. I've been keeping tabs on you, you know."

"Yes, I did notice that. I thought it was a bit strange at first, that you would care so much about me when no one cared where I was for years. Maybe I was wrong; maybe it was sweet. But now I think it's just fucking suspicious."

"Language!" he chided. She noticed his eyes were darting about, and he looked distinctly jumpy. Was he beginning to sweat?

"Here. Something I found interesting in the bookstore today." She dumped the armful of her father's books on his desk, sending the dean's papers and pens sprawling. He made an aborted move to pick them up and instead shrank back in his chair.

"My father's books for sale. Not cheap either. With reprints in the last half a dozen years, at least. These are required reading for at least five classes at this university. How many students per class, per year, are buying these books? And that's only on this campus. What about across the country? Other countries? All this time, I've been thinking academic publishing must be peanuts; whatever my father might have earned when he was alive was lost long ago. Famous Professor Raine and his famous books. But now I'm thinking all those students buying his books for all these years—that adds up to quite a lot, doesn't it? Even after you subtract the publisher's cut, and even if you're deducting a literary agent's cut—but even after that, it doesn't quite add up to nothing, does it? So what I would like to know is this—where did the money go?"

She was breathing hard, but her tone was flat and level. The dean was definitely sweating now, his whole bald, round head shining with it. He was making a little panting noise and clumsily stacking the books on his desk, as if making the sight of them neater might somehow help the situation.

"Jane, Jane, that's not . . ."

"Who's pocketing his royalties? Tell me."

"It's not that simple . . ."

"Tell me who or I start making phone calls to the publisher."

"The university!" he squeaked at last.

"What?" Jane stopped short. "How can the university be taking the money?"

"You have to"—he wheezed—"you have to understand. When your father died, he left no instructions behind. It was very stressful! I had co-ownership of a trust with him, where his book-related income went. His intention was to donate at least part of it to a scholarship fund for the university, for incoming students of academic merit. That's why I was co-owner."

"Then there's a scholarship? I'll be needing one come September."

"It was his intention, he told me as much, but there was no documentation for it. When he died . . ."

"When he died, you got all the money." Jane felt her stomach sour. "And you didn't even create the scholarship fund. Or give the money to me, his daughter who might reasonably be interpreted as his natural and only living heir, in the absence of a will."

"You were underage." He pulled at his collar, his face now pallid. "You couldn't have received the funds at that age. My intention was to hold on to them until you were eighteen, then I'd supply you with half and use the other half for the scholarship."

"Very generous of you. So where is it?"

"My dear, this is very troubling for me, very embarrassing . . ."

"I'm going to ask you one more time: Where is it?"

He gaped at her like a fish, blinking rapidly. "2008," he mumbled.

"What?"

"2008. The recession. So much loss. The university had, ahem, dabbled in the markets with part of an endowment fund, the strict parameters of which forbade such investments . . ."

She stared at him, uncomprehending. Ten years ago. Ten years ago when 2008 decimated Bay Street and Edward was sold into marriage to save a failing firm. Ten years ago when stock markets failed, when she was still a teenager and didn't know what that meant. Ten years ago when an endowment fund was invested in the stock market, where it wasn't supposed to be. Wasn't *allowed* to be.

It clicked together.

"You used my father's money to cover your losses. Losses *you* incurred *illegally*."

"You're too young to understand! When 2008 hit, the devastation was astronomical. Funding was being cut left, right, and center; bright young professors were being laid off. And before that things were already tight; there were discussions of raising tuition fees just to break even. It is my moral duty to protect the university and its students."

"And in protecting them you sacrificed me. And did something illegal."

"Questions of legality are not so black-and-white."

"Save it," Jane snapped. "I've heard attorneys quibble terms better than you. I've dealt with Bay Street lawyers that would eat you for lunch."

Her composure that she so long prided herself on was gone. "I went into foster care. Five years of it. Then I worked as a waitress for eight years. Shopping at the Goodwill, worrying about rent. And I tried not to mind it, really, because I thought my father couldn't help dying, that this was just the hand life dealt me, and there was nothing to do but get on with it. But it wasn't; it was the hand *you* dealt me so you wouldn't have to cop to your sneaky dealings. So you could sit here in your plush office and pretend to be wise and to care about young people. You sat here in your leather chair, in your lovely office, while a young woman, *your friend's daughter*, scraped burgers for over eight years, barely living above the poverty line."

Never in her life had she'd been so incandescent with rage. Never had she felt so powerless, so murderous, so ready to tear down every palace of privilege and person who claimed to know better than her, with her bare hands. Edward was right, when he used to talk about the firm and the kind of people he wanted to fill it with, too bad for the "usual sort." High or low people were all alike. They proved their worth by their actions, and nothing else meant as much. Edward had lied in a misguided attempt to protect her, to be with her and take care of her, and in remembering that she often softened his errors.

This man, this man had lied to her to rob her.

"Jane, Jane, I had no idea you were suffering so. Of course I would have reached out to help you. I've helped you now, haven't I? With the job and the courses. I've been checking in on you . . ."

"You've been keeping tabs on me because you were worried I might figure it out. Just stop lying. You know what I think? I think on some level you were always planning to keep that money." He watched her beadily, still making his small gasping motions, still sweating. "I think you tell yourself the recession forced your hand, but I think as soon you saw that money, and no one able to claim it, you considered it your own. You felt entitled to it. You're a thief and a liar." He flinched. The air was pregnant with the pause.

"I can make it worth your while."

"Excuse me?"

"What's done is done." He breathed deeply, trying to calm himself, then steepled his fingers and leaned back in his chair. The self-important confidence of his pose was ruined by his copious sweating and the pulse Jane could see jumping in his temples and his neck. She was flabbergasted. In no way had she expected him to try bargaining.

"What recourse is open to you now? You could sue me for restitution, but the money is gone; it would be a long and arduous process to try to get it back. Lawyers are expensive, and as you say, you're already short of funds. Think of the cost, the labor, the uncertain result. I can offer you, instead, a lifetime of free tuition. You could go all the way to PhD—you're a smart girl—and never have to pay a dime. Graduate completely debt-free, and I'd hire you on as a professor with an elevated salary. I own a little house just off campus—it's lovely. I can transfer it to your name. Think of that." He leaned closer, his ratlike eyes focused hypnotically on hers. "An entire house in your name, an elevated career path, a guaranteed income. Your father's daughter in more than name, the life you had as a child back again."

Now it was Jane's turn to breathe heavily, transfixed, as the picture he painted opened up before her. Forget all those unhappy years, the foster care, the waitressing, even Edward. It could be like she never left the campus, and everything else was a bad dream. Security, real security for the first time in her life. Her own four walls. Income. A respected, elevated profession . . . Walks under the trees and lectures and evening concerts with friends. Her father's life. Her life, back again.

And then everything snapped to, and she was suddenly reminded of what she told herself all those months ago when she accidentally burned her blouse before her first day at Rosen, Haythe & Thornfield.

Lying to myself is a luxury I simply don't have.

Her father would still be dead. Edward would still be married. She would still be haunted by foster care. And every day she would have to walk onto campus and encounter the dean, knowing that all she owned and achieved was a lie and a false bounty condescendingly bestowed upon her by this man, whose very presence she now loathed.

"No," Jane said, and it echoed in the room. "If I never see a dime, it'll still be worth it for everyone to know what you did.

And where do you get off, thinking this is all yours to offer? You could die; you could be fired. You're an old, sad man; you have nothing to give."

He stared at her tremulously, his false bravado rapidly receding. "What are you going to do?"

Just a little bit, the tiniest bit, of her rage started to recede. She had the power now. What he did was unethical, illegal, and unbelievably selfish. And now he would have the board of the university and whoever was involved in the endowment fund to contend with, not to mention what the lawyers could do to him on her own behalf. She'd lost years, but she could recover; she had time. The dean was old. This would be the end of him. She had the power now.

"Jane, the money may not even be recoverable. Please, I'm a friend of your father's . . ." he pleaded.

"No, you aren't. He would have never wanted me to be treated this way. He loved me." She exhaled, hard, trying to purge however much negative emotion she could leave behind in this room.

"I have nothing more to say to you, except this: better lawyer up, asshole."

She left the room, the dean's gobsmacked secretary staring after her.

Aaron Sorkin really owns the best exit lines.

Chapter 23

It took several laps of aggressively speed walking around the campus and several primal screams into her pillow in her apartment before Jane felt any degree of returning calm. She rather wished she had the old iron fire escape around her Port Credit apartment to clang up and down to get rid of this energy. The "what could have been" of this would haunt her for maybe the rest of her life. Stoicism could not stifle the gross injustice of this, nor resilience fully overcome it. But Jane's temperament wasn't built for rage. In the aftermath of her screaming and then crying, she found herself exhausted. She would like to wring the dean's neck, but more than that, she wanted to sleep.

She slept and couch surfed and ate comfort food for two days. She called in sick to work and skipped at least one of her classes. And at the end of it, like she had after Edward's big reveal, she told herself life needed to resume, simply because it did.

She had high hopes the money would be recoverable, and if not, then at the very least she would make sure she received all future royalties and the dean was exposed. The big worry of her life was money; perhaps this could still partially solve it. His threats were nothing more than threats, until proved otherwise.

So solving the rest was up to her. Nothing new there. In fact, Jane thought as she cleared the debris from last night's extra-cheese pizza and began to make herself a chicken salad, she was getting better at this. Instead of looking at this as another decimation, standing in the rubble of her hopes, as per her new narrative view of her own life, it was just another obstacle that she could and would overcome. If anything, she was getting faster at getting back up again. There was a kind of twisted comfort in that.

Nothing but myself, my own two feet, and the ground I stand on. That's what she had said to Edward. *My own two feet are steadier than I realized.*

She knew now she couldn't stay at this campus, not long-term. She would finish her summer courses and, using those grades and references, apply elsewhere for the fall. She was determined to get her degree, and to embrace what career opportunities or future came with it. The dean could pant and blow and cower in his office awaiting her next move. She was not going to slink silently off ever again.

I am not a damaged person.

What she had said to Edward that horrible day, that they were both damaged people, was wrong. Jane had always rationalized her past to herself: that the universe was cold and indifferent, that bad things happened to people all the time, that parents died and betrayal existed, and expecting otherwise was stupid and a waste of time. She had thought that an eminently logical way to view it. But looking back now—to say that expecting otherwise was stupid, was really a way of telling herself that *she* had no right to expect otherwise, wasn't it? It was a way of saying that she was owed nothing, and that just wasn't true. She had been a child; she was owed care and protection. The adults in her life owed it to her to look out for her and think and plan ahead for her future. Her father had failed in many respects, but now she knew he hadn't left her destitute. The dean was at fault. And now that she knew it definitively, she could finally realize that *none of it was her fault*.

Because like all traumatized children, some dark, hidden corner of her mind had assigned blame to the only person left standing to receive it: herself.

It wasn't that the universe owed her nothing; it was that she owed *herself* something. She owed herself more than languishing in that waitressing job for so many years, hoping to go unseen. More than a lonely, isolated life. More than believing heartbreak was the only possible outcome for her relationship with Edward.

Betrayal had seemed more logical, more expected, at the time, than the fact that a man could really love her and want to start a family with her, to make a home together.

During her self-imposed quarantine—read meltdown— Edward drifted through her mind, more often and with more license than she had consciously granted him. The ripple of pain, of loneliness, of longing was still there. Now it was also tinged with curiosity. She had such an urge to talk to him, to ponder how both their lives had been thrown off-balance by a financial crisis, and the greed of two men who should have looked out for them. It was an irresistible train of thought that always led straight back to him.

What was he doing out in Vancouver? Was he throwing himself into his work? Was he meeting new people? He didn't know anyone out in Vancouver, she didn't think, being a Toronto boy and a Montreal alum. He never mentioned any desire to go to Vancouver. Was he in hiding because the story of his wife was outed? Was he missing her, like she was missing him?

The urge to call Adele, to hope some sparse tidbit of information on him might be available, was overwhelming. Back in classes and at work, she picked up and put down her phone a dozen times a day, raising a curious eyebrow from Daniel who had clocked the new tic.

"Expecting a call?" he asked over a coffee after class.

"Resisting making one," Jane replied, turning her phone facedown on the table again.

"Date not call you back?"

"Friend I'm worried about."

"I'm shocked . . . I didn't think you had any other friends but me."

Jane rolled her eyes at him but smiled at his rare display of humor, then flipped her phone screen side up, and then back down again.

Things were, if not fully mended, then decidedly en route to being back to normal for them after their tiff. It seemed so long ago to Jane, so inconsequential compared to the shattering episode that had come next. When Daniel texted a few days later to ask her opinion on something they were both reading, she recognized it for the peace offering it was. She couldn't deny her guard was slightly up around him now, in a way it hadn't been before, but she also acknowledged to herself that though his input had been misguided, it was well-intentioned, and as self-sufficient and independent as she had been all her life, she had perhaps overreacted to his meddling.

"If it's a friend then why can't you call and check on them?" he asked.

"We're not speaking at the moment," Jane hedged. "He—"

"Oh, it's a he," Daniel interrupted her. He turned to glance out the window, obscuring his expression.

"A 'he' from what feels like a long time ago. I'm not sure I can reconnect."

He nodded and didn't pry further, which Jane appreciated.

"Are you busy tomorrow night?" he asked, abruptly changing the topic and turning back toward her. "There's a dinner being held for visiting scholars, and as a new transplant I've been included. I have a plus-one. I thought you might like to come."

"Go to a dinner. With you?" She startled.

"Yes, I believe that's the nature of the invitation I just expressed."

"Okay." Jane regained her composure. "Okay, yes, that sounds nice. Thank you for asking."

He nodded at her acceptance, showing neither surprise nor pleasure on his aristocratic face, and resumed their earlier conversation about Mary Shelley.

Chapter 24

The visiting scholars dinner was being held in one of the old-est campus buildings, Hart House Hall (Jane wondered how something could be both a house and a hall, but that was cam-pus life for you). It was a funny little stone building, almost like a bungalow, in that it was only one story and very flat, reaching out far and around. There was a terraced outdoor garden smack in the center of it, as if the building were built on the model of a square donut, and arched doorways from all sides looked out onto the terrace.

The long, white-clothed table, laid out to seat twenty, had been set up through one of the archways so that one end of the table's guests were inside with a view to the outdoors, and the other side were outdoors looking in. Though the evening was cooler, there was still a heavy heat and the setting sun slanting down, so Jane would have infinitely preferred to be seated at the indoor side of the table, but there was a little pre-arrangement, so she and Daniel were obliged to take their seats outside.

Droplets of sweat trickled down her back, and she re-gretted wearing her light-colored blue summer dress; a dark color would have hidden the sweat stains better. Her carefully smoothed hair was starting to lift and frizz. Daniel's only concession to the heat was to remove his jacket and sling it on the back of his chair; otherwise he looked cool and collected, as always.

Jerk, Jane thought good-naturedly. It'd be nice if just once he showed some sweat stains or mismatched socks or flubbed his lines too.

The dinner was in theory being hosted by old Professor DeGroone, who occupied some minor position within the faculty administration that made this his purview. He was so old and wizened that when shaking his hand at the beginning of the evening, Jane had a sudden fear that she might have crushed it, and she loosened her grip immediately, having a mental image of the parchment paper–thin skin and delicate bones crumbling to dust beneath her fingers. *Gee, sorry, here's your hand back.*

"What, what's that?" He cupped his ear and bent toward her, wild white eyebrows beetled behind thick glasses.

"JANE RAINE," Daniel enunciated, repeating the introduction, louder than before.

"Jolene? Didn't take you for a Dolly Midler fan, old boy. Ha ha!" Daniel simply sighed and, cupping Jane's elbow, moved her down the line.

There were one or two expat Brits like Daniel hoping for a permanent position, a visiting professor from India, two PhD students from Iceland who had showed up in jeans and looked like they were thoroughly regretting that decision, and a retired emeritus professor from Australia who was in town only for a few weeks to give a series of lectures on something they were particularly studied in, which Jane later found out was the obscure field of ecogastronomy. Adding to that complement were several of the university's usual faculty chosen for one reason or another, and a scattered number of plus-ones like Jane. She had hoped that Karian and Camila might come, but apparently not.

There was also a tall man whose presence spoke of gravitas. This, Daniel murmured in her ear as they were making the rounds before dinner, was Professor Kwame James, and apparently he was a man worth impressing; he held several positions on various committees in the university.

I wonder what he thinks of the dean.

Daniel shook hands firmly with him, and then presented Jane with what, on a less austere man than Daniel, she might have called a flourish.

"And this is Jane Raine," he introduced her. He put no audible emphasis on her last name, and Jane wondered if she had grown so paranoid of the notoriety of her surname that she was imagining his triumph by just saying it.

"*The* Professor's Raine's daughter?" Professor James asked, shaking her hand. "I had heard a rumor you were on campus."

Jane smiled politely and then to change the topic said, "I like your waistcoat," indicating the deep green garment he wore. She felt Daniel ever so slightly stiffen beside her, no doubt at this lapse into frivolity, but Professor James laughed and thanked her.

"My wife says it's too old-fashioned, but when I was a boy, all the dignified men at the university wore waistcoats."

Jane smiled. "I knew a law professor who insisted on wearing bow ties. I asked him why once, and he said it was to show off his skill that he could tie one. I always thought he looked very dapper."

Professor James threw back his head and laughed. "Well, I'm glad to have someone who appreciates my fashion at the table."

Jane sensed more than saw Daniel's confusion at this warm rapport but also his approbation. She mentally patted herself on the back.

The food was decent, if slightly wilted in the heat. The salads and mains had been dressed up with an excessive number of garnishes to look fancy, but Jane, who had been enjoying the more upscale dining scene of Toronto with Edward, knew better enjoyment could be derived from food that was less showy and more tasty.

It astounded her to even think such a judgment, but even her short stint on Bay Street, with its pinnacle of manners and unspoken rules and formality, had rendered an academic dinner that might once have given her anxiety . . . easy, for lack of a better word. This was no battleground, like so many of those Bay Street scenes. Conversation was rather stilted, so deep in their area of knowledge each of them, almost to the exclusion of other information, that to observe a science professor try to chat with a music professor was almost painful to watch, although everyone's friendliness and goodwill seemed to go a long way.

Daniel was an active participant in the conversations floating around, though always mindful to let others speak and curtail himself, in his usual courteous way. Jane would have preferred to stay quiet and observe or speak to individuals one-on-one, rather than join the fray, but Daniel seemed at pains to draw her out and ensure her inclusion.

"Oh yes, Jane and I were at the concert. We particularly enjoyed—what was the movement, Jane? . . . Jane was recently living in Toronto and attended the symphony there . . ."

"Jane is working for Professor Karian. She could probably tell you what the Classics Department is considering about that conference . . ."

"Yes, Jane's a big fan of the Victorian novel. She should really tell you herself what she thinks of . . ."

Jane thought that last one was a bit rich, considering their quarrel. She was relieved when the conversation turned from literature to the latest on the California wildfires.

The sweat continued to pool between her shoulder blades and on the backs of her thighs where her dress stopped and bare skin pressed against the stifling suede of the chair. Jane felt herself falling back into her old ways of being: her smile polite and expressionless, her answers factual and to the point. She envied old Professor DeGroone, who apparently found the conversation boring enough that halfway through the entrée he turned off his hearing aid, pulled out a book, and proceeded to read through the rest of dinner, ignoring everyone else.

She couldn't put her finger on why, but throughout the dinner she had the strangest sensation, one that could only be likened to a growing resentment at being asked to perform. It was beyond her father's name; it was conversational marks that perpetually put her learning, her scrapings of being cultured, her time in downtown Toronto (which in this more remote town held a kind of social currency) on display with a follow-up need for her to fulfill the claim, to demonstrate her worth. Had she been less schooled in controlling her emotion, her cheeks might be burning with indignation. As it was, by the time the dessert was brought around, she was thoroughly miserable.

And thoroughly pissed off with Daniel, who in this light appeared to her as her chief torturer, or rather her handler, bringing her out like a trained animal for display. He clearly made the same exacting demands of himself: careful to subtly trot out his education at Oxford, his friendly associations with notable professors on campus, and his erudite (and Jane thought clearly rehearsed) opinions on a recent paper.

He clocked Professor James's reaction to every one of his or Jane's conversational points, and Jane was somehow more irritated to see that they were in fact gaining ground and favor.

She took a vicious satisfaction in thinking about how she had already decided she wouldn't be staying at this campus, and that rather than a feted academic's daughter as a feather in the university's cap, she was in fact sitting on a proverbial grenade. She wondered what Professor James and Daniel would think if (*when*, she corrected herself) she exposed the dean for his fraudulent ways. *Finish the semester, get your grades, and get out*, she reminded herself. *Then I will sue the hell out of them.* She didn't know what further tactics the dean might try, but she wasn't about to give him an immediate reason to "lose" her transcript or anything else that could be held back as a bargaining chip to stop a court case. Better to let him think she was cooling off. Then she nearly had to smother a laugh to think that Daniel, for all his posturing for Professor James, had no idea that Jane herself had a personal relationship with the dean of the entire university, and that in that last explosive scene, he had cowered before her.

That's what Bay Street and academia have done for me. I'm power mad. She snorted at her own thoughts.

"What are you smiling about?" Daniel asked.

"Oh, nothing," Jane replied airily, and discreetly tried to lean forward so that the chair wouldn't continue to press her sweaty dress into her back.

They were at last on the final round of tea and coffee. Professor James gently clinked his glass and stood up to make a toast.

"To our friends from abroad"—("Ha! Broad," said Professor DeGroone, apparently having tuned in again)—"whether you're visiting or staying," Professor James continued as if he hadn't heard a thing, "our community is so much richer for a diversity of voices. We hope that you find our campus, our students, and our staff as welcoming as can be." He sat down again.

It was possibly the shortest and most on point speech Jane had ever heard. Edward would have infinitely approved.

Waiters came to clear the last of the table, and people began to amble away. Professor DeGroone shoved two miniature honey jars meant for tea into his pockets, along with the unfinished rind of his mousse-filled tart, and without saying a word of goodbye to anyone, got up and walked away.

"That man is my hero," Jane said very seriously to Daniel as she watched him go.

"There's much to admire about Aaren DeGroone." Professor James had come up unexpectedly behind them. "Independence of spirit and of thought is not something that can be taught, but it's worth its weight in gold."

"Absolutely, couldn't agree more," Daniel said. "Indepen-

dence of thought is crucial to scholarship. It's what keeps de-
bates so lively between Jane and me." He placed a hand on the
small of her back. Jane took a tiny step forward. And not just
because her back was sweaty.

James shook hands with them both and then graciously
offered, "I enjoyed having your company this evening. There's
an English Department luncheon I organize at the start of the
fall term, for a few people. I'd be delighted if you both could
join. The seventh of September."

"Thank you, we'll both be there," Daniel answered.

Jane bit back her reply that by the fall she'd hopefully be
out of here.

Chapter 25

They said their good nights and exited into the slightly cooler night air. Jane tugged and flapped her skirt about her, trying to waft some breeze onto herself and bring the temperature down.

"You could wait until we're out of sight to do that," Daniel said calmly. Jane immediately dropped her handful of skirt.

They walked in silence for a few moments, headed toward her apartment where Daniel habitually dropped her off before continuing to his own home.

"I think that went well," he said at last, as if he'd been weighing the pronouncement in his head and determined the conclusion solid.

"Food wasn't great," Jane replied.

"I meant our rapport with the other faculty, our impression on Professor James."

"Oh," Jane said.

"I suppose we could have touched on more modern authors, but you know . . ."

"Are you . . . are we actually doing a play-by-play, like a report card of tonight?" Jane asked incredulously. She was no stranger to strategy and the undercurrents of social situations, knowing from the firm that the personality communicated in every handshake was important, but something about tonight was rubbing her raw.

Daniel sighed. "Is it not important to you that we're perceived well by faculty?"

"When did we become a packaged set?"

Daniel sighed again, and Jane wondered what it was about her that he found so very wearying. They were in the midst of passing through a lush, green lawn–covered quad, with little footpaths crisscrossing through and dotted with benches. It was relatively deserted.

"Perhaps we should sit and talk," Daniel said with his typical calmness. He led her to one of the benches and sat beside her. Too close beside her.

"Jane, we've both been disappointed in love."

"You dumped your girlfriend because she liked reality TV and didn't suit your career ambitions. Your disappointment is on you."

He gave her a look that ordinarily would have schooled her back to solemnity and made her feel bad for interrupting, but after tonight's little display, she suddenly had a childish urge to sidestep and thwart his every unspoken demand.

"We both want academic careers. We're both intelligent, hardworking, pragmatic. And I think we've both experienced how hard life can be on our own, without a partner. Having to take on every obstacle yourself, rely on only yourself for guidance, for decisions, no one to confer with."

"There are lots of people like us." Jane shrugged, unwilling to concede to the pairing he was putting before her until she knew where this conversation was going. She thought she knew, but it seemed so unlikely . . .

"It may come as a surprise to you, how much I like you. That's my fault. I've been cautious in showing my feelings. I've been your class instructor these past few months; it would have been unfair for me to show favoritism, and inappropriate to initiate a romantic relationship while you were my student."

Oh. So we are going there.

Jane was getting an uncomfortable déjà vu being on the receiving end of yet another declaration that started with a lesson on power differentials. Only while the first one had filled her with hopeful joy, this one was inciting cold dread.

"But I do like you, very much. And I think we could accomplish a lot, together. As a couple."

"But you *don't* like me," Jane blurted.

And until the moment it was out of her mouth, she hadn't realized how true it was. He didn't like her. He wanted to correct her and educate her and shape her, until she was at her maximum potential. Her maximum utility to him.

"Yes, of course I do."

"No, quite frankly, you don't," Jane said, punctuating her words with that flat, blunt quality favored by Edward when delivering his rudest epithets to opponents. The quality that turned every word into a rising stone wall against his opponent.

"You like that I'm Joseph Raine's daughter. You like that we perform well at dinners, that I have Toronto experience, but that you're still ahead of me career-wise. You like how I complement your résumé. This isn't a romantic declaration; it's a proposed merger."

310

She was breathing hard by the time she was done with her list, feeling sure of her truth, but at the same time exhilarated with adrenaline. Like she was about to fight something off, like Daniel's slow, insidious stranglehold over her, that she hadn't noticed until now. The gentle corrections, the subtle frowns. All the minute pressures that she, with her lifetime of servitude, had thoughtlessly responded to, with adjustments, with pulling in, with a dampening down of those same livelier spirits that Edward had helped set free.

Fuck that.

Daniel was very calm while she talked, his thoughtful, studious expression unwavering. His hands rested gently on his knees; his posture was upright but still relaxed. He now laid a hand over hers. His palm was cold. Her speech had not in the least bit disturbed his composure.

"I'm sorry if I'm not being romantic enough for you. I'm not a hero from Brontë or Austen. I won't go running across the moors madly. But that's not real. This is. You think I don't like you, but I do. We care for each other. We're attractive people . . ."

Jane snorted. They both knew that she was not really in his league looks- or polish-wise.

He ignored her snort. "I'm already established as an instructor. I can help with the scholarship applications, with your studies, guiding you . . ."

Jane laughed. She couldn't help it. Amazing, really, how many men in the last year were offering her the security she had been searching for since her father died—Edward, the dean, Daniel—and how ill-equipped any of them were to give it to her.

But the dean wanted to silence me; Daniel wants to control me and use me. Edward just wanted to love me and be with me.

Here, on this strange night with this strange proposal from this strange man, because they *were* strangers in all the ways that counted, ways that Daniel couldn't understand, Jane missed Edward with a ferocity that couldn't be subdued and . . . what else was it? She felt color-blind to her own emotions for a moment. They moved within her, yet she couldn't identify them. What was this? Was she angry? Bored? Weepy? It just felt like . . . like these weeks dancing to Daniel's tune, and trying to impress the university and please the dean before she found out the truth, and now thinking about next steps, it was all . . . distraction. Fussing. Everything kaleidoscoped into something new inside her. A new vision of how things could be. There was suddenly a clarity to her thoughts, an impetus to movement that had first propelled her out of that restaurant.

She was leaving campus. She would fight the dean in court. She would not be Daniel's creature. And she was hopelessly in love with Edward, and probably always would be.

She understood now, how easy it was to end up in a relationship that was more merger than love, and not know how you got there. She had wrenched herself back from this precipice with Daniel, but Edward had married Julie, and no doubt felt every bit as manipulated and suppressed by her and his abusive father as Jane felt by Daniel and the dean. And Edward was still being manipulated, still having to dance to Julie's tune, unable to get free. When he'd called himself a sniveling idiot for marrying her, Jane hadn't recognized that what he was expressing was a victim's misplaced sense of shame. It didn't excuse his lying to her, but she understood it better now, his desire to hide it and pretend it hadn't happened to him, that it didn't define his future.

And she understood herself better now. Her terror over Edward one day leaving her, that overriding fear that had been the stinging chaser on the cocktail of hurt and betrayal that day, finally slacked its hold. Her greatest fear, she realized, had already happened—she was out of his life—and here she was still standing, more resilient than ever. Stronger and wiser every day. Throwing off the Daniels and the deans of the world. She didn't need the paperwork of a marriage to make her feel secure. Edward saw her like no one else did, loved her like no one else did, and if it ended in heartbreak again, that was worth the risk. She trusted herself to get back up again.

"Listen, Daniel . . ."

He gave his mild, reproaching eyebrow raise at being cut off.

God, had he still been talking?

Whatever. Jane couldn't find the will to care.

"This isn't going to work. I'm really sorry that . . . no, scratch that, I'm not sorry. I understand that you think you've been kind to me, and that this is a good deal, but you haven't. And it isn't. I really hope you find someone . . . suitable for you, and that your career goes well, but you are so far from what I want in a man, what I want in a relationship and a life, that this whole conversation is a dumpster fire."

Daniel jerked back from her. He didn't quite wrinkle his aristocratic nose in distaste, but it was a near thing. Something acidic was leaking through his persona at her repeated rudeness to him. She could almost see him silently mouthing the words "dumpster fire" in scorn.

"'Dumpster fire.' An idiomatic expression of a thing that is disastrous. Personally, I find the term quite poetic."

"If that's how you feel." He turned away from her, his color heightened.

"It really is."

She stood from the bench and flapped her skirt about her aggressively, in the exact way he had stopped her from doing after dinner, and walked away.

Chapter 26

*E*xams were the very next week. With a herculean mental effort, Jane shoved everything else aside to study, and study and study. Professor Karian even quizzed her on poetic terminology when Jane was ostensibly doing her job for the Classics Department, helping her create acronyms for the many terms for the meters and the volta, running potential essay questions as practice.

The week after that, two weeks since the disastrous faculty dinner, final marks were posted. She had passed with flying colors. *Good.* Now she had a transcript to go on.

That was her fledgling academic career sorted; now for the mess that was her personal life. The conversation she wanted with Edward could only be done in person, but was he still in Vancouver? Would he even talk to her?

She called Adele.

"Chérie!" Adele said, picking up on the first ring. She sounded nervous, surprised.

"Adele. I'm sorry to put you in the mess of this, but . . . I have to know. Is he still in Vancouver? Is he okay?"

No need to clarify who "he" was. Adele exhaled long and hard at her question.

"Then you know. Are you all right?"

"What?"

"I wanted to call you. I nearly phoned you dozens of times in the past few days, but I didn't know if I would be doing more harm than good. C'est tragique, mais . . ."

"Adele. I don't know anything. What's going on?"

There was a long silence over the line. Jane gripped her battered cell phone tighter. She was sitting at home, at her desk, the grades for classes still pulled up on the computer in front of her. She had dialed Adele immediately after seeing them.

"Mr. Rosen"—Adele hesitated—"things went from bad to worse. I told you about the blowup fight with his wife. All the partners finding out . . . He was not himself after you left. Not grumpy. Dangerous. The board decided it would be best if he went to cool off. The cover was checking on the Vancouver office, and après ça, a sabbatical. Secondment to the law school, to teach there for a while."

"They kicked him out of the firm? Can they do that?"

"Non, he still owns . . . je ne sais pas." Adele always slipped further into her native French when upset. "He still owns, still directs the firm, but he is not—eugh, lawyering. He is teaching. Not forever, but . . ." *But until the board thinks he's got his shit together, if ever.*

Jane pressed her fingers hard against her temples, trying to absorb the news. He must have been humiliated. Exposed, kicked off Bay Street, benched for all intents and purposes. He still had control of the firm, could still implement his plans to make it into a model of corporate social responsibility, but he was removed from its day-to-day, from the clients and the partners. He was teaching. What was that like? She breathed quietly on the line, while Adele waited patiently.

"Chérie, are you okay?"

"I'm okay," Jane said.

"There's more. Have you been watching the news?"

"More?" Jane rasped. "No, no, I've been studying and . . . distracted. Why, what's on the news?"

"Mon dieu. The California wildfires. The wife, Julie, she refused to evacuate. She died."

The room spun.

Oh, what an awful way to go. What an awful, horrible, tragic way to die. Jane had no immediate thought for anything beyond horror at the loss of life. She couldn't reconcile the sultry teasing tone on the phone, the icy blonde in the photo on the website, with someone who could be wiped from the face of the earth so quickly. It was so sad.

And Edward. What was he feeling? Cut off from the firm he had sacrificed so much to protect, at odds with Gerry (because she knew the reveal of his deception would put them at odds), and now his wife was gone. The woman he had loved and then resented. He was so protective over everyone's welfare, even people he didn't like. He would feel guilt over this, and responsibility. And no one was there to tell him that a forest fire a country away was not his fault.

A little boy with a reset arm and parents who left him alone and retreated to their opposite corners rather than speak. He would be alone again, his life in pieces. She couldn't leave him like that, couldn't stand the thought of it.

"Adele, where can I find him?"

Chapter 27

It was the most romantic, impulsive, bold thing she had ever felt compelled to do. It was also the stupidest.

The rush of urgency, of needing an answer face-to-face and that wild feeling of kismet, sustained Jane through the purchase of the ticket (why was the price of flying within one's own country so eye-watering?), the hasty packing of an overnight bag, and the trip to the airport. Action gave no time to think.

But five hours in the air gave her too much time to think. In movies and books, racing off to confront one's former lover was usually a headlong rush of romantic impetuosity, but Jane was now thinking of the editing process that must have eliminated all that time sitting in a cramped airplane and picking through the duty-free catalog. Two weeks had passed since her epiphany at the faculty dinner, when the stark contrast of Daniel to Edward had brought clarity, and only a single day since her call with Adele had added urgency to a reunion. She'd felt so confident, but now? What if he'd moved on? Maybe he wasn't alone at all. Maybe he hadn't contacted her because he'd found someone new. Someone who had been happy to ignore the specter of his wife and could now simply enjoy his newly single status. This felt too lighthearted a way to describe his widowhood. But was he really a widow in the traditional sense? Maybe he'd found someone new while he was in Vancouver, teaching. Maybe . . .

Too many maybes. That's why you're going. To find out one way or another.

She focused all her attention on a neck brace that also transformed into a sock, featured in the magazine, and refused to let her thoughts wander.

Four more hours to go.

The Vancouver airport was modern and airy, the people more relaxed than those who populated Toronto's Pearson Airport. She stepped out of the arrivals gate to the taxi stand and felt a breeze of cool air tinged with a scent of the ocean, balmy and refreshing after the Ontario heat she'd left behind. Under any other circumstance, she'd be marveling to be so far from home; she'd never before left Ontario, let alone gone to the far side of Canada.

The University of British Columbia law school was only twenty minutes away according to the map on her phone. Her heart was beginning to pick up speed in her chest as she whizzed along the city streets and finally was deposited in front of a large, square green-and-white building.

"I'm looking for the faculty wing, Professor Rosen's office?" she asked a passing custodian.

The door to his office was slightly open and gave her a glimpse of a room one-third the size of his former office. He was wearing a rumpled white button-down with the sleeves rolled up as per his custom, and his dark, messy head was bent over the desk, writing.

For one jolting minute, it was like seeing something imaginary, like a mirage in the desert. Four months felt like four years had passed, which Jane could only think was the bizarre effect of such an intense experience and connection being cut off so abruptly. He was better-looking than the memory she'd held in her mind, and in the aftereffect of Daniel's cold, calculated version of affection, the mere presence of Edward seemed to radiate a warmth for her, and softened the anger and hurt of their last meeting. He was just a man, a flawed man who made mistakes, and she loved him.

Jane rapped her knuckles on the door and stepped just inside the threshold. Edward looked up with a start, and the brief expression of elation went a long way toward soothing her worries, until it was followed by an immediate wall of guardedness.

"So, Mr. Rosen is now Professor Rosen," Jane said, voice only slightly wavering. He swallowed hard, and when he spoke his voice was husky.

"Yes, Professor Rosen. I have to mind my manners a lot more now. But surprisingly, I like it, more than I thought I would." He wet his lips. "How are you, Jane?"

"I'm sorry that your wife died," she replied instead, approaching the matter head-on.

"You know it wasn't a real marriage."

"Still, you believed you loved her once."

"Yeah." He cleared his throat. "Her brother phoned me after . . . A beautiful, tragic soul, he called her. And all I could think about was why wouldn't she just fucking leave. Steven and I had both pleaded with her to evacuate. She laughed, asked where my assistant had gone, taunted me about her latest lover. What was I supposed to do, go physically move her? Keep her safe against her own will?" He scrubbed both hands over his face and blew out a deep breath. He looked suddenly weary. "Years of scrapping to be free of her, and this is how it happens."

"Edward," Jane said softly but firmly, "there was nothing more you could have done. I'm so sorry. I wish she'd long ago given you a divorce, but I never wished her dead."

"I did," he said, brutally blunt as always. "Many times, particularly these past four months, and now I've got that horror to carry on my conscience as well." He sighed. "How are you, Jane, really?"

"How am I?" She pretended to think about it. "Well, I'm a student. I'm potentially moderately wealthy. I'm confused. And I'm cold because summer in Vancouver is chillier than summer in Toronto."

"A student?" He brightened a little. "Good, I'm glad. Clearly, you've spent your time much better than me, but then you always were the more mature person."

She smiled her thanks, and then he paused and she could see him mentally rewind her list of clauses.

"Why are you confused?"

Now they were at the crux of the matter.

"I'm confused . . . because when I heard that your wife had died . . . I didn't hear it from you."

He sat up straight, alert, his eyes darting over her face like this was a logic puzzle to work out and he suddenly wanted to win. "You told me not to contact you."

"Yes, I did, and thank you for respecting that. But as a lawyer, I thought you might recognize the difference between a decree nisi and a decree absolute." She paused and took in his rapid blinking. "Okay, that metaphor doesn't exactly work, but you know . . ." She huffed out a breath. *Brace for rejection and don't cry.* "Edward, I was hurt and angry and scared and heart-broken, but I heard about your wife because I called Adele to find out where you were, because I needed to see you again. You have to know . . . I still . . . love you."

There was dead silence. The words took time to land.

Suddenly, he was up out of his chair faster than a lightning crack, faster than a baying bloodhound that just caught the scent. He came to a nearly overbalanced stop two feet away from her and stood there, radiating barely controlled energy.

"I didn't think you'd give me a second shot."

"Why don't we think of it less like a second shot and more like something new? On more even footing this time."

He stared at her.

Jane had to ask, though she cringed to hear herself say it. "Do you . . . still love me?"

"Jane, I . . ." His face split with a blinding grin. The wearied-looking man of five minutes ago was no more, and in his place stood *her* Edward. Passionate, wild, loving Edward.

He swore loudly, making her jump, and in a single swoop crossed the remaining distance and gathered her up. Jane threw her arms around his neck and welcomed his enthusiastic round of kisses.

When he finally drew back, she was laughing and crying at the same time.

"Every time I kiss you and tell you I love you, you're crying! Damaging to a man's ego, Raine."

"That's only happened twice. You should do it plenty more times and then I promise I won't cry." She burrowed tighter into his embrace, eyes never leaving his. "And this doesn't solve everything; you know we still have to talk about the lying thing, and some healthier communication habits." He nodded rapidly, eagerly.

"Yes, ma'am." He kissed her again and again.

She could feel the minute his brain flicked back on, and he pulled back slightly. "Wait, what do you mean you might be moderately wealthy?"

She laughed at his inability to let any detail go.

"Well, it turns out my father's books made quite a lot of money that was meant for me, and the university went and spent it all."

"Spent it?!" He made one of his bizarre, grimacing facial expressions. Jane had missed him so much. "Are you going to fight them for restitution?"

Jane nodded and smiled. "Know any good lawyers?"

He grinned and bent his head to kiss her again.

"Wait, is that Lamp? You brought Lamp across the country to law school?"

Epilogue

The sun was shimmering down on the waves, the mountain range looming in the distance on the far side of the water, and Jane paused frequently from her book to admire the stunning Vancouver views from the living room's sweeping windows. The late-afternoon autumn sun limned everything in a warm copper-colored glow.

She was ensconced on the couch, a massive plush leather sectional big enough to accommodate even Edward's frame, though Jane's toes couldn't touch the ground, with her notes for her essay spread out on the cushion beside her, and a dog-eared copy of Edith Wharton's *The Custom of the Country* open on her lap. A crisp breeze ruffled the pages from the patio door left ajar, but she was cozy and warm in a white cashmere sweater she'd bought impulsively just last week, and half-covered by a soft gray throw blanket. A steaming cup of tea sat on the end table beside the couch.

It was peaceful and still.

Too still.

"GODDAMNED IDIOTS!"

Ah. Edward was home.

"OF ALL THE IDIOTIC, FLAMINGLY MO-RONIC . . ." The front door slammed, echoed by the crash of their heavy oak coat stand toppling over for the third time this week, and then more swearing and clattering as Edward grappled to tip it back upright. "CALL YOURSELF A COAT STAND WHEN YOU CAN'T EVEN STAND UP! Why did we even buy this ridiculous . . . JANE! Jane, where are you?!"

Jane stretched contentedly like a sleepy cat before resettling into her warm nest on the couch. "Marco," she called out lightly.

"Polo!" he boomed back.

Really, their condo wasn't so large, although it was much bigger than Jane's former apartment and *so much* nicer. She'd done her best to tamp down on Edward's usual predilection for being extra when they first started looking for a place together, still plagued by fears of financial inequality. ("Really, Jane, you know I appreciate your little-match-girl persona, but en suite laundry and a concierge for security are the minimum requirements, not the height of luxury.") But she had relented once she fully grasped the extent of her newfound wealth.

The lawsuit she'd initiated, with Edward's and Gerry's help, had been grueling and public. A daughter long forgotten suddenly reappearing and claiming money invited skepticism. It was only after documentation of the dean's dealings, emails and bank transfers that showed him not only covering his losses but continuing to drain the well dry afterward, had come forward that the tide had turned. The university had been quick to distance itself from the dean, and quick to agree to a settlement. On top of that, the publishers, who shamefacedly admitted they had never questioned their payment arrangement to the "estate" of her father, negotiated a new contract with Jane for a reprinting of the books, now with a foreword from his daughter, Jane Raine, full-time student at the University of British Columbia. For the first time she felt able to revisit his works with something like pride.

So with a bank account that meant freedom, it was harder to scale down Edward's real estate choices, and when they walked into the two-bedroom lower penthouse with the breathtaking views and wraparound windows, cream walls, crown molding, and a gleaming kitchen, she crumbled. Edward was equally in love with it, though he continued to threaten her with five-bedroom upper-penthouse units until they signed the lease.

It was the first time in a long time either of them had a real home, and he was seized with a fit of decorating madness that was more enthusiastic than wise, which had resulted in his nemesis the coat stand.

"Marco!" Jane called again, and he rounded the corner, crumpled shirt, crumpled hair, and a sheaf of crumpled papers covered in angry red markings clenched in his fist.

"What's the rumpus, ace?" she asked playfully. "Mean old coat stand take a swing at you again?"

"This, this is the rumpus." He brandished the papers at her. "This is what passes for scholarship these days. This is a third—not a first—a *third*-year law student's paper on tort law!"

"Uh-oh," she said calmly, "did they have a typo?"

"If she spelled her name right it'll be the only thing in the whole fucking essay that's correct!"

He collapsed on the sofa next to her with a massive exhale, sending her notes and his essay flying before hauling her—blanket and all—into his lap for a kiss.

"Remind me again why I'm still a professor?"

"You decided you liked it."

"I thought it was because I was booted from my own firm in disgrace."

"That too." She smoothed his hair back and kissed his temple. "But then they decided to let you back onto their playground and you chose to stay and teach, so that's on you."

"Such comfort from my loving girlfriend."

Jane snorted and kissed him again, and this time he extended the kiss by trapping her in place with an arm wrapped around her waist.

It was still amazing to her that they'd gotten to this place of jokes and teasing about their rocky past. Edward hadn't been expelled per se; it was as Adele said: he'd been sent to Vancouver to cool off after his marriage was outed. That the other partners were unimpressed with his complicated arrangement with his wife was an understatement, but her death had significantly deflated the issue. They were quite happy to have him back at the firm and the past swept under the rug, rather than change the letterhead and "air the dirty laundry on Bay Street," as Adele put it.

Everyone but Gerry and Jane was shocked when Edward expressed a desire to stay in Vancouver and continue as a law professor.

An arrangement was made: Edward would work out of the Vancouver office part-time as a consultant. He would retain a stake and a say in the leadership of the firm, particularly its pro bono and charitable work, and its recruitment of new talent. He called it keeping his hand on the steering wheel. The rest of the time he was teaching and thoroughly enjoying it, despite his grumbling.

Repairing the relationship with the firm partners had been relatively easy. Repairing the relationship with Jane took longer.

Overjoyed to be reunited, still, Jane hadn't been kidding when she'd told him that day in his office that they needed to talk about open communication. It took time and many conversations to fully rebuild the trust they'd once enjoyed. Jane felt he needed to better understand her hurt, her reasons for leaving. He in turn explained the panic and helplessness that had led to such, as he put it, spectacularly boneheaded decision-making.

It was worth it, Jane thought, to be sitting here in their home, wrapped around each other at the end of a long day.

"Well, your loving girlfriend would like to know what's for dinner."

"I'm feeling ambitious tonight. How about eggs Benedict?"

"You only mastered poached eggs last week. Is this graduation day?"

He tackled her down onto the couch, tossing the shield of her blanket aside while she shrieked.

"Traitor! Questioning my skills! I am cracking good at all things eggy; you should be egg-static, you should be—stop laughing! It makes it difficult to kiss you or come up with more egg puns."

She tugged him in by his ears for a long, thorough kiss,

which only ended when she suspected he was forgetting all about dinner.

"Go, make me these amazing eggs, then." She laughed and gave his chest a firm shove, which didn't move him an inch, but after another kiss he obligingly hauled himself to his feet with a grunt.

"Eggs Benedict coming right up."

She gathered her fallen papers, resettled her blanket nest, and resumed her work, now with the comforting sound of Edward cooking in the background; the cheerful whistling, the angry curses, and the clattering utensils all soothing and familiar as she worked through another chapter and the sun slowly set.

"Raine," he called at last, sounding gleeful, "dinner is served! Come look at my amazing Benedicts!"

She joined him in the kitchen to see him brandishing a plate in each hand, containing two eggs Benedict each.

They actually looked pretty drunken; of the four he'd made, only one was still sitting precariously on its English muffin base, while another two had slipped off and were swimming in a veritable sea of incredibly lumpy-looking hollandaise. One had clearly been assembled in the wrong order, the bacon between the plate and muffin.

"They're beautiful," Jane cooed, always grateful when Edward's cooking was still distinguishable from a burnt hockey puck. She reached across the kitchen island for a plate, but Edward had frozen and was suddenly looking wide-eyed at the Benedicts in his hands.

"Uh, Rosen, still admiring them? Or are we eating them?"

"I . . . I don't know which one is yours."

"Uh . . . okay, does it matter? I'll take the Benedict reinterpretation." She reached for the plate with the bacon base layer, but Edward jerked both plates back toward him, a look of panic overtaking his face as he wet his lips. His ears were quickly turning red. Those were both his major tells: the last time Jane had seen them teamed up together was because a student had turned one of his rants into a meme that had gone viral.

"What have you done?" she asked.

"What?"

"Edward William Rosen, what have you done?"

"It was a surprise."

"A surprise?"

"In the hollandaise. I think. Or maybe wedged under the bacon?"

"Okay, so there is a surprise probably in the hollandaise," Jane reasoned. That would explain the extreme lumpiness and volume. "Which plate?"

"If I goddamned knew that, Jane, we wouldn't have a problem!" He looked panicky.

"Okay, honey, it's fine. What's the surprise?"

He stared at her, his eyebrows upturned high in his stressed forehead, and then his expression softened to resignation. There was a long pause before he admitted quietly, "A ring."

"A ring," Jane repeated.

Then it clicked.

She felt her cheeks heating and a ludicrous smile stretch across her face. Her eyes were brimming with tears. "*That* kind of a ring?"

Edward nodded, his own helpless grin curling up in response to hers.

"And you thought sticking a ring somewhere in a messy eggs Benedict plate was a good idea?" There was an explosion of joy taking place in her chest, and she was losing her battle to contain her tears.

"Well, our meet-cute left me doused in coffee after you bewitched the coffee machine, and our declaration of love was while flinging our sweaty selves down a sixty-five-story stairwell during a fire drill; I thought an eggy surprise proposal might be . . . calmer and closer to normal? But now it's messy and it's just become . . . our style," he croaked.

Jane laughed even as she started to cry. "Oh my god, you're such a handful. I love you so much."

He dropped the plates on the counter with a clatter, rounded the kitchen island, and pulled her into his chest, kissing her hair, her cheeks, her chin, before pulling back.

"Jane, will you"—he held up two forks—"go digging with me?"

"Yes."

Acknowledgments

I wrote much of this novel during COVID lockdown, watching as shops, restaurants, and little locations that peppered the book went out of business or were transformed by the effects of the pandemic on Toronto. They are fondly remembered here in *Jane & Edward*.

My gratitude to my agent, Melissa, for her exceptional guidance, and to the team at Stonesong.

With thanks to my very wise editor, Kate, and the team at Berkley.

And finally, full reverence to Charlotte Brontë, whose Jane Eyre remains the most remarkable of heroines.

Jane & Edward

A MODERN REIMAGINING OF *JANE EYRE*

MELODIE EDWARDS

Discussion Questions

1. Knowing *Jane & Edward* is a modern reimagining of *Jane Eyre*, what similarities to and differences from Charlotte Brontë's novel did you find intriguing? What contemporary updates did you appreciate? Why do you think the author decided to set most of the novel at Rosen, Haythe & Thornfield LLP? How is the high-end law firm like Thornfield Hall? How are the modern Jane and Edward like the original Jane and Edward and how are they different?

2. Jane has been waitressing for several years and seems to have normalized its highs and lows. She has learned to "fit in" to that life. Mandi chatting with her friend cannot be the first time Jane has heard someone talk about routes to post-secondary education. So why does it spur her to action *now*?

3. Jane is understandably risk averse, and yet she makes many brave decisions throughout the novel. What do you think drives her courageous behavior and her resolve to change her life no matter how intimidated she is? What qualities does she possess that make her successful? Think about a time when

you took a big risk or a leap of faith for yourself. What factors were you considering and what prompted you to "go for it"?

4. Why is Jane capable of working with Edward when so many of his previous assistants have left?

5. Why does Jane slowly redecorate her apartment?

6. Education, wealth, and social status might be obvious barriers for Jane and Edward's romance, but what do they have in common that forms and strengthens their bond?

7. In so many ways Daniel Holland, PhD Oxford, is pretty dreamy, yet Jane finds him unsuitable. Why? What's wrong with Daniel?

8. Jane's efficacy and advocacy for herself are unshakable when she confronts Edward but much more so when confronting the dean. What's changed in her since enduring or dodging the creepy table-nine guy at the restaurant?

9. We talk a lot about how relationships must grow and strengthen over time, but perhaps not enough about how partners must make space to grow and thrive as individuals. How do Jane and Edward change as individuals throughout the novel? How do they help each other to thrive?

Melodie Edwards has a BA from the University of Toronto, a master's degree from McMaster University and Syracuse University, studied comedy writing at the Second City Training Centre, and works in communications. *Jane & Edward* is her first novel.

CONNECT ONLINE

MelodieEdwards.com
🐦 Melodie_Edward
📷 MelodieWritesEdwards

Ready to find
your next great read?

Let us help.

Visit prh.com/nextread

Penguin
Random
House